WARNINGS

Sheila's eyes told her that Lord Rande's striking good looks were but part of a vanity that extended to his perfectly cut clothing and the elaborate knots in his cravats.

Drawing room whispers told her that Lord Rande was infamous for the number of ladies of easy virtue he had bedded, and duels with angry gentlemen he had won.

Sheila's brother Brian told her how Lord Rande had forced him to drunkenly lose his land and his money in a game in which the cards were clearly stacked against him.

Brian's friend and mentor, the handsome Sir Jasper Tennant, told Shiela how much better off she would be with a good and faithful suitor like himself rather than a rogue and rake like Lord Rande.

But when Lord Rande took Sheila in his arms, she discovered that though she was forewarned, she definitely was not forearmed. . . .

The Irish Heiress

More Delightful Regency Romances from SIGNET

		(0451)
☐	THE UNRULY BRIDE by Vanessa Gray.	(134060—$2.50)*
☐	THE ACCESSIBLE AUNT by Vanessa Gray.	(126777—$2.25)
☐	THE DUKE'S MESSENGER by Vanessa Gray.	(118685—$2.25)*
☐	THE DUTIFUL DAUGHTER by Vanessa Gray.	(090179—$1.75)*
☐	RED JACK'S DAUGHTER by Edith Layton.	(129148—$2.25)*
☐	THE MYSTERIOUS HEIR by Edith Layton.	(126793—$2.25)
☐	THE DISDAINFUL MARQUIS by Edith Layton.	(124480—$2.25)*
☐	THE DUKE'S WAGER by Edith Layton.	(120671—$2.25)*
☐	LORD OF DISHONOR by Edith Layton.	(132467—$2.50)*
☐	A SUITABLE MATCH by Joy Freeman.	(117735—$2.25)*
☐	THE NOBLE IMPOSTER by Mollie Ashton.	(129156—$2.25)*
☐	LORD CALIBAN by Ellen Fitzgerald.	(134761—$2.50)*
☐	A NOVEL ALLIANCE by Ellen Fitzgerald.	(132742—$2.50)*

*Prices slightly higher in Canada

Buy them at your local bookstore or use this convenient coupon for ordering.

NEW AMERICAN LIBRARY,

P.O. Box 999, Bergenfield, New Jersey 07621

Please send me the books I have checked above. I am enclosing $_____ (please add $1.00 to this order to cover postage and handling). Send check or money order—no cash or C.O.D.'s. Prices and numbers are subject to change without notice.

Name_____

Address_____

City_____State_____Zip Code_____

Allow 4-6 weeks for delivery.

This offer is subject to withdrawal without notice.

The Irish Heiress

Ellen Fitzgerald

A SIGNET BOOK

NEW AMERICAN LIBRARY

NAL BOOKS ARE AVAILABLE AT QUANTITY DISCOUNTS WHEN USED
TO PROMOTE PRODUCTS OR SERVICES. FOR INFORMATION PLEASE
WRITE TO PREMIUM MARKETING DIVISION, NEW AMERICAN
LIBRARY, 1633 BROADWAY, NEW YORK, NEW YORK 10019.

SIGNET TRADEMARK REG. U.S. PAT. OFF. AND FOREIGN COUNTRIES
REGISTERED TRADEMARK—MARCA REGISTRADA
HENCHO EN CHICAGO, U.S.A.

SIGNET, SIGNET CLASSIC, MENTOR, PLUME, MERIDIAN and NAL BOOKS
are published by New American Library,
1633 Broadway, New York, New York 10019

First Printing, July 1985

1 2 3 4 5 6 7 8 9

PRINTED IN THE UNITED STATES OF AMERICA

1

AFTER DAYS, ACTUALLY years, of anticipation, Sir Brian Corbett stood amid the small crowd in the stern of the *Mary Kathleen* watching the coast of Ireland recede. Some of the passengers aboard the packet wept at the sight. Others, aware that they would not reach Liverpool for eight long hours, were beginning to look queasy. The winds were rough and the high waves swelled beneath the craft. Sir Brian, however, seemed in high good humor, a mood that increased as the ship sailed onward.

Miss Sheila Corbett, leaning on the railing a few paces away from her brother, did not reflect his exuberant mood. She drew her cloak tighter about her shoulders but conversely lifted her head to the fresh, cool breeze. Her hood had fallen back and her dark curls were whipped forward. A young man nearby stared at a face both lovely and piquant, noting that her eyes were dark blue, almost the color of the sea on this particular day. If she had been standing in the prow, she would have made an admirable figurehead, he thought. However, she was gazing steadfastly at the rocky coast and her expression was regretful, he decided as he turned away.

Sheila Corbett was not really regretful, or she reasoned, she ought not to be. Oddly enough she, who had only once set foot out of Ireland, was returning to the country of her birth. She had been born in England during the first of the two Seasons her parents had spent in London. Sir Brian, on the other hand, had made his entry into this world, a scant six months after the beautiful Miss Moira O'Neill became Lady Corbett.

Sheila wished she had not thought of that, for rather than viewing the scenery, her gaze turned inward and she saw her mother weeping. "He laid so long a siege to my heart, I thought he loved me, and Father so set against the English, remembering Drogheda and all."

Sheila's lips firmed. She had heard a great deal about the Siege of Drogheda from her grandfather. His own great-uncle had been one of those guarding the city when Cromwell's forces finally succeeded in forcing an entry. The inhabitants had been put to the sword.

"Not excluding the babes in arms, dashing their brains out and gutting their mothers like so many fish," her grandfather had said, speaking as if those events had taken place yesterday rather than in 1649 and also reminding her that her own father was English.

She unleashed a rueful sigh. She had determined not to think of Lord Carlingford, dead these eleven months, whom she missed most dreadfully.

"Gathered to my ancestors, lass. Hunting the red stag in the forests of the Fianna, that's how 'twill be," he had whispered at the last. She closed her eyes for a moment, envisioning the stylized rendering of his favorite legend that hung in his library at Dahna, the estate being named after an ancient Celtic goddess. It was her library now, she thought with a sense of unreality. Her library, her house, her acres, horses, farms. She stole a look at Brian, glad that he was not party to her thoughts. He would have accused her of gloating over her good fortune. She sighed. He had been extremely disappointed not to have received so much as a share of Dahna, but, she reasoned, he owned Corbett Manor, his . . . *their* father's estate. It was strange how often she thought of Sir Matthew as Brian's parent and not her own. At any rate, the manor, enriched by her poor mother's dowry, ought to compensate him for what he considered an inexplicable bequest.

It was not inexplicable to Sheila, however much she might decry it. She had an explanation, one she had never shared with her brother. As she thought of it, she could hear her grandfather's deep bass voice reverberating in her ears. "You've got a backbone and you'll not be casting your heart at the feet of the first man who gives you the eye, like my dear Moira. Better for you not to be wed at all than to suffer as she did, poor little lass."

" 'Tis a fine dowry he's left you," that had been the regretful comment of her great-aunt Maeve, who had always had a soft spot for handsome young men—Brian in particular. She could not imagine why her brother had passed over her charming grand-nephew, who, moreover, had managed the horse farm. "He must have been daft," she had snorted, with a glare at Sheila, as if she had believed it her doing.

It was not a dowry, Sheila could have told her indignant aunt. It was to keep her from needing to marry anyone for anything save love, an emotion in which neither she nor her grandfather believed.

" 'Tis not meant for us to be loved for ourselves alone, *macushla,*" Lord Carlingford had told her more than once. "Your mother learned that too late and I, myself, too early. While you—"

"I think I was born knowing it, Grandfather."

"Aye." His choleric blue eyes had softened. "Of that I'm certain. 'Twas in your mother's milk."

Sheila nodded agreement with the tall, white-haired man who occupied the darkness behind her eyes. She had grown to the age of eleven to the accompaniment of Lady Corbett's sighs—as she wrung her hands at Sir Matthew's frequent absences. These were rarely shorter than a month and generally ran to three or even four months with no more than a courtesy visit to his wife. He remained in London most of the time. His excuse was the Prince Regent, who demanded his presence there. His real purpose was to be with the mistress he had loved before his marriage, retaining and maintaining her in a Chelsea snuggery all the while he wooed Moira O'Neill, bedding her then wedding her when she was too ill to enjoy the wedding, unhappy Moira, not quite eighteen when Brian was born and gratefully dying at thirty-one. Ironically enough, Sir Matthew had succumbed the following year

along with his faithful mistress when his curricle over-
turned in the midst of a race with a wild young marquess.

Sheila straightened her shoulders and pulled her hood
over her windblown curls. In spite of her strong prejudice
against her father, she was glad she had inherited his
inches. Men were invariably indulgent to little women.
They petted them. She loathed that attitude and could
recall Sir Matthew on his brief sojourns at Dahna, patting
her mother's red-gold hair as one might stroke a favorite
dog! She glared at her brother's tumbled auburn locks. He
resembled their mother while she took after Sir Matthew,
at least in her dark hair and creamy skin. She preferred to
believe that her eyes were a legacy from her grandfather.
Sea-colored eyes, he had called them—blue at one moment
and gray at another. She stared into the water—gray, now,
under the massing clouds.

The wind was blowing more strongly, she realized and
shuddered slightly, remembering that a packet ship had
sunk with all hands and a full complement of passengers
not three months ago.

"Sheila, let us go forward," Sir Brian suddenly said.

"Not yet," she demurred. "You go."

"I'll not leave you behind." He frowned. "There are
too many looking at you."

"I did not notice that."

"You never do," he smiled. " 'Tis well I am with you,
for sure you'd get in trouble alone—not even your famous
set-downs would suffice in this crowd." He put an urging
hand on her arm. "Come along now, please."

"Do you not want to say farewell to the green hills and
the rocky coasts of Ireland?"

"I've said my farewells," he spoke a shade bitterly. "I
wish to fix my sights on our own country now."

"Your country," Sheila corrected quickly.

"I beg you'll not be so set against it," he pleaded. "Wait
until you know it better."

"As well as you do?" she inquired sweetly, and immediately regretted that taunt. "I am sorry, Brian," she said
contritely, putting a hand on his arm. " 'Twas no fault of

yours that your plans have been delayed. 'Twas not easy to find a manager as capable as you at Dahna. I do wish you'd share it with me."

He shook his head, saying firmly, " 'Tis time and past that I took on the reins of the manor, but we'll not dwell on that." His eyes, a greeny gold, gleamed. "First there's London and"—he winked—"Miss Letty Martyn waiting for you."

Sheila stuck out her tongue. "Why should I need a chaperone at twenty," she sniffed.

"You've been too free and easy in Galway—riding from Ennis Abbey to Spanish Point without even a groom to follow you. You'll be shocking the English, quite."

"Be careful how you describe *your* countrymen, dear brother."

"And yours," he reminded her, "for all you're an Irish landowner."

"Oh, my, I begin to think you hold that against me completely," she sighed.

He put an arm around her. "Of a truth I do not. If you can tease me, why may I not do the same to you?"

"You may, of course." She tweaked a lock of his hair, feeling relieved. She really adored Brian and did not like to think that their grandfather's will had erected a wall between them. After all, Lord Carlingford had bequeathed the larger part of his fortune to Brian. A slight smile curved her lips as she remembered that Brian was also her guardian until she reached her twenty-first birthday, which would take place as early as March. "If you insist," she continued, "we may go forward, though 'twill be a long time before our horizon will be filled with England."

"And a longer time before we see Erin again."

She did not argue, but nor did she intend to stay in England any longer than was absolutely necessary. However, she withheld that confidence. She had already dampened her brother's enthusiasm with her unavoidable mention of their grandfather's will. Brian loved Ireland as much as she did. The slight contempt with which he had overlaid the words "the English" strengthened an opinion she had long held. Brian, she was positive, shared her own prejudices against the country they would be visiting. However, he, with an English baronetcy, must suffer more from his divided loyalties than herself, who had no feeling for England at all. She had agreed to accompany him mainly because she had not wanted him to feel lonely while he was settling into his new estate—his new environment. She felt a lump in her throat, knowing that she would miss him once she was back at Dahna. However, there was no use borrowing trouble—time did not move that swiftly and they would be in England until her birthday, at least.

Brian plucked at her sleeve. "Come, then, my dear."

Standing in the prow of the small vessel peering into the misty distances, Brian said, "I wonder if Lord Rande will be in town."

"Ah!" Sheila exclaimed with a frown. "I wondered when you'd be mentioning him again."

"And why should I not mention him? 'Tis odd for you to have developed a prejudice against someone you've never met. He's an extremely well-spoken man. 'Tis a pity you were not at Dahna when he arrived."

"With his doxy at his side," Sheila commented tartly.

"She was a charming little bit o' muslin," Brian grinned. "Graceful, too. An opera dancer, unless I miss my guess."

"Papa's mistress came from the corps de ballet, if you'll remember."

" 'Tis not unusual. And he's nothing like Papa."

"How can you deliver any estimates of his character when you met him only once, when he came to purchase Balthazar?"

"I pride myself on the fact that I know character," Brian asserted. "Such address he had . . . and his garments were the very crack of fashion."

"His garments?" Sheila pounced. "Clothes make the man, then?"

Her brother favored her with a sulky look. "He dresses

in high style but not ostentatiously. 'Tis the cut of his coat.
I must know his tailor!''

"Why did you not inquire his name when Lord Rande
was there?''

"It would not have been seemly, but''—Brian's eyes
shone as he added eagerly—"he's invited me to call upon
him in London. I have his direction.''

"There! A golden opportunity. And what else do you
wish him to teach you? The art of catching a mistress?''

"Sheila!'' Brian sounded both shocked and reproving.
"I pray you'll put a bridle on your tongue when we're in
London. A young female should not express herself in that
forthright manner. You should not even know about such
things.''

"I am twenty and I have heard about mistresses since I
was nine!''

"Mama should not have confided in you,'' Brian said
indignantly.

"She needed a sympathetic ear and no arguments,''
Sheila reminded him, not without a trace of bitterness.
"She was not used to receiving that from gentlemen, and
though Grandfather was sympathetic enough, he was also
inclined to lecture her on the folly of encouraging Papa's
attentions when he'd strongly advised against it.''

"Still, she should not have filled you with her
prejudices.''

"She did not. I have my own,'' Sheila retorted.

"Well''—Brian produced a conciliating smile—"I
cannot blame you for them. And I am glad you are not
vulnerable like Mama. You'll not fall prey to a fortune
hunter, surely.''

"Or to anyone,'' Sheila declared. "I shall live alone in
single blessedness.''

"A most regrettable decision, ma'am, especially for so
beautiful a young lady, even with sea foam gilding her
brow.'' A tall, slender man in a three-caped coat turned
toward her. His teeth, very white against a sun-browned
visage, were exposed in a beaming and admiring smile.

Meeting Sheila's astounded and far-from-welcoming stare, he inclined his head. "I pray you'll excuse the liberty of my commenting on your statement, but I could not help overhearing you any more than I could refrain from producing an immediate rebuttal. My name, by the way, is Tennant, Jasper Tennant." His eyes, dark and brilliant, rested on Brian's lowering countenance. "I think I must be addressing your brother and again, sir, I apologize for my temerity. I hope you did not find my remarks too personal? I must add that I am rarely so impulsive."

"I would hope not, sir," Brian said coolly.

"I do apologize," Tennant repeated. "But 'tis a long and rather tedious voyage for those of us who must often travel to Ireland. I am always hopeful of being able to converse with my fellow passengers—if they will allow it. If you'd rather I absented myself, I shall withdraw immediately, never fear."

"No." Brian flushed. Much to Sheila's annoyance, he added, "I take it you are from London."

"From England," Tennant amplified. "I have a home in the country and a small house in Chelsea, which, as you know, is not far from London."

Sheila said, "I do find it very windy here. Shall we go below, Brian?"

Her brother regarded her in pained surprise. "To the *cabins*?"

"If you'd not mind."

"But I would," he responded. " 'Tis monstrous stuffy below, I'm sure of it. I would prefer to remain up here as long as possible."

"I feel that I have intruded," their new acquaintance remarked with a regretful look at Sheila.

She did not contradict him, but Brian said quickly, "Oh, no, sir, I assure you . . ."

"But I see that I have," Tennant insisted. "I should not have spoken out of turn. I beg that you'll excuse me." Bowing, he strode away quickly.

"My God, Sheila," Brian began, "you were not half-pleasant to him and he was very well-spoken."

Sheila glanced after him. "Did you think so?" she said coolly. "I found his comments far too personal. And I did not like his smile."

"I know a gentleman when I see one," Brian said stubbornly. "Did you notice his garb? I feel like a country bumpkin beside him."

"Oh, Brian," she said in some exasperation. "That is the second time you've measured a man by his dress."

"And by his address." Brian gave her a mischievous look. "But perhaps you are right. I expect he should not have praised you quite so highly upon such short acquaintance."

"On no acquaintance," Sheila said tartly.

"Well," he admitted, "that's true enough, but perhaps he could not contain himself. You are beautiful, you know. And at least he had the courtesy to take himself off."

She nodded and looked down at the swirling waters. She longed to inform her brother that it was through no fault of his that the stranger had departed. However, experience had taught her that Brian would not profit from her reproof. He would only resent her comments and would not scruple to remind her that she was twenty-three to her twenty and ought to be her mentor rather than the other way around. She also feared that he was still resentful over the will and that would render him considerably less receptive to her advice. She wished that her grandfather had left them the property jointly—wished, too, that Brian had accepted her offer to share it with him. She shook her head slightly recalling that he had turned bitter and loftily refused what he called "largess." And when scolded for that, he had turned the matter into a joke, saying that he sensed Lord Carlingford's restless spirit must come back to haunt him were he to accept his sister's offer.

"He prided himself on the fact that there were no family specters or even a banshee. Imagine how annoyed he'd be if he were summoned to assume that position himself? No, my dearest sister, let matters stand as they are."

Sheila lifted her gaze from the waves to the horizon, wondering anew what awaited her in England.

* * *

Though the breeze was steady and the waters of the Irish Sea less turbulent than they had anticipated, it was close on five when the packet docked at the Liverpool docks. By that time Sheila had ceased to question her future in England and was only pleased to set foot upon dry land and to breathe air which still carried the salty tang of the sea but which did not reek of the odors that had entered her nostrils when she had gone below to the large common cabin. Such had been her state of mind upon returning to the deck that she had lent a more than interested ear to Brian's suggestion that they purchase a yacht for future crossings. She could also agree that she was in no mood to cross back to Dublin in the near future. Though she had not been seasick, she was one of the few who had not succumbed to the motion of the vessel or to the sight of others less fortunate than herself. If she had remained any longer aboard the boat, she had no doubt that she, too, would have been dismally ill. She still felt slightly queasy and was inclined to seek the nearest hostelry rather than heed Brian's suggestion that they hire a hackney and find a comfortable inn.

At length, she yielded, for even with the hood shading her face and the cloak concealing her shape, she was aware of many interested glances and leers. She was equally aware that the streets were crowded with a preponderance of rough-looking men, many of them the worse for drink. Though her brother would be well able to protect her from one or even two of the louts, she decided that it was her turn to follow his lead rather than the other way around, as was generally the case.

"Now, is that not all right and tight?" Brian inquired, using his favorite expression, as they settled back in the comfortable post chaise with their own coachman, Paddy O'Shea, at the reins and Mickey, his son, acting as postboy.

"I never should have questioned you," his sister allowed, clinging tightly to the strap hanging by her window. "These streets are monstrous uneven and"—she wrinkled her nose—"I never did smell so much tar."

"Nor I, though I suppose I must have. My memories are a bit vague when it comes to this country."

"Not surprising when you were but four when we left it," Sheila murmured.

"Imagine not returning for nineteen years," he marveled.

"If London is anything like Liverpool, I would let another nineteen pass before I'd set foot in it again." Sheila rolled her eyes.

"Liverpool's no fit introduction to England, so says Sir Jasper Tennant."

Sheila said with a tinge of annoyance, "You've furthered your acquaintance, I see."

"We spoke briefly while you were below. He gave me his card. He's a pleasant fellow and very knowledgeable about London—not surprising, since he has lived there for the past eight years. I beg you'll not look down your nose at him, Sheila. 'Twill be helpful to have an acquaintance with him."

"As long as I am not inflicted with his company, I expect there's no harm in it," Sheila said. She could say nothing else, she reasoned. She could hardly tell Brian that she did not like the man. She had exchanged no more than a few words with him. Her prejudices were based on feelings alone. She had learned to trust these, but she could not explain anything so amorphous to her brother. His expression, she noted regretfully, was already sulky.

"You certainly do arrive at your conclusions hastily," he complained. "I happen to think that you are much . . ." Whatever else he was going to say by way of criticism was interrupted as the wheels of their vehicle hit a large pothole. He quickly put his arm around Sheila to save her from a jolting, and by the time they had reached a smoother stretch of road, his mind had leapt forward to lodgings for the night. "The Red Crown is considered a pleasant inn," he said.

Sheila decided against asking if he had received this information from Sir Jasper. Probably he had, and she could only pray that the baronet would not be joining them that night.

Her prayers were answered, and being bone-weary, she went to her room after no more than a bit of cold chicken and a dish of tea. She could wish that she had not dispensed with the services of Bridget, her abigail. Just before leaving, she had caught the girl lolling about half-tipsy, and with one of the grooms, in the stable loft.

Though she was fully capable of dressing and undressing, she was tired, dispirited, and though she hardly liked to dwell on it, regretful over her brother's decision to remain in a country she equated with her father's selfishness and her mother's misery. For reasons she could not quite fathom, Sir Jasper reminded her of Sir Matthew—perhaps it was only that they bore the same title. No, it went far deeper than that. Her father had been dark like Sir Jasper and he had had the same fixed gaze when confronting a woman—a woman who was not her mother. His glance had rarely fallen on poor little lovesick Moira O'Neill.

Sheila tugged angrily at her small buttons, succeeding only in ripping two of them off and rendering her traveling dress unfit for tomorrow's journey. The contents of the sewing box were, alas, a mystery to her, who had spent nearly every waking hour in the saddle or at her books. She would have to send for Bridget—because, tipsy or not, she needed her. She was glad that she had only left her behind rather than dismissing her out of hand. Perhaps it would be punishment enough to subject the girl to the crossing, though undoubtedly she would be drunk all the way. Sheila's thoughts ceased the minute she put her head on the pillow.

Sheila and Brian had often heard it said that Dublin was a miniature London. However, confronted with the city, she, at least, was in deep disagreement. She disliked the place on sight. It was too big, too crowded—the streets were so full of drays, wagons, lumbering coaches, post chaises, curricules, and even a sedan chair or two that they all moved at a snail's pace. Furthermore, it was very warm. September, it seemed, was a warm month in England. In Galway, fires were already glowing on hearths. Here she felt as if she might melt in her cloak and cotton gown! And the place was so noisy! The cries of street vendors and the plaints of beggars could be heard even above the horns of the coachmen and the whinnying of the horses as well as the clatter of wheels over stones and the cursing of, again, coachmen, their equipages stalled in streets that were never meant to suffer so steady a stream of traffic.

By the time they had reached their destination in Albe-marle Street, Sheila had forgotten the exigencies of their journey from Liverpool—the indifferent inns, the jostling of the carriage, the heat, the dust—and was ready to undertake it again . . . immediately! The experience of London was all the more difficult because she must needs keep her feelings to herself and furthermore must pay attention while her brother rhapsodized about the ugly city.

Of course, Brian was not dwelling on the noise or the traffic or the crowds. In essence he was already changing his countrified clothes for the garb of the man of fashion he aimed to be. He had praised Sir Jasper's tight unmentionables, his brocade waistcoat, his collection of gold fobs, and his admirably well-fitting coat. He had also spoken of his shining Hessian boots, champagne-polished to a high shine, with gold tassels looking as if they were new-minted. He had had other words of praise for his cloak and his curly-brimmed beaver hat, and wonder of wonders, Sir Jasper had also divulged the name of his tailor—so it would not be necessary to ask Lord Rande to be equally informative. Brian had confessed that he was glad of that, for he did not doubt that Lord Rande could vie a fellow a sharp set-down were he of a mind to do so.

This last comment had disturbed Sheila. She had not met Lord Rande, but he had bought Balthazar, which proved him an astute judge of horseflesh. The animal was not a showy steed, but for muscle and sinew, for strength and endurance, he was the prize of the lot at Dahna. According to Brian's description, the earl held himself aloof, and not only filled him with awe but elicited his respect.

Sir Jasper, on the other hand, had been far too fulsome and, in her estimation, too anxious to make friends with the naive young man from the country. Much as she loved Brian, she was fully aware that he lacked town polish as much as she did, but it was not her ambition to cut a dash in London society and mingle with the *ton*. She had but one friend in the city—Lady Farnall, who before her marriage had been Fiona McErney. Sheila smiled to herself. Until Fiona's marriage to Sir George Farnall, she had been violently anti-British and had soured the air with her curses once she learned that her elder brother, Sean, sent to Oxford instead of Dublin's Trinity College—and a fair shame that —was bringing a classmate home for the winter holiday.

"And will I not make him rue the moment he set foot on Irish soil," Fiona had vowed on the very morning of his arrival. That afternoon, as far as Sheila could discern, she had fallen madly in love with the vile enemy.

"They are not all the same," had been her defensive response to Sheila's teasing. She had added, "You yourself are part English, and you are my best friend."

It had been the first time Fiona had ever alluded to this deficiency. However, since her removal to London, her letters described several friendships formed among the "enemy," each reflecting a naïve surprise that, on their home ground, the English were actually tolerable.

Sheila's eyes gleamed with anticipation. She longed to see Fiona again. She had missed her lively chatter these two years past, and now Fiona was the mother of Timothy, who was a year old and, from all reports, adorable. She was eager to see Timothy. She loved children. That was the one problem in her decision not to wed. However, she reasoned, she could always be an aunt to her brother's brood, unless, of course, she found someone who did love her. But how could she ever be sure of that? The man in question would have to be richer than herself—but wealth was no guarantee. A rich man could be just as dazzled as a fortune hunter by her broad acres in Ireland. And if she were to wed an Englishman, they would come into his keeping. The same would be true if she were to marry one of her countrymen—Ireland *was* her country in spite of her father's heritage.

A hand was on her shoulder. "Sheila," Brian muttered.

"Yes." She gave him a startled glance.

"Lord, but you were far away, *macushla.*" He laughed. "Do you not wish to descend the stairs?"

"Stairs?"

"The stairs which Mickey has just put against the side of our chariot. We've arrived, do you see."

Sitting next to the curbside of the post chaise, Sheila looked up and out and saw a white-columned portico leading to a large square house of red brick, fronted by a square of garden and enclosed by an iron fence. On the street near the place where Paddy had brought the horses to a halt stood a pole bearing a gas lamp, a felicity not yet to be found in Dublin. Other than that, the dwelling looked no different than the elegant town houses of what she preferred to call her "native" city if not her birthplace. However, it was not a time to dwell on her patriotism or her prejudices.

Sheila climbed stiffly down the three steps held firmly by young Mickey O'Shea. His gaze grew worshipful as she thanked him both for his small service and because his freckled visage and mop of curly red hair was a comforting sight in this great city to which she had come so reluctantly and which filled her with an unexplainable foreboding. Probably there was no explanation save the fact that the house, standing there so solid and imposing, suggested permanency—as if, indeed, she were going to remain there rather than leaving after her requisite year in England. That, of course, was ridiculous. She would be back at Dahna in a matter of . . . twelve months, and the house did not belong to them, after all—it was hired only for the Season. The rest of the time would be spent at Corbett Manor.

"Only for the Season . . . only for the Season," the phrase danced through Sheila's mind as she and Brian entered the large hall on the ground floor to be met by a small slender lady with dark wavy hair, slightly streaked with gray, and big sparkling dark eyes. Back of her loomed the bulky form of Sean O'Flaherty, their butler, and with him were Kevin and Tim, the two footmen who, in company with Mrs. O'Malley, the cook, had come ahead to help put the house in order. There were two parlormaids from Dahna, Maggie and Grace, both young and evidently excited by their new quarters. There was also Mary, the abigail they had provided for Cousin Letty. Exchanging greetings with the staff, Sheila felt unexpectedly homesick and near to breaking into tears at the sight of these familiar faces in this distinctly unfamiliar setting. However, she could not because Cousin Letty, her English connection, was waiting to be greeted. Before she could open her mouth, however, Letty Martyn had come forward to reach up and hug her.

"My dearest Sheila, how you have grown, and into such a beauty! You'll have a grand success—and Brian, lad, if you are not the very image of your dear, dear mother, whom I did love. Oh, I am delighted to see you both—and in London at last!"

She fluttered from one to the other, standing on tiptoe to kiss Brian as well. "I have been on tenterhooks," she continued. "I have been imagining all sorts of mishaps, from the boat sinking to the carriage overturning, but the weather's been very clement, though one must always remember that there are squalls even in summer. Still, here you are, tired no doubt from the road and inns and I chattering like a magpie or, perhaps, a parrot when I should only say, 'Welcome, my dear cousins!' "

It was impossible not to like her. Prejudice faded in the wake of her exuberant greeting. Sheila smiled as she followed Miss Martyn up a swirl of stairs to the first floor and into a hall brightened by the light from a crystal chandelier. Standing on a console table was a huge bunch of roses charmingly arranged in a Chinese vase and reflected in a mirror.

"I do hope neither of you is afflicted with rose fever. I do love flowers and the roses are especially lovely this year." Miss Martyn looked a trifle anxious, as if, Sheila thought, she feared a scolding. She recalled that her cousin had, for the last twenty years, kept house for her brother, a vicar. Lord Carlingford had known her as a young girl, which was one of the reasons Sheila had decided to enlist her services as a companion and chaperone. She remembered her grandfather saying, "Of all your father's family, I think I like his cousin Letty Martyn the most. She once visited here with her brother, Jeffrey. He was a stern, joyless soul, but she fluttered about like a butterfly, a pretty and engaging little thing, as I recall, but much put down by the vicar."

She was still engaging, and Sheila regretted the touch of apprehension she read in a face that must once have been very pretty. She said, "The roses are lovely and so beautifully arranged."

Miss Martyn flushed with pleasure. "Do you think so? I am pleased but, of course, 'tis not difficult to arrange roses —they really do it themselves just by being what they are."

"'That could not be entirely true, Cousin Letty," Brian said.

Sheila was pleased. Brian could be obtuse on occasion, but in common with herself, he had taken the measure of their cousin and arrived at the same conclusion.

With a smile for Brian, Miss Martyn said, "My dears, you must be weary. Let me show you to your rooms. And I expect you will want to rest. You'll need a great deal of rest, for I am positive that two such glowing young people will be the toast of the town."

A sharp set-down quivered on Sheila's lips. She wanted to impress upon her cousin the fact that she, for one, would not be the least interested in partaking of town pleasures. Only Hyde Park beckoned and not at the fashionable hour of five, when, according to Fiona, the ladies of quality and that sinful sisterhood known collectively as the Fashional Impures were wont to fare forth in their carriages to see and be seen. She, Sheila Corbett, would exercise Aldebaran, her stallion, at five in the *morning!* Brian would probably ride with her. If he did not, it would not matter; she would go alone, as she had at Dahna. She sent a defiant look around the hall—she might have arrived in London, but her outlook remained unchanged. Her heart was and would forever remain in Ireland!

2

THE CLOAKROOM AT Almack's was not crowded at the late hour of nine—only two young ladies remained. The maid who presided could not make up her mind which was the prettier: the dazzling young matron in a gold silk that set off her ruddy locks to perfection and seemed to add its glow to her huge gray-green eyes—or her friend, a lovely brunette in turquoise blue trimmed with gold at hem and at the bodice, which was cut fashionably low.

Used as she was to the highborn young women who were granted vouchers to this most august of Assembly Halls, the maid could not help but be surprised by such a barrage of beauty. Most of the debutantes who crossed the threshold of the cloakroom were no more than passably presentable, however much the gentlemen might extol their charms. Generally, those charms lay in their dowries or their family connections. And, oddly enough, these two ladies seemed to be the best of friends, even though one of them wore a wedding ring! The maid grimaced. Were she married, she would not cultivate such a beauty for a friend. To the best of her knowledge, the sacrament of marriage did not blind a husband to the charms of another. A second later, she thought she had a reason for their obvious attachment. Their conversation had revealed that they were both Irish, and as everyone knew, the Irish were a different breed entirely—as witness the late Lady Hamilton!

"Oh, I am delighted to see you." Lady Fiona hugged Sheila and moved back, saying regretfully, "I am devastated that I was not in town last week when you first arrived. I should have designated myself your official guide. I expect you've seen everything by now."

"Not quite everything," Sheila said teasingly. "I have been to quite a few mantua makers and milliners and, of course, Cousin Letty insisted that Brian and I view the Tower of London, St. Paul's, and Hampton Court."

"Oh, dear, how dreadfully instructive." Lady Fiona wrinkled her small nose.

"We did not stay long," Sheila said in apology.

"Nor did I, I can assure you. Have you gone riding in the park?"

Sheila nodded and said crossly, "But with Paddy O'Shea guarding me. I would much prefer to go alone, at five in the morning, but I thought Cousin Letty would have a fit of the vapors when I suggested it."

"My dearest Sheila!" Lady Fiona put a small hand to her bodice. "You will see me in the same condition! This is not Dahna. You would be ostracized!"

Sheila's eyes glinted. "I know."

"Oh, dear, I can see you are spoiling for some mischief. Do promise to be good. But you are teasing, of course, are you not?"

Since Lady Fiona actually appeared anxious, Sheila said soothingly, if mendaciously, "Of course! I am not minded to set society by its collective ears."

"You should not be," Lady Fiona said on a breath of relief. "You have started out so well—with a voucher to Almack's within a week of your arrival. 'Tis quite amazing."

"I am told that 'twas because Papa was such a particular friend of the Prince Regent and"—Sheila grimaced—"thus English blood tells."

"Do not say it that way."

Sheila raised her eyebrows. "I was not aware of saying it any way."

"Ah, hah, you are giving me a set-down. Well, I shall not accept it from you," Lady Fiona giggled. "My . . . your fires are not quenched in the slightest—for all you are in the enemy camp!"

"Should you think they would be?"

"As to that, I am of two minds, and I think you must be also."

"Which mind would you prefer?"

"Well, there are English, and English, my love. You will see what I mean when you've been here longer. I hope you mean to stay in London for a long time."

"We are, as I wrote you, here in England for twelve months. We expect to be in London for the Season, but I do not think we'll spend all our time in the city. Brian's most anxious to see the country house."

"Let him go by himself," Lady Fiona exclaimed.

"My own curiosity would not allow that, and I do not believe we will be leaving London in any great hurry. Brian has just recently been accepted into Brooks."

"Oh, has he? And who is his sponsor?"

"Lord Rande."

"You'll never tell me that," Lady Fiona exclaimed.

"Do you know him?" Sheila inquired.

"I am slightly acquainted with the gentleman. George knows him better and likes him, I believe, in spite of his reputation."

"His reputation?" Sheila repeated. "Does he . . ."

"Sheila, my dearest, what are you about?" Miss Martyn hurried into the cloakroom. "You cannot spend the whole of the evening in here."

Sheila, her curiosity piqued, was inclined to remain behind with Lady Fiona but her friend said hastily, "Oh, dear, and I expect George will be wondering what happened to me." She fastened her gray-green gaze on Sheila's face and said in a voice pregnant with meaning, "We shall talk later—tomorrow, perhaps, if not this evening."

"We must." Sheila frowned. To her cousin, she continued, "Have you met Lady Farnall, Cousin Letty?"

"No, I have not had that pleasure." Miss Martyn smiled shyly. "And dear Sheila has mentioned you so often." She put out her hand.

Lady Fiona clasped it warmly. "She has mentioned you to me, too. I am glad we meet at last."

"And I . . . You will come to call, will you not?"

"Indeed, I shall."

"Gracious," Lady Fiona exclaimed, "I was near forgetting. Sheila, my love, you must want to waltz, do you not?"

"Oh, yes, I do love a waltz."

"Then, we will have to see Lady Jersey. You must have her permission or that of the dear Princess . . . but I really know Lady Jersey better. I see her over there near the door. She, by the way, knew and admired your father. Come!"

As she was being propelled toward the lady in question, a cold-eyed woman of an uncertain age and extremely dignified, Sheila felt very nervous. Her nervousness was not alleviated by Lady Jersey's chill inquiring stare. However, she listened graciously to Fiona's introduction, and some of her hauteur left her as she heard the mention of Sir Matthew's name. She had heard the Regent speak of him, she acknowledged—and he had been much cast down at his death. Shortly after this recollection, the coveted permission was grandly granted.

Dismissed from the august presence, Lady Fiona, releasing a caught breath said, "There, that's all right and tight. And I do not hesitate to predict that you will soon be surrounded. Come, love, I will take you back to Miss Martyn."

Joining that lady, Sheila followed Miss Martyn into a large room with a shining expanse of floor. Its ceiling was hung with a row of chandeliers. Tall windows, partially concealed by the flowing draperies that masked them from the curious gaze of pedestrians, rose on either side of the high platform containing the orchestra.

Sheila, with the beguiling strains of a waltz in her ears, found her foot tapping as she paused to watch what Miss Martyn breathlessly described as the "very cream of the *ton.*" She truly loved to dance and in the Assembly Rooms at Dublin she had always found partners eager to encourage her in this particular pastime. Momentarily forgetting her prejudices, she looked yearningly at the whirling dancers.

"Come, dear," Miss Martyn prompted, her gaze on the spindly chairs against the far wall where sat the chaperones and those young ladies who had not been claimed as partners.

Sheila would have gone with her, but before she had taken so much as a step toward that unhappy coterie, she was surrounded by gentlemen all eagerly demanding her as a partner. Going by the theory of first come, first served, she had promised a waltz to a tall, nice-looking youth whose name, Hazelwood, she inscribed on the spokes of her little ivory fan. Immediately following his request a country dance was promised to a Mr. Willoughby and she was entering Sir Bertram Ratliffe's name on a third spoke when Brian, in company with a tall, slim man, somewhat older than himself, pushed determinedly through the group around her. "My dear Sheila, here is Lord Rande, who has said he would like to make your acquaintance."

Sheila, glancing up, met amused eyes beneath dark winged brows. Their color was arresting—they were gray but seemed to have the sheen of silver. His gaze was singularly compelling, and for a moment she, much to her annoyance, could not look away. It was with something less than her usual composure that she said, "I am delighted, my lord."

"The delight is mine," he responded. He had a pleasant voice, deep and edged with that same amusement that sparkled in his eyes. "May I hope that I am not too late to claim a dance, Miss Corbett?"

"The next three are promised," she said.

"Oh." Brian appeared annoyed. "That is a shame."

"Not if your sister will put me down for the fourth. I think it is a quadrille. Our esteemed patronesses will always include more quadrilles and cotillions than waltzes."

It was on the tip of her tongue to tell him that there were waltzes as yet unclaimed, but that would have seemed forward and probably he was aware of it himself—his name was undoubtedly inscribed on someone else's fan. She contented herself with saying, "It is a shame they do not allow more waltzes," as she dutifully inscribed his name on the fourth spoke. She was immediately regretful for that statement, realizing that it sounded rather provocative.

"At this moment, Miss Corbett, I find that omission particularly regretful." Taking her hand, he pressed a brief kiss upon it. "I shall return immediately the quadrille is announced," he assured her, and moved away, Brian close behind him.

She looked after him. She had been rather confounded by his manner. Though he had been perfectly polite, she had had the distinct feeling that he had found her amusing —though why this should be she did not know. She also retained no clear image of his features—only his gray eyes remained in her mind. Recalling her interrupted conversation with Fiona, she wished she could find her friend and question her about his lordship's reputation, but that was impossible and, besides, Mr. Hazelwood was leading her out for the promised waltz.

The ballroom was warm and the waltz was followed swiftly by the cotillion, and after that came the country dance. To all intents and purposes, Sheila should have been winded, but once she was on the floor, such discomforts meant very little to her. As was her wont, she gave herself entirely to the music. Consequently, when Lord Rande came to claim her for the quadrille, she greeted him with a gaiety that appeared to surprise him.

"You seem to be enjoying yourself, Miss Corbett," he remarked as he led her toward the other couples already assembled for the dance.

"Oh, I am," she agreed. "I have been so much in the country of late that I'd half-forgotten the pleasures of the floor."

" 'The pleasures of the floor,' " he murmured. "That is most felicitously, not to say uniquely, expressed, Miss Corbett. And it is a revelation to hear such a sentiment expressed at Almack's. You must beware that Mrs. Drummond Burrell does not accuse you of enthusiasm.''

She caught a sardonic inflection in his speech, but before she could dwell on it, the music had begun. Lord Rande was a graceful dancer and he seemed to enjoy himself, but once the quadrille was at an end, he thanked her and relinquished her to her next partner with an alacrity that caused her to believe he had asked her to dance only to please her brother. She sent another searching look across the floor, but she did not see Fiona. Her friend must have gone home, she decided regretfully, and then she forthwith put Lord Rande out of her mind as another country dance was announced.

On the morning after the ball, Sheila slept late, awakening at noon to the timid knock of a much-chastened Bridget. ''Come,'' she called sleepily as the knock was repeated.

''If you please, Miss Sheila, 'tis herself who's wantin' to see you.''

''Herself? I pray that you'll be more explicit, please.''

''It's sorry I am, Miss Sheila,'' Bridget said nervously. '' 'Tis Miss Fiona . . . uh, Lady Farnall.''

''Oh.'' The mists of sleep dispersed like morning dew at the stroke of sunlight. ''Do show her in.''

''You'll not be comin' down?''

''Let her come up,'' Sheila said eagerly, not wanting to waste any time in dressing. ''And you may bring us both chocolate and rolls.''

''Yes, Miss Sheila, at once.'' Bridget withdrew.

Left alone, Sheila frowned. That her eagerness to see her friend was partially based on their interrupted conversation of the previous night was something she preferred not to admit even to herself. However, her curiosity concerning Lord Rande loomed as large in her mind as it had last night. On the way home, her brother had been very enthusiastic about his lordship. He had, affirmed Brian, done her a signal honor in asking her to dance. Sir William Caulfield, a new acquaintance, had told him that Rande seldom deigned to favor young females with his attentions.

"I must inscribe that in my journal," Sheila had answered caustically, "or I should, did I keep one."

Her response had annoyed him. "Lord Rande is my good friend. I hope you will keep that in mind."

"He is a bit old to serve in that capacity, is he not?" she had asked.

"He is not above thirty, which you cannot consider ancient."

"He seems older, and certainly he is far more sophisticated."

Brian had given her a sulky look. "Well, he has been here longer. He has not been spending his days on a blasted farm schooling a lot of horses."

"I thought you enjoyed that," Sheila had said.

"I did." Brian had turned away from her abruptly to stare out of the window at the dawn-touched sky. Over his shoulder he had added, "But 'twas a waste of time, after all. I would have been better off attending to my own concerns."

Sheila had not responded. She had been unable to think of a proper answer. Indeed, there was nothing she could say that would console Brian for the loss of Dahna. It had been a bitter blow. However, if he had not been so weary, she was sure he would not have mentioned it. To give credit where credit was due, he had been doing his best to write off that loss and concentrate on his English holdings. He had already visited the firm of solicitors patronized by Sir Matthew and soon he would be leaving for the country.

A knock on the door interrupted her thoughts. She glanced up eagerly. "Yes?"

Bridget opened the door. "Lady Farnall, Miss Sheila."

Fiona was garbed in a Nile-green walking dress of French washing silk that flattered her admirable coloring. It also demonstrated to Sheila that her friend had either acquired the coveted town polish or received some excellent advice from one who knew. Much as she adored Fiona, Sheila had early conceded that her sense of style had been sadly wanting. She had always favored bright colors that had clashed with her hair and she was far too addicted to showy jewelry. However, even as a compliment trembled on her lips, it was forgotten when Fiona said dramatically, "It is outside of enough and I pray you will find some way of giving him one of your most withering set-downs, for sure he deserves it. If I knew him better, I would tell him so myself, though George would not like it. The worst part of it's that other people heard him— gentlemen I mean—and 'twill be going the rounds!"

"What is?" Sheila demanded, postponing her questions concerning Lord Rande in favor of probing the mysteries of Fiona's outburst.

"A 'bucolic beauty'! That is how he described you."

"My dearest, do sit down and give me the name of this villain," Sheila begged.

"Lord Rande, of course. George told me and it has caught on. Oh, dear Sheila, I do hope you'll not take it too much to heart. At least, it means that you have captured the notice of the *ton* and will be in demand. And I do not think you are in the least countrified and certainly you did not seem so last night. I do not know how to account for his remarks, do you?"

"I do wish you'd begin at the beginning," Sheila said, pausing as Bridget came in with the requested repast. After the chocolate had been poured and the abigail sent down stairs, Sheila continued, "How did he happen to make this comment?"

"George said that a Mr. Hazelwood had remarked that he had danced with you and praised your beauty to Lord Rande, to which he readily agreed. He did readily agree, Sheila. George assured me of that. But then that horrid Lord Rande said, 'A bucolic beauty, indeed.' And, of course, they all laughed and called him a great wit."

"Lord, it does not take much to acquire such a reputation," Sheila commented coolly.

"No, it does not, at least among the English, who are not known for their sparkling repartee. But what could you have said to Lord Rande to elicit such a response— can you remember?"

"I can remember everything I said to him, and 'twas not much."

"Tell me!"

Fiona, her chin cupped in her hands and an intent expression in her eyes, listened closely as Sheila obliged. "And that was all?" she questioned. "Are you sure?"

"That was the whole of it." Sheila shrugged.

"I expect it was telling him that you *liked* to dance," Fiona said after some silent cogitation. "In his set no one really likes to do anything. They are all far too world-weary."

"An affectation, I am sure," Sheila commented caustically.

"Probably, though I believe Lord Rande might be war-weary. He fought both in the Peninsula and at Waterloo, and was decorated for bravery."

"Well, that's to his credit," Sheila acknowledged somewhat reluctantly. "However, you know something more about him. You mentioned his reputation last night . . . before my cousin came in. What did you mean?"

"I was referring to Brian, mainly. Lord Rande cannot be good company for him. From what I remember, dear Brian is often very easily influenced."

"That's true." Sheila frowned.

"Well, Lord Rande is a practiced gamester. He has won fortunes on the tables, and consequently, he might lead Brian into deep play. I cannot think he is as cautious or as cool as Lord Rande. You know he's been called the rakehell. And he did not earn that nickname lightly. He's very reckless. He rides fast horses and makes mad bets. He's often seen with Fashionable Impures. He once spent an entire evening in Harriette Wilson's box at the opera. He was half-drunk, I'm told, and they both laughed so loudly that the singers could scarce be heard. But 'tis not only courtesans he cultivates. Last year, Lord Meridan challenged him to a duel. That, I might tell you, does not happen very often because he's an expert swordsman and he's equally expert with pistols and—"

"Who won the duel?" Sheila interrupted.

"Oh, it did not come off. I imagine Lord Meridan changed his mind. I know his lady went to the country and has not been seen in polite circles since."

"Dear me . . . And has Lord Rande never been wed?"

Fiona shook her head. "The *on-dit* is that he was badly disappointed in his early youth and has had no respect for females ever since. 'Tis a well-known fact that no single woman's safe with him."

"Gracious, it seems I escaped very lightly," Sheila commented. "Though I do not imagine that even his enterprising lordship could seduce me on the dance floor."

"Sheila," Fiona exclaimed, "you must not be so outspoken."

"Not even in the company of my best friend?" Sheila regarded Fiona quizzically.

"Yes, of course with me, silly. But you'll certainly need to guard your tongue here among the English."

"You sound like Brian, who chastised me in practically the same terms," Sheila complained. "Neither of you seems to believe that I have any degree of common sense."

"Of course we do, my dearest, but you also have a quick temper and can be very impulsive upon occasion. Actually, though I first advised you to give Lord Rande a set-down, I think 'twould be better if you ignored his remark."

"I'd not give him the satisfaction of letting him know that it affected me, which it did not," Sheila assured her. "And I do not anticipate that we will be seeing much of each other."

"Probably not," Fiona agreed. "He runs mainly with the Prince Regent's set."

"Oh, dear, I could wish that Brian had never met him."

"Perhaps you could tell him . . . warn him, I mean . . ." Fiona said tentatively.

Sheila gave her an unhappy look. "I can tell him very little these days. I wrote you about Grandfather's will."

"Yes." Fiona regarded her worriedly. "But sure he cannot hold that against you. Certainly, he must have more common sense than that!"

"I expect that when he's settled on his own acres, he'll feel less resentful—at least I hope so."

"Oh, I am sure he will. Still, he ought to be warned about Lord Rande," Fiona said. "He's the last person who should be sponsoring Brian in society."

"I will make the effort to speak to him," Sheila sighed.

"I think you must, my dear—and as soon as possible."

Unfortunately for Sheila and Fiona, their well-laid plans had like those of the mouse in the poet Burns' poem already gone "agley." Even before Fiona had arrived, Sir Brian, notwithstanding the scant three hours' sleep he had had the previous night, was riding side by side with Lord Rande bound for a mill featuring one George Cooper, who had defeated the great or, rather, once-great Molyneux in a matter of a mere twenty minutes in March of 1815. If Sir Brian were a little sleepy, he had no intention of apprising his companion of that fact. That his lordship had deigned to invite him to watch the fight was an honor he had not anticipated. They were now riding over a narrow bridge, and since Rande was in the lead, Sir Brian had the opportunity of admiring his excellent seat on a horse as well as comparing his beautifully cut garments to his own, which, though he had patronized Sir Jasper's tailor, lacked the finish that marked those of the man in front of him. His admiration for Rande was in the ascendancy again, and if one were to stand Sir Jasper beside Lord Rande, the latter would definitely pale by comparison. He was almost in agreement with Sheila when it came to their shipboard acquaintance.

Thinking of Sheila, he was reminded of the main reason for his pleasure at Lord Rande's invitation. Since Rande was obviously wealthy, he could have no ulterior motives in cultivating Brian to ingratiate himself with Sheila. He was not dangling after an heiress. In fact, Rande had already made it abundantly clear that he had no interest in his sister. Brian's teeth showed in a pleased grin. He could guess Sheila's reaction when he informed her that Rande had dubbed her the "bucolic beauty." She would be hurt and angry, especially since she prided herself on her sophistication.

He had watched them last night. Even though they were both dark, they had looked well together. In fact, he had been quite concerned. It would not do for her to become interested in Lord Rande or in any other man. It was her intent to remain single, and that was one plan that pleased him greatly. Unfortunately, he was of the opinion that she would change her mind before she was much older. Still, as her guardian, he could forestall any such plans, at least until March. And who knows what the future would bring? He himself had several plans in mind for his sister. It only remained to select the one that must prove the most effective.

"Lord, man, what has occasioned such gloom?"

Brian glanced up hastily and found they had reached a broader stretch of road. Meeting his companion's inquiring glance, he said, "A sudden twinge in my shoulder. I was tossed from the back of one of our colts last year. I fell on my shoulder. It still aches at odd moments."

"Then, should we not seek an inn?"

"No," Brian quickly demurred. "I would not miss one moment of that fight—and I feel quite fit, really."

"You are sure?"

"Quite sure, my lord." Brian spurred his horse forward to catch up with him. He was pleased at Rande's evident concern. He was a very pleasant fellow and he had access to some equally pleasant little friends. When he got to know him better, he would ask him for an introduction to one of the girls in the corps de ballet at the King's Theater. An image of the charming little creature who had accompanied Rande to Dahna danced before his inner vision. It would be better if his lordship had tired of her. She was a real beauty, slim as a reed and with clusters of golden curls to frame a most bewitching countenance. She had gazed at her protector with her heart in her eyes, but those girls were not above entertaining other men in the absence of their "friends." Very likely, her adoration was predicated

on the sovereigns he poured into her lap. Two could play at
that game. Brian smiled, glad that his lordship could not
peer into his head. He stole a glance at him and found him
staring into the distance. He wondered jealously if Rande
were dwelling on the charms of the opera dancer—
Marie, he recalled her name was.

It would have surprised and discomfited him if he had
had the power to divine the thoughts of his companion, for
Rande was pondering on the look he had glimpsed on the
young man's countenance. It had not been one of pain.
Unless he were very much mistaken, Brian had been in a
fury. He wondered what had occasioned it. He did not
think that the anger was directed at himself, but neither
had he liked what he had read in the lad's face. He had
seen such expressions on the visages of the French soldiers
who had rushed at him in the thick of battle. He had no
doubt that their wild anger was mirrored on his own face
as he confronted them, but Brian's anger was more than
wild, it was murderous. He gave himself a little shake. He
doubted very much if this charming youth were bent on
murder.

Yet, almost defensively, his thoughts left Brian to center
briefly on his sister. She was a pretty girl, more than pretty
—quite lovely, even though he himself did not admire
dark-browed beauties. But her eyes were not dark, he
recalled. They were blue, the blue of deep rivers and moun-
tain lakes or loughs, as they were called in Ireland. Elsie
had had sky-colored eyes. He winced and substituted an
image of Marie, whose eyes were green. Better to think of
Marie, who did not activate the flames of an old desire, a
dead desire, he thought bitterly. Marie was as different
from Elsie and, he guessed, from Miss Corbett as night
from day. She was an adorable child, greedy in the way
that a child is greedy, giving kisses for comfits—the
comfits in question being a pair of diamond earrings or a
ruby necklace. He was glad he had convinced her that
rubies were too flashy for her delicate loveliness. She had
been just as pleased with the emeralds. He cast a glance
behind him to the bridge they had just quit. They were

leagues out of London and he felt a fool for desiring Marie as much as he did, wishing it were she who rode beside him, her dark hair caught by the wind and her dark, stormy blue eyes . . . but Marie was *fair*, he reminded himself angrily, fair, *green*-eyed and *golden*-haired, a condition she augmented with lemon and sunlight unless he were very much mistaken. Marie was enough—more than enough to satisfy his needs!

His dear friend Lord Byron had had the right idea, "Man's love is of man's life a thing apart; 'tis woman's whole existence," he had penned in *Childe Harold*. Lord Rande had another bitter smile for that and a sigh for Lord Byron, now gone to Italy, driven from England by public opinion coupled with his ridiculous ill-advised marriage to that beautiful statue of a woman, Anabella Milbanke, who, unlike the fabled Galatea, would never take on the semblance of life in anyone's arms. Byron had been a fool to wed her. Marriage was not for him, nor was it for himself!

"We must be nearing the place of the mill," Brian called. "I see a very large crowd assembled."

"Eh?" Lord Rande stared at him vaguely.

"The mill." Brian pointed.

"Oh, yes, the mill," he murmured.

"He's a coming man, I've heard. Tom Stokes, I mean, who'll be closing with Cooper."

"Yes, I have heard the same," Rande agreed. He was glad to be thinking about the match rather than Lord Byron and whoever else had been cluttering his mind. Yet, at the same time he was weary of these diversions, weary of mills and gambling and wenching. He needed a change. He thought of the Continent—of Vienna, Paris, and Rome safe for traveling now that Bonaparte was on Saint Helena.

"What did you say his weight was?" Brian pursued, and was rather discomfited by his companion's merry laughter as well as by his response.

"I would think he'd lost at least a stone."

"Do you mean he's out of condition?"

"Very much so, I would think," Lord Rande replied.

"Then, should I lay my blunt on Moore?"

"By all means, back the champion," Rande advised, coming down to earth and scanning Sir Brian's face, which was, he decided, most unlike that of his sister. He wondered whom she resembled, but it did not matter. She did not matter! He could not understand why she figured in his thoughts at all. She was beautiful, but there was a naïveté about her, an artlessness that, at this age, he could no longer appreciate. He had been right when he had termed her "bucolic." As for himself, he had reached a time in life when he much preferred the hothouse rose to the wild, blue-petaled Pimpernel!

3

ON THE WAY to the King's Theater, Brian was full of the mill he had attended last week with Lord Rande. He had talked of little else since it had taken place. And once more he was illustrating what must have been a very bloody combat with gestures and with descriptions that made his sister heartily grateful that she had not been a spectator at something that sounded more like willful slaughter than sport. As Sheila listened to him, her opinion of Lord Rande sank several more notches. She was extremely sorry that they would be seated in his box. She also wondered if, by the evening's end, his lordship would have thought of another adjective with which to characterize her appearance or would "bucolic beauty" suffice?

Though the description had been circulating only for the last week, it had already come to the attention of the cartoonists, and she had been depicted as an immense milkmaid in a country setting augmented by equally immense cows and chickens. She had brought the caricature to her brother's attention when he had mentioned the theater party. He had been surprised that she had heard it, saying kindly that he had hoped to keep her in ignorance both of the caricature and of the sentiment, which had been uttered when his lordship was in his cups. However, he also begged her to overlook the matter for this one evening when they would be Lord Rande's guests at a performance of Handel's *Alcina*. It was, he had explained, the closing night of the current opera season.

The fact that it was the closing night was what had prompted her to accept the invitation. She loved music, and being possessed of a singing voice herself, she was particularly fond of opera. Furthermore, she would be seeing and hearing it from a well-placed box, she was sure of that, recalling that his lordship's mistress danced in the corps de ballet at the King's Theater. Still, now that she was on her way to the Haymarket, she was filled with second thoughts. It was a lack of pride to accept his invitation, but unfortunately, it was also too late to turn back. Their carriage was caught in the crush of vehicles bound for the opera house. She frowned, annoyed with herself for having yielded to temptation. She had not only yielded to one temptation, she had decided to show his lordship that, bucolic or not, she could be as fashionable as anyone he was likely to meet in London!

Consequently, she had had a gown made for the occasion, not in her favorite blue, but of white lace over a pale-pink silk underdress, which her mantua maker had assured her was the very latest from Paris. At the last fitting, the lady had added several encomiums, clasping her hands over a full and palpitating bosom as she exclaimed, "Ah, but *mademoiselle est très, très belle!*" in an accent more redolent of Hammersmith than Paris.

Sheila had doubted her sincerity as one always must with a modiste. However, her abigail had been equally enthusiastic and so had Miss Letty. Brian, too, had joined in the praise, though he had commented that the lace looked as if it had been rather dear. He had frowned when she had admitted he was right. He had also said, though lightly, "As your guardian, I feel impelled to curtain your expenditures, my love, but as your brother, I must say you do look ravishing and 'twas worth every guinea you must have spent on it."

Sheila smiled to herself. If anyone required a guardian, it was Brian. She had expressed that particular sentiment and he had readily agreed with her, saying he knew full well that their grandfather had not expected to die within six months of making his will. "He was in the best of health when he had the notary to see him. And you must know that I am only teasing . . . I have no wish to assume the duties and vexations of a guardian.''

The post chaise drew to a stop—with Paddy explaining that he was as near to the opera house as he could get and that they must walk the rest of the way. Neither Sheila nor Brian dreamed of disputing him. Paddy O'Shea had been coachman to them since they were children. Dutifully, they clambered out of the carriage, and with little Mickey forcing a passage through the crowds, they reached the columned facade of the theater.

They were still hard put to find a way into the lobby, and then as they finally squeezed inside, a familiar voice said with considerable pleasure, ''But it is Sir Brian and Miss Corbett! Well met by moonlight, if I may paraphrase the bard.''

Sheila looked up and, recognizing Sir Jasper Tennant, said coolly, ''Good evening, sir.''

'' 'Tis a very good evening, ma'am, now that you and your brother have enhanced it. Will you be in the boxes or the pit?''

''We will be in the boxes,'' Brian replied. ''We are the guests of Lord Rande.''

''Ah, indeed?'' Sir Jasper raised his eyebrows. ''He is often here, a regular habitué of the opera, one might say.''

''Do you have an acquaintance with him?'' Brian asked.

Sir Jasper inclined his head. ''We have, shall I say, mutual friends, without being particularly close ourselves. But I must go. I hope I may come to see you during the interval?''

''Of course,'' Brian responded. ''We should be delighted.''

Sir Jasper's dark gaze was on Sheila's face. ''It is I who will be delighted—and may I say, I hope without offending you, Miss Corbett, that you are looking most beautiful this evening? Indeed, you outshine all others.''

''I thank you, Sir Jasper.'' She managed a smile.

''Rather I must thank you for adding to the glamour of the occasion.'' He bowed and moved away.

"Oh, I do not like him," Sheila muttered.

"Why not?" Brian stared at her in some surprise. "He was certainly complimentary."

"I prefer honesty to compliments."

"I think he was both."

"That, my dear, is why you cannot be my guardian," she admonished lightly and moved ahead of him.

Taking her place in the front of Lord Rande's box, Sheila had not expected that her second meeting with their host would be free of constraint, but fortunately she was not called upon to say much beyond their initial greeting, during which she had the satisfaction of seeing his lordship's eyes widen and what she privately characterized as a haughty look change to one of sincere appreciation. She was pleased about that. Her gown had been dear, but it had had the desired effect. She was rather sure that the earl could tell a French import from its domestic counterpart. Thus reassured that she did not appear countrified, she settled down in her chair while her brother conversed with Lord Rande.

She was very glad that she was not called upon to join their conversation. Aside from the resentment she was still experiencing, she was interested in her surroundings. The house was far more opulent than its one counterpart in Dublin, but it was not the paintings, the ornate plasterwork, or the statuary that claimed her attention, it was the audience. The boxes were full, and not all the occupants were from the upper echelon of society. Some ladies, glittering with jewels and surrounded by admiring gentlemen, were quite shamelessly dallying with them. Their gowns, she noted with a blush, were cut extremely low, exposing a great deal more of their bosoms than was seemly. Even as she looked, one young lady's plump breast popped out of its meager confinement. The girl laughed loudly and Sheila swallowed a gasp as she saw one of the gallants at her side return it to its silken nest. In looking away, she stared down and blushed as she met a battery of quizzing glasses turned on herself. Among the interested observers was Sir Jasper Tennant, who waved at her. She did not return the salute. She swiveled around hastily and met Lord Rande's silver gaze, now bright with amusement. Sheila wondered if he had observed her discomfort and put it down to her "bucolic" background.

He said, "Your brother tells me that 'tis your first time in this theater, Miss Corbett."

"Yes, it is, my lord." She felt it incumbent upon her to add, "It was very kind of you to invite me. I am particularly fond of Handel's music."

He seemed surprised. "Are you? I wish I could say the same. I find him rather repetitious."

Sheila's eyes glinted. "Well, he can be," she allowed. "But still there are passages which are heavenly, and they make up in some part for the endless repetitions."

"The endless repetitions, yes." His smile broadened.

Brian had heard the end of the conversation and he visited a quelling look upon Sheila. "My sister's not as well-acquainted with the opera as she is with plays," he observed in a deprecating tone of voice.

A hot denial sprang to her lips, but she swallowed it as Lord Rande said gently, "I have been happy to learn that your sister and I are quite in agreement of certain aspects of Handel's music."

"Oh, are you?" Brian flushed. "Well, I am happy to hear that. Sheila is fond of music."

"So she has been telling me. We share that fondness. I am indeed sorry that Madame Catalani is no longer in London. I feel that you would have enjoyed her in the role of Alcina."

"I am sure I should have." Sheila nodded. "We were in the country when she appeared in Dublin." She quelled an impulse to slip in the term "bucolic." She was enjoying the conversation and sensed the reference would only succeed in embarrassing him.

"That is a pity. 'Tis a most remarkable sound."

"My teacher used to speak of sound rather than voice. Have you studied music?" Sheila asked interestedly.

"Very little. I had an uncle who was musical and he gave me a few lessons on the pianoforte. I take it you have studied music."

"A bit." She nodded.

"Sheila has a very nice little voice." Brian's tone sounded patronizing to his sister's ears. She longed to give him a set-down he would remember, but now was not the time.

"So you sing," Lord Rande exclaimed. "I do hope that I will have the opportunity of hearing you, Miss Corbett."

She said with some constraint, "I sing mainly for my own pleasure, my lord. I am not sure that I could give the same to others."

"I have a distinct feeling that you are being more modest than truthful, Miss Corbett."

"You've not heard me, my lord."

"I am hoping to rectify that omission. Since I can play the pianoforte, I could accompany you if the selection you chose was not too difficult."

"Perhaps one day," she allowed, and hoped he would not be in any hurry to set a time. She was shy about her musical accomplishments. Only her friends had heard her, and while they were far more flattering than her brother, she was unsure of her ability and not anxious to make a fool of herself. Fortunately, the clamor in the house was dying down, for the orchestra had filed in and the opera was about to begin.

Madame Fodor was singing the title role, and at the interval Lord Rande told her that the prima donna had been compared favorably with Mrs. Billington, a popular artist who had disappointed a host of admirers by retiring in 1809. In the earl's opinion, Madame Fodor's top notes were shaky. He was less critical of the tenor Mr. Braham, who, he said, had started singing at the age of thirteen and, since he had made his debut in 1787, was now in the twenty-ninth year of his career. Lord Rande, who seemed to know the artist, added that he was a good man, not at all swell-headed or Italianate in his gestures. "Since the King's Theater is the home of Italian opera, you may even find the English members of the company speaking with an accent.''

It was not to be expected that Brian would take kindly to Lord Rande's discourse on an art he found not at all to his taste. He had listened with growing impatience, and as his lordship paused for breath, he said, ''Would you not care to walk out?''

Before Rande could answer, Sir Jasper Tennant had arrived. His greeting of his lordship was pleasant but cool, and Rande was equally cool. Despite all the warnings Sheila had heard in regard to her host, she was distinctly regretful to see him rise and courteously offer his chair to the new arrival. If he were a rake, he was still pleasant company, she decided, whereas she was hard put to produce so much as a smile for Sir Jasper, whose ways she found ever more insinuating and effusive. Brian, however, seemed uncommonly glad to see him, holding him in conversation for several minutes before Sir Jasper turned to Sheila inquiring, ''I hope you are enjoying yourself, Miss Corbett.''

''Very much so, sir,'' Sheila replied.

''My sister's fond of music,'' Brian said as if he were making an indictment. ''She sings ballads and selections from the opera as well.''

''Really? I, too, love music. I should like to hear you, Miss Corbett.''

''My brother omitted to mention that I sing only for my own pleasure,'' Sheila emphasized with a quelling look at Brian.

'' 'Twould also be for mine, I am sure. Your speaking voice falls very easily upon the ears.'' Sir Jasper's dark gaze lingered on her face.

''You are collecting quite an audience, my dear,'' Brian teased. ''First Lord Rande and then Sir Jasper. We must plan a musicale.''

''Lord Rande?'' Sir Jasper cocked an eyebrow. ''I had the distinct impression that his lordship favored Terpsichore over Euterpe.'' He glanced toward the stage. ''The situation of this box is particularly felicitous for the viewing of the ballet, especially now that the practice of amorous young gallants strolling upon the stage is in disfavor.''

Sheila, looking down, noticed for the first time that they were within two boxes of being directly over the stage. "He does seem to love music," she commented.

Sir Jasper smiled broadly and remarked, "I'd say he does not pay over twelve hundred guineas a season for the privilege of merely listening to the scraping of the violin, the blowing of horns, and the bleating of a few scruffy Italians."

"Twelve hundred guineas a season!" Sheila repeated. "That seems uncommonly dear."

"I'd vow he does not regret the outlay," Brian murmured.

"Not a bit of it," Sir Jasper agreed.

This mysterious exchange suddenly made sense to Sheila. She remembered Brian's hypothesis concerning the girl who had accompanied Lord Rande when he came to purchase Balthazar. Brian had said that she might be an opera dancer. She ought not to be surprised, she decided. The practice was widespread among nobles and gentry alike. It would be a very indifferent or homely dancer who needed to depend on the pittance paid by the theatrical management. Yet, she would have thought . . . She had no time to pursue that particular speculation, for Lord Rande returned, and immediately he sat down, the music resumed.

She would have quizzed Brian about the situation during the next interval, had they been left alone, but her brother left the box hastily and she accepted the earl's invitation to stroll along the corridor and thence to the Coffee Room, where he purchased a lemonade for her and a coffee for himself. As they stood there, Sheila was aware of many inquiring glances from men and women both, the latter being, she was amused to note, frankly envious. Lord Rande introduced her to several of those importunate ladies and to a few gentlemen as well, but such was the noise in the lobby that she was quite unable to hear, much less remember, the names of anyone. She was considerably relieved when, at last, they returned to the box.

"Ah," he commented as they took their seats, "your brother has not yet returned—he'd best hurry, else the fate of Alcina must remain a mystery to him."

"I expect he'll be back soon," Sheila assured him, feeling annoyed with Brian for this breach of conduct. Then, an imp of perversity stirred and she added, "Though I must admit that he is rather fonder of the ballet than the opera. Would you have a similar preference?"

"No, I find ballet pleasant to watch, but the opera is, to my mind, considerably more rewarding. Do you not agree?"

"Indeed, I do," she said, feeling slightly ashamed of herself for having voiced what he, fortunately, had not perceived to be a loaded question.

"In fact," Lord Rande began, but whatever else he might have said was muffled by the return of the orchestra.

Sheila, casting an annoyed glance at Brian's empty chair, reasoned that he would return for the ballet. He liked dancing or, more specifically, dancers. He, too, had been involved with an opera dancer—a certain Molly Gogarty, who displayed her shapely limbs on the stage of Dublin's Theater Royal. Their grandfather had been quite distressed over what proved to be a very short-lived attraction. Sheila did not doubt that Brian would find other similar attractions before he was ready to settle down. She stopped thinking about him and gave herself up to the enjoyment of the music.

Sir Jasper arrived at the box only moments after the opera ended. Sheila, in the midst of applauding and agreeing with Lord Rande that Madame Fodor had astonished her by a truly astounding display of vocal pyrotechnics during her final scene, saw him with regret. She was even more regretful when the earl immediately rose and gave his seat to Sir Jasper. Until that moment, it had seemed to her that he intended to remain and converse with her, a circumstance that would have pleased her far more than listening to Sir Jasper's stream of compliments.

Her attention wandering, she noted Rande among the visitors to the box of a lady; she could not have been the notorious Harriette Wilson, since she was well on in years and, judging from the number of obviously high-ranking men and women about her, a person of considerable distinction. She was quite heavyset, but, Sheila guessed, she must have been a great beauty in her youth. She also noted that Lord Rande was enthusiastically greeted both by the coterie surrounding her and by the lady herself. She also guessed that he was fond of her. His attitude was most attentive and several times he said something that caused her to laugh and tap him playfully on the arm with her folded fan. Sheila doubted that Sir Jasper would have spent two minutes conversing with a woman so advanced in years. Truly, there were facets to the earl that she could approve, even though his response to her still rankled and for reasons she would as lief not consider.

"Do you not agree, Miss Corbett?" Sir Jasper inquired.

Sheila turned and felt her cheeks grow warm. She had no idea what he had said. "I beg your pardon, Sir Jasper," she murmured. "The heat in here . . . I fear my attention wandered."

There was a frown between his eyes, but it vanished quickly. "It is indeed warm, Miss Corbett. Fortunately, the ballet will be of short duration and you will be able to leave. I hope we can meet soon again." He bent over her hand.

Embarrassment moved her to reply, "It is my hope, too, Sir Jasper."

His eyes gleamed. "And one I can gratify, Miss Corbett, and will as soon as possible. Until then, I bid you good evening."

"Good evening, Sir Jasper." Sheila managed a smile as he left, but with a sigh to follow. He would not, she knew, have been pleased had he seen her press the back of her hand to her gown to wipe away the moisture left by his kiss.

A second later, Brian returned, putting her thoughts to flight. "Where were you?" she demanded edgily. "I must think you sadly wanting in manners to have remained away during the whole of the final act.''

"Lord." Brian rolled his eyes. "Would you have had me suffering through that caterwauling, and in a language I could not understand?"

She regarded him quizzically. "You speak as if you'd never heard an opera before," she chided. "As you are quite aware, they are nearly all in Italian."

"That does not mean I have to like them," he retorted.

She saw no use in reminding him that he had liked opera tolerably well until this evening. He was obviously in one of his contrary moods. "Where did you go?" she asked.

"I went out for a breath of air. The theater's monstrous warm. 'Tis a wonder they keep it open so far into August."

" 'Tis only the tenth. I've heard it usually closes on the fifteenth of the month."

"Ah, then we should really be stifled. And where's our host? Was he so discourteous as to leave you all alone?"

She heard a taunting note in his voice that annoyed her. "I was not alone. Sir Jasper was here to entertain me."

"But you did not entertain him and so he left?"

She had never felt quite so out of accord with Brian, and obviously his mood matched her own. Indeed, he was extremely edgy. It occurred to her that he was not being truthful with her. She also had the impression that, rather than wandering about downstairs, he might have had a specific destination in mind. However, before she could speculate further, their host returned.

"Ah, Sir Brian, I was thinking we'd lost you," Lord Rande said lightly.

"I was uncommon warm," Brian explained.

Lord Rande nodded. "Yes, it is a bit heavy in here this evening. Lady Melbourne told me that she'll not return for the ballet, but I hope you are not of her mind?"

"Oh, no," Brian said eagerly. "Vestris is dancing. I have always admired her. Is there a chance we might go to the Green Room to meet her after the performance?"

"If you wish," Lord Rande said.

Sheila had managed not to reveal her surprise at Brian's statement. To her certain knowledge, he had never seen Eliza Vestris dance. He must have another reason for wanting to go backstage, one he chose not to divulge. As for herself, she would have preferred to follow the example of Lady Melbourne. She glanced across the house and saw that the elderly woman to whom Lord Rande had been speaking had gone and felt a little thrill of excitement. Lady Melbourne's fame had crossed the Irish Sea. Who had not heard of her notorious daughter-in-law, Lady Caroline Lamb, and of her own friendship with Lord Byron, whose involvement with the same Lady Caroline had rocked British society. Sheila, who had devoured the poet's works, quite longed to ask her host if he knew Byron, gone from Britain's shores, some said, forever. It was a pity to have missed a possible sight of him by no more than six months!

"My dear Miss Corbett," Lord Rande said, "you seem very pensive. I hope 'tis not the company."

She regarded him in some surprise. "Oh, no! I was only thinking of Lord Byron. 'Twas your mention of Lady Melbourne brought him to mind."

"Ah, many ladies turn pensive at the thought of Byron. Are you an admirer of his verse?"

It seemed to her that he was teasing her. However, she said staunchly, "I am. However, I must admit that I cannot like all of it. Some is beautifully lyrical, though."

"And some," he smiled, "is a trifle tortured." Clearing his throat, he declaimed:

"If changing cheek and scorching vein
Lips taught to writhe and not complain.
If bursting heart and madd'ning brain
And daring deed, and vengeful steel
And all that I have felt and feel
Betoken love—that love was mine . . ."

On finishing that glib quotation he added, "Am I wrong in assuming that such extravagance is not entirely to your taste?"

She laughed. "No, indeed, you are not wrong. I do not know that particular passage, but I do find it exceedingly overwrought. Still there is much charm and wit to be found in his poetry."

"Indeed there is," he agreed. He looked as if he might have something more to say but he was silenced by the lifting of the curtain and the wild applause as the darkly lovely and incredibly graceful little Eliza Vestris came tripping on stage, surrounded by a bevy of equally lovely nymphs—one of which, a slender blond girl, slight of figure and very graceful, raised huge eyes in the direction of Lord Rande's box. Sheila read distress written large on her countenance, and wondered at it. Then, she whirled away, following the patterns of the dance. It was impossible, however, not to note how very often her gaze returned to that box.

Sheila sighed and was immediately annoyed with herself for the regret that had occasioned her reaction. She knew Lord Rande was involved with an opera dancer, had known it for months. It was ridiculous to wish . . . But she preferred not to dwell on her wishes in this particular matter. She did not hope that the evening would come to an end soon. She did not believe she wanted to see Lord Rande again and prayed that her brother would not insist upon it.

She fastened her eyes on the charming Miss Vestris, who was known to sing as well as she danced, and had, earlier this season, undertaken the role of Susanna in *The Marriage of Figaro*. However, she could not keep her mind on the dancer. It *was* uncommonly warm in the theater. She would have liked to follow her brother's example and take a stroll outside. She longed to be alone and smiled wryly. Only certain types of women walked the London streets alone. Not for the first time, she wished she might have been born a man. Men were free to do as they chose—women were very little more than bond-servants. If only the ballet would end and the evening with it, but she recalled regretfully, they were going backstage. Obviously, Brian had an eye on some graceful member of the corps de ballet—and she would be hearing about her charms *ad infinitum* until he tired of the chit. She wondered, too, how long Lord Rande had been involved with the golden beauty on stage. A second later, she was angrily wondering why she was wondering! If he had been the dancer's protector for ten months or ten years, it could make no difference to her! Her head had begun to throb and she wished once more that the ballet would end. She guessed that the dancers might share that desire. From where she sat, she could see that their faces were streaming with perspiration and that their flimsy gowns were plastered against their bodies. Poor things, they ought to be spared the crowd of visitors who would be besieging them directly the curtain fell. If she had the opportunity, she would draw Brian's attention to that fact. She would also mention that she had developed a bad headache.

Any hope that she could inveigle her brother into taking her home was flouted by his rapt expression as the dancers made their bows. His heart, she could tell, was set on going backstage. He would not rest until he had, and were she to protest, he would be in a dreadful mood for the rest of the night and on into the morrow. Since she was in no state of mind to contend with his humors, she swallowed her protests. The curtain had not been down half a second when Brian reminded their host of his promise.

With an indulgent smile, Lord Rande nodded. He, Sheila guessed, was even more eager than Brian to repair to the Green Room. He did have the grace to ask Sheila if she minded going back with them.

Aware of Brian's compelling stare, she said, "No, not in the least. It might prove very interesting. I have never been in a Green Room."

"Ah, then you do have an experience of sorts awaiting you," he commented. "But I warn you . . . the magic is snuffed out with the footlights."

"I should think it would be. They must be very weary."

"They are, but they'll not be unwelcoming. Adulation is meat and drink to a performer." He offered her his arm, adding, "You'd best stay close to me, Miss Corbett. There will be a crush when we arrive."

"I thank you, my lord." Sheila, taking his arm, found herself flushing and hoped he had not noticed. If he had, no doubt he would attribute it to the heat, which seemed to have grown even more intense since the curtain had descended. However, she reasoned, he would not notice for, in common with Brian, his mind was fixed on the delights he expected to encounter in the Green Room.

The walls of the Green Room were actually green. Lord Rande obligingly explained the reason for that hue. " 'Tis for the comfort of the actors whose eyes are weary from the stage lights."

The area, oblong in shape and quite large, was extremely crowded. In addition to those members of the audience who had come back, there were also the relatives of the performers and some of the singers and dancers, too. On seeing them, Sheila found that they were quite a bit older than they had seemed on stage. Mr. Braham, for instance, had amazed her with his youthful appearance in *Alcina,* but off stage he looked a good forty-two and even more. She did not immediately spot the dancers and guessed that they must still be in their dressing rooms. Brian, too, had disappeared. Probably he was lingering near the small door that, Lord Rande had explained, opened onto the corridor containing the dressing rooms. She wondered which of the dancers had taken her brother's eye. Molly Gogarty, she recalled, had been almost as fair as Lord Rande's dancer. Sheila suddenly turned cold as she recalled the praise Brian had lavished on her. Yet, she could not imagine that Brian would have the audacity to pursue one who was committed to a man he called friend as well as host, unless he had originally had an ulterior motive in cultivating his lordship. Brian, unfortunately, could be quite ruthless when it came to attaining his ends.

Molly Gogarty, she recalled, had been kept by one Shamus O'Rorke, a well-known pugilist who had waxed quite ugly when her brother had dared to flirt with Molly.

He had gone as far as to threaten Brian, who had forthwith spoken with a justice of the peace—with the result that poor Mr. O'Rorke had been transported to New South Wales. Sheila had remonstrated with him, whereupon Brian had insisted that the man was dangerous and his threats had embraced her as well as himself.

She loosed a quavering breath, wondering why she had suddenly remembered that episode. At the time, she had preferred to believe that Brian had been speaking the truth, but she had had doubts, even though Molly Gogarty had seemed to welcome his attentions. Tonight, the little dancer had seemed distressed, but of course, one could have nothing to do with the other. She was, she decided, only borrowing trouble.

"My dear Miss Corbett, I fear you are in danger of being trampled here," Lord Rande said. "Let us find a place near the wall."

"I thank you . . ." She let him lead her to the spot in question and once more she scanned the crowds, still not finding Brian. "I cannot imagine where my brother has gone," she said concernedly.

"Oh, no doubt he'll pop to the surface soon enough," he said. "If he does not, I will send out an alarm."

"You are teasing me," she accused.

"I admit it. You are, I think, teasable. Most serious people are."

"Oh, dear." Sheila made a little moue. "Do I seem serious to you, then?"

"If you do, 'tis not a fault, Miss Corbett, nor was it meant as a criticism. You seem a lady of many moods, however. I cannot believe I am wrong about that."

There was an intensity to his tone that surprised him. She had suspected him of whiling away the time until his opera dancer appeared by dallying with her, but on looking up, she found his gaze matched his tone. He had offered an observation, she recalled. She said, "I expect that all of us are creatures of moods, my lord."

"Some more than others, I think. And I find . . ." He paused, startled as a girl cried shrilly, "But, monsieur, I pray zat you do not me follow . . . I 'ave tol' you . . . you are very *méchant* . . ."

"Damme," Lord Rande muttered, and turning, looked toward the small door he had mentioned to Sheila. "Marie," he called, starting forward.

"Oh, *mon chéri,* I am here . . . and *cet homme* . . . this man . . . I 'ave tol' 'im *c'est impossible,* but he me does not listen to . . ."

"Oh, Lord, I beg you'll not make a Cheltenham tragedy out of this!"

Sheila tensed, recognizing Brian's voice. She had not been mistaken. He had stupidly dared to press his attentions on the little dancer. He must have frightened her badly, else she would not have made such an outcry. Sheila could well imagine that Brian, intent on the gratifying of his wishes, would not have considered the effect he had on the girl. The room, she noted miserably, had grown very silent and all eyes were turned in the direction of the doorway, where the dancer, still in her costume, stood with Brian behind her, a hand on her shoulder.

"If you will excuse me, Miss Corbett," Lord Rande murmured, moving away from her.

"Of course," she said woodenly, wishing that she might sink through the floor.

Then there was a rustle and a stepping aside as Lord Rande started toward the couple. He did not walk hurriedly. Instead, he strolled up to the pair, and looking down at the tearful little dancer, he said casually, "But what is amiss, my dear?"

Brian began, "She seems to think—" The words died on his lips as he received an icy stare from Lord Rande.

"I believe I addressed Miss Hiver," he said.

"But . . ." Brian began and paused as with a rush of words, the dancer cried, " 'E came back, *mon ami* . . . me, I am alone and . . . and 'e try to . . . but I say 'tis impossible . . . and now . . . he comes again and—"

"Enough, my dear," Lord Rande said. "I understand."

"You do not understand. I thought—" Brian blurted.

"Please." Lord Rande lifted his hand. He looked at the

girl and then removed his evening cloak and handed it to her. "I think we must go now, my dear. You can remove your makeup later."

Hiver meant winter, Sheila thought. Mademoiselle Winter was her name, but the cold was emanating from Lord Rande. She could not see his eyes, but she had seen them and could compare them to twin icicles. She was aware of a strange little pain at the base of her throat and also a throbbing.

"*Mon ami.*" The dancer looked up at Lord Rande. "I wish to leave . . . *vite, vite* . . ."

"Yes, we will leave quickly, my dear," Lord Rande assured her.

"Now!" she urged.

"In a minute, *ma belle.*" His eyes fell on Brian's flushed face. "Because you were my guest, I will not call you out, or rather, let us say that for your sister's sake, I shall refrain from exercising my prerogatives in this matter, but I do not expect that we will meet again, Sir Brian." Slipping his arm around the dancer's shoulders, he drew her out of the room.

There was a moment of silence and then laughter swiftly followed in Brian's wake as he strode toward Sheila. His face was flushed and his eyes bright with fury. "I charge you," he muttered. "Do not say anything. I do not want to hear a catalog of my errors—just come with me."

She nodded and let him escort her into the corridor and thence to the stage door.

"Paddy will be in the front of the building," Brian said between his teeth. He took her arm, holding it in a painful grip. "Do you understand that I do not wish to hear any reference to this incident—not tonight, not ever?"

"I understand," Sheila told him over the myriads of words piled on her tongue. Leading them all was one that if she had spoken it aloud at that moment, must have sounded like an epithet. It was "Folly."

4

"OH, I DO wish I had been there," Fiona breathed, looking at Sheila with wide eyes. "We had intended to go to the last night of the opera, but George's sister was ill and so we went to the country instead. I was never so disappointed. Everybody attends the final night, no matter what the offering." She shook her head and then added solemnly, "Brian had a narrow escape. Lord Rande is deadly with his pistols."

"Brian was a fool!" Sheila, seated in her friend's pretty, cretonne-hung back parlor, glared at an unoffending chrysanthemum, part of a border painted on the wallpaper. In her mind, she was reliving the scene in the Green Room, now some five days back in time but still fresh in her memory. She continued indignantly, "Imagine laying siege to that girl in her dressing room and he knowing full well that she was Lord Rande's mistress!"

"Oh, well," Fiona said dismissively, "he's young."

"He is two years older than you," Sheila pointed out, "thought not half so intelligent. I begin to think him sadly wanting in the upper story."

She received a narrow look from her friend. "I've never known you to be in such a pet, my love. If this Marie's as beautiful as you seem to believe, 'tis not unnatural that the sight of her would turn Brian's head."

"You've always had a soft spot for my brother." Sheila rose and took a turn around the room.

"And you have not? When I quit Ireland, you and Brian were much in sympathy."

"Brian's changed." Sheila frowned. " 'Twas Grand-father's will, I know it."

"Oh, my dear, surely you are mistaken." Fiona raised distressed eyes. "He is wealthy in his own right."

"And bound on losing the lot. I have warned him . . . and he tells me that he is my guardian, not the other way around."

"He cannot take that stipulation seriously! He must be teasing you." Fiona laughed.

"I expect he is, but be that as it may—have you found out anything about Sir Jasper Tennant?"

Fiona shook her head. "I asked George directly I received your note, but he's of little use. He never frequents Brooks or Boodles. He prefers the House of Commons and listening to those interminable speeches. However, he has promised he will make further inquiries, though I should not count on it, my love. He will probably forget."

"Oh, dear, I wish he might have been more informative. However, I cannot believe I am wrong about him."

"And I, my dearest, cannot think you are any proper judge of character. You did like Lord Rande, and after all I have told you!" She added inconsequentially, "That blue lutestring is particularly becoming on you."

"I beg you will stick to the point," Sheila said impatiently. "Are you so sure that all you have heard about Lord Rande is true?"

"I could tell you any number of poor little moths who've singed their wings in his flame. Talk about Byron and the Lamb, they are two of a kind, my angel."

"One has heard that Lady Caroline's downfall was of her own engineering."

Fiona sighed. "I was forgetting that you had a penchant for Byron, too. My love, I cannot say that I am sorry your acquaintance with Lord Rande has been cut short. You are a babe in the woods when it comes to these London bucks, and I am moved to remind you what Rande said about you."

"I assure you I have not forgotten that, but on speaking

to him at the opera, he seemed much different than I had expected. And he appears to be very well-liked, too. Lady Melbourne—''

"Lady Melbourne!" Fiona exclaimed. "My love, that woman has a soft spot for all handsome men. In her youth she was even more accommodating. 'Tis said that her son, William, who is unfortunately wed to Lady Caroline, is the image of his father, Lord Egremont, with whom Lady Melbourne enjoyed a long liaison before changing to Wyndham . . .''

"You cannot be sure of that."

"Ah, you'll defend even the scandalous Lady Melbourne, poor Sheila. I am sorry. You have met so many gentlemen . . . Imagine, this is the first free moment you could spare for poor me—what with your rides in the park and routs and whatever. Do none of these equal Lord Rande in your eyes?''

Sheila glared at her. "I am *not* in love with Lord Rande, if that is what you are suggesting. I found him different than I'd expected, different than you'd led me to believe, that is all.''

"And that, my dear love, is why he is so dangerous," Fiona said sagely. "I am told he wears many faces and can charm any female he chooses to favor. Indeed, I am glad this contretemps took place. I cannot believe him fit company for either you or Brian!''

"I expect you are right," Sheila conceded reluctantly. "I have been told he is a gamester and a rake—by others also. But I cannot believe that Sir Jasper Tennant is the sort of individual Brian should call his best friend in London. He's taken him to so many hells.''

"But you say that Brian his won," Fiona pointed out.

"That winning streak cannot last forever. And what strikes me as strange is that Brian insists that Sir Jasper has given him pointers on how to win at piquet and has himself lost to Brian. 'Tis not often the teacher is so soon bested by the pupil. I cannot help but fear that he has an ulterior motive.''

* * *

Had she but known it, Sheila's feelings concerning Sir Jasper were being echoed some eight hours later to Lord Rande as, on entering Brooks, he was hailed by Lord Paxton, one of his close friends. "I vow, Ivor, you'll receive no thanks here for having loosed that Irish cub upon these premises."

Rande's glance was frosty as he asked, "What's amiss?"

"He's in the card room and looks half-drunk to me. Furthermore, he's challenging all and sundry to a game of piquet. When he's refused, he accuses them of being afraid of what he calls the Corbett Luck."

"And have none of those accused responded with a challenge of a different nature?"

"Bless you, no!" Paxton laughed. "They're all aware that he's one of Tennant's sheep."

"Tennant . . ." Lord Rande frowned. " 'Tis a great pity he still has access to this club."

"And to young Corbett, I agree. I know you've no cause to love him, but still, he is a bit of an innocent. I hope the lad doesn't land in the Marshalsea like Sir Humphrey Laidlow. And there was poor young Fosdick, who blew his brains out. He'd have been better advised to turn the pistol on Sir Jasper."

" 'Tis a great pity that the Prince still finds him amusing," Lord Rande remarked.

"He's always had a fondness for loose screws. In my father's day it was Sir John Lade and that wife of his, Letty. Ugly as sin she was, and with a mouth like a sewer. She'd been the mistress of Sixteen-string Jack, the highwayman who finished on a rope at Tyburn."

"I know." Lord Rande nodded. "And 'tis where Sir Jasper ought to finish, too. He's a highwayman of another sort."

"Indeed—and 'tis my opinion Tennant will soon close in and lead this young lamb to slaughter. It's too bad you couldn't drop a word in his ear."

"I doubt if he'd accept my words, even were I inclined to spend them in his cause." Lord Rande shrugged.

"I know. He repaid you ill for all your kindness. The

thing of it is that Tennant's got an eye on the sister, too. She's an heiress with a very comfortable fortune and—''

"I know the sister." Lord Rande frowned again.

"I, too." Paxton's eyes brightened. "I rode with her and her cousin, Miss Martyn, in the park yesterday. She has a splendid seat on a horse and she is beautiful. It's times like these that I could wish I were not burdened with a wife."

"I have never noticed that you found that particular weight too heavy. You and your Lucy have caused me to conclude that not all marriages are made in the counting-house."

"Confound it, Ivor." Lord Paxton flushed. "Yes, I love the wench, but 'tis not fashionable to prate about it. And I could wish she were not in Scotland visiting her mother."

"Ah, that is why you went riding with the fair Miss Corbett?"

"And her cousin," Lord Paxton said. "I have some small acquaintance with the family."

"Yet, not enough to drop a few words of wisdom in the brother's ear?"

"No, others have done so . . . but he's bent on trying his wings."

"And like Icarus ventures too near the sun?"

"I look for the wax that bonds his feathers to be melting soon," Lord Paxton sighed. "I expect you are in no frame of mind to say anything?"

"As I have told you, I doubt he'd listen to me were I of a mind to do as you ask, which I am not. What he needs is an object lesson."

"Which he will receive from Sir Jasper, I have no doubt. He's a bad man."

"Water seeks its own level." Lord Rande shrugged. "I will bid you good evening, John—and try my luck." So saying, Lord Rande strolled into the card room.

The tables in the long salon at Brooks were not quite full. It was early in the evening and consequently Brian could sit alone at a table near the fireplace, a pack of cards in front of him, a wineglass and bottle reflecting the flickering flame of a candle in a tall holder. To his left was a candelabrum, its five tapers as yet unlighted, their wicks still a pristine white suggesting that the would-be gambler had not yet found anyone to meet his challenge.

That he had been drinking was evident. His eyes were unnaturally bright and his face was flushed. Evidently, Rande decided, Sir Jasper had failed to inform his pupil and protégé that though cards and wine might be a heady mixture, they were not a healthy one for the serious gamester.

Several people murmured a greeting as Rande entered. He had not expected that Brian would form one of that company, but much to his surprise, the young man waved a hand at him, calling in a slightly slurred tone of voice, "Ah, Rande, what do *you* say to a game of piquet?"

Rande heard an explosion of laughter from one table and muttering from another. Aware that the opera incident had gone the rounds, he gathered that some of the assembled players were as surprised as himself at the invitation. He stepped to Brian's side and stood looking quizzically down at him. "You are challenging me?" he asked.

Brian regarded him with no little defiance as he said, "I have been told that you are an expert player."

"I'd not say that," Rande murmured. "I have had some luck, however."

"And so have I," Brian smiled. "A great deal of luck, in truth."

"So I have been informed."

"Ah, have you? I suppose you would not play with me, then."

"On the contrary," Rande replied. "I would be delighted."

"You would?" Brian regarded him owlishly. "Thought you wouldn't . . . thought you were angry still."

"Not in the least," Rande assured him. The half-formed resolution that had been in his mind after his conversation with Paxton crystallized. He pulled out a chair and sat down across from Brian. Raising his hand, he summoned one of the waiters.

"Your lordship," the man moved softly to his side.

"The candles." He indicated the candelabrum. "Light them if you will and please bring us some fresh packs of cards."

"At once, your lordship." The man produced a waxen taper and, holding it to the single flame on the table, ignited it and lit the candelabrum.

The resulting glow illuminated Brian's face and surprised an expression that was singularly baleful. Though it vanished in a second, Lord Rande was reminded of another time he had caught such a look on young Corbett's visage. He could not quite remember the circumstances, but it hinted at depths he himself would not care to explore. Moreover, he had an impression that Brian was less intoxicated than he appeared. Possibly, he hoped to reap some manner of revenge for the embarrassing incident at the opera. That, of course, was not unnatural and there was the distinct possibility that Marie, for all her seeming distress, had enlarged upon Brian's importunities.

It was to Marie's advantage to retain the appearance of being faithful to him alone. He doubted that she could be. The only woman whose word he could accept without question was dead. He shrugged that intrusive memory aside and fixed his attention on poor Brian, buoyed up by Sir Jasper's false assurances and insidious advice. Here was a sheep for shearing indeed! And, as Paxton had said, it was not the first time, nor would it be the last. However, for his sister's sake if not for his own, Brian would be one brand snatched from the burning and taught a lesson he would not soon forget. Rande was rather sure that there was no other teacher more qualified and less grasping than himself.

Reaching for a pack of cards, he broke the seals and shuffled them. Placing them down on the table, he said pleasantly, "Let us cut for the deal."

* * *

"Hell and damnation," Sheila exclaimed, and snatching another book from the library shelves, she hurled it across the room, where it fell close to two other volumes, which had not flown there on their own accord. "Blast him!" she added.

"My love." Letty Martyn looked at her with wide eyes sunk in dark hollows. She had not had enough sleep the previous night. Nor had Sheila, but of course, the young seldom revealed the ravages of white nights. She continued pacifically, "Please, the poor books are not to blame."

"Oh, dear, I am sorry, Letty." Sheila crossed the room and retrieved the fallen trio, carefully replacing them in their accustomed niches. "But"—she whirled away from the shelves, her anger claiming her again—"our father's house, Letty—rather Brian's. And Actaeon, the horse Brian trained and was to enter at Newmarket, all wagered, all lost! That monster, to take so cruel a revenge, and all for the sake of that damned doxy that warms his bed."

"My love," Miss Martyn protested, "if anyone were to hear you—"

"They would understand. In a night, not even a night, in a matter of five measly hours! He was fleeced, picked clean as a hen for stewing!" Unmindful of this mix of metaphors, Sheila reached for a vase only to have it daringly snatched out of her hand by Miss Letty.

"No, no, no! I cannot allow it," that lady cried, cradling the threatened child against her spare bosom. " 'Tis Dresden ware and there are cupids and white roses on it. 'Twould be a shame to treat it so!"

"Oh, dear, I expect it would be." Sheila had a commiserating look for her distressed old cousin. "I am sorry to vent my vile temper on you. 'Tis not really on you, dear Letty, you know that. 'Tis that creature!"

"I know, dear," Miss Letty murmured. " 'Tis a terrible thing to happen. Poor Brian. Oh, goodness gracious, whatever will he do now?"

" 'Tis not what he will do," Sheila said bitterly. "We must wait to see what course his blasted lordship chooses to pursue. And to think that I thought I liked him!" She stamped her foot and looked about for something else to hurl. Not finding it, she sank into a chair instead. Ever since Brian had come home or, rather, had been practically borne home by a shocked, pained, and horrified Sir Jasper Tennant, who, since Brian was three-parts intoxicated, had had to give her the terrible news that had kept her up most of the night, she had been in a condition alternating between fury and despair.

" 'Twas our father's estate. It has been in the family—"

"I know, my love," Miss Martyn murmured. "Queen Elizabeth was entertained there on one of her royal progresses, and Charles the First by the marquess, at least he was a marquess at the time but later he lost his title because . . ."

"Because he sided with Oliver Cromwell!" Sheila said. "And he damned well deserved to lose it. Blasted traitor!"

"My love, he was your great-great-grandfather."

"Through no fault of mine!" Sheila said roundly. "Just think," she observed with some satisfaction, "he died a plain mister. 'Twas not until the reign of Queen Anne that the Corbetts received their baronetcy, though why that woman would grant them such a title when her great-great-grandfather was murdered by Cromwell's hand, I do not understand!"

"I do believe it was Charles the First who suffered, not Lord Darnley, as least he did not suffer beheading—he was blown up in the Kirk o' Fields."

"And did I not say Charles the First?" Sheila demanded crossly.

"No, my love, you said 'twas Queen Anne's great-great-grandfather, who would have been Lord Darnley. Her great-grandfather was James the First and Charles the First was her grandfather and James the Second . . ."

"Do you imagine that I wish to hear the chronology of England's monarchy at a time like this?"

Tears appeared in Miss Martyn's faded eyes. "I am sorry, my dear," she murmured.

"Oh, dear Letty, so am I." Sheila rose and hugged her cousin. "Bear with me. I am being horrid, I know."

"I do not blame you for being angry, Sheila. If only anger could mend matters, but as I am sure you are aware, it never does."

"You are right." Sheila ran her hands through locks already disordered by several similar treatments. "But what are we to do? How could it have changed hands so quickly? Brian's estate and . . . Actaeon . . . how could he have been fool enough to wager them? And how could Lord Rande accept so heinous a bet? I would not have thought it of him."

"And why would you not? 'Twas you who warned me about him in the first place." Brian, looking considerably the worse for his night of drinking, stood in the doorway wrapped in a red-and-gold dressing gown. The colors did not flatter his sallow complexion and bloodshot eyes.

Sheila moved toward him swiftly. "Oh, my dear"—she put her arms around him protectively—"I am so sorry."

"Yes, my poor boy," Letty mourned. "If only you'd stayed away from that horrid place . . . So many, many poor young men—"

"Poor," Brian groaned. "Yes, I am poor." He moved away from the two women and half-fell into a chair near the bookcases. "Oh, God." He buried his face in his hands, but a split second later he looked up at his sister. "He has it all, Shee, the lot of it, and Actaeon, such a sweet goer . . . Oh, God, God, God, what am I to do?"

"My dearest, you must not be in such despair." She knelt beside his chair. "You have been unwise—"

"Unwise? Mad! But 'twas not my fault! He challenged me. A gentleman cannot refuse a challenge, can he? I was waiting for Jasper, who was late in coming, then Rande strolled in. I thought he must avoid me, but to my amazement he came directly to my table and 'twas as if the episode at the opera had never taken place. He was uncommonly cordial and asked me if I would like to play a game of piquet and—"

"And you, being tipsy, which he must have known, acquiesced," Sheila cried.

"That was the way of it . . . I was a bit tipsy." Brian

shuddered. "He kept winning and winning . . . It was as if he knew exactly how the cards would run—"

"He cheated!" Miss Martyn gasped.

"I'd not say that." Brian shook his head. "But he did ply me with wine."

"The monster!" Sheila exclaimed. "Oh, that I were a man. I would call him out."

"And be slain for your pains," Brian groaned. "Sir Jasper says he is a dead shot and ruthless."

"Ruthless and cruel," Sheila agreed.

There was a knock at the library door. "Yes," Sheila called.

The butler appeared in the doorway. "If you please, ma'am."

"What is it, Sean?" Sheila asked, and was about to remind him that they were at home to no one when he announced, "Sir Jasper Tennant."

"I have said that we are not at home, Sean."

"No, we are at home to him," Brian spoke quickly, adding, "I want to see him, Sheila."

"Very well," she said reluctantly, "you may show him in, Sean." She expelled a short impatient breath. The animosity that his name always occasioned filled her again. Had it not been for Sir Jasper's having introduced Brian to the dubious pleasures of gambling, he would not be in this ghastly situation. However, her sense of fairness intervened. It was not Sir Jasper who had first brought Brian into Brooks. That had been Lord Rande! Had he been planning her brother's downfall even then?

Sir Jasper, looking grave and concerned, strode into the room. "My dear Miss Corbett," he began in low commiserating tones, "I cannot tell you how miserable this circumstance has made me. If only I'd not been detained last night, none of this would have taken place."

"And why were you detained?" Brian demanded belligerently. "You told me to be there at nine o'clock. I was there on the hour, but you did not arrive until midnight."

"My boy, my apologies, I did not see you!" Sir Jasper

moved quickly to Brian's chair. "I was on my way to the club, and it being a fair evening, I'd decided to go on foot. Unfortunately, I was set upon by thieves."

"Oh, how dreadful!" Miss Martyn exclaimed. "One hears that they grow bolder by the minute."

"Aye, they do," he agreed. "And Bow Street cannot cope with them."

"Were you hurt?" Sheila felt it incumbent upon her to ask.

"No, Miss Corbett, I was not." Sir Jasper smiled grimly. "Ask, rather, what happened to my attackers. I am never abroad without a pistol for my protection. I produced it, and one of the ruffians lies at death's door in hospital; the other's in the hands of the constables. But the altercation took time and there was the matter of my needing to explain the matter to the magistrate. Subsequently, I was forced to return home, my clothes being mired, for they'd tripped me up, do you see?" He sighed deeply. "Were it not for that, I should have been in good time to prevent another robbery."

"Another robbery?" Miss Martyn exclaimed. "Where?"

"At Brooks, ma'am. I am speaking half-metaphorically, of course. Yet"—a frown darkened his brow and narrowed his eyes—"I think I can easily describe it as a robbery, and not his first, I might add."

"You are speaking of Rande?" Brian rasped.

"Of course," Sir Jasper assented, and took a turn around the room, pausing beside Brian's chair. "And here I was thinking that his so-called pride would have kept him from addressing Brian, but seeing the lad half-tipsy, he would not resist the temptation of challenging him to a game. As I have said 'tis not the first time he's acquired a fortune in this manner, and unless he's stopped, 'twill not be the last."

"You are suggesting—" Sheila began.

"I am saying that Rande is a hardened gamester who does not know the meaning of the words 'ethics' or 'mercy.' Time and again he has fleeced young men newly arrived in London, charmed by his address and, of course, his lineage and title. 'Tis not often an earl is so accommodating as Rande has been to your brother.''

"They had met before in Ireland," Sheila said.

"Good Lord, are you excusing him?" Brian demanded harshly.

"No, of course, I will never excuse him," she retorted bitterly. "I was merely saying that you had met—"

"And no doubt you, Brian, were impressed by his extreme charm of manner." Sir Jasper shook his head. "There's no one more charming than the Earl of Rande when he puts his mind to it."

As he was speaking, Sheila was remembering Fiona's words: "He has won fortunes on the tables," she had said. She had also said, "He might lead Brian into deep play," and he had—so deep that he was drowning!

"I have heard that they call him the rakehell," she said.

"Aye, they do, ma'am—and many other names as well, which he has earned as he has that one. But, of course, he rejoices in the friendship of the Prince Regent."

"Evidently the Prince is not very discerning," Sheila observed coldly.

"My love," Miss Martyn protested, "the dear Prince . . . such a handsome young man as he was. Jeffrey visited Brighthelmstone for his health—the sea-water baths, you know, and I saw the Prince with Mrs. Fitzherbert, a beauty, though a Papist of course, with such pretty blond hair, and Jeffrey much annoyed with me for staring at what he called 'a woman no better than she should be,' but they were married, I do believe."

"I am sure they were," Sir Jasper said kindly. "But the Prince, though I, too, can call him friend, is not always discerning."

"I cannot see what the Prince's friendships or the lack of them have to do with my predicament," Brian snapped. "Have you any suggestions?"

"Is there no way of appealing to Lord Rande's sense of fair play?" Miss Martyn interrupted, clasping her thin little hands together.

"Bless you, ma'am, he has no sense of fair play," Sir

Jasper scoffed. "Else he would not have cheated this poor lad of his birthright."

"Oh, God," Sheila groaned. " 'Tis outside of enough . . . in a single night to—" She broke off at another tap at the door of the library. "Yes," she called.

The butler appeared again. He was holding a silver tray and on it reposed an envelope. "This was brought by messenger to Sir Brian," he announced.

"I will take it." Sheila moved toward him.

"Er, Miss Sheila, an answer is requested. The messenger says as how he'll wait."

She tensed and stared at the envelope. It bore a crest and Brian's name was written distinctly and distinctively, a handwriting that was large, flowing, and black. Even without prior knowledge, she would have associated it with Lord Rande, she thought, and immediately wondered why but preferred not to dwell on reasons. "Very well," she responded. "Have him wait."

As the door closed on the man, Brian said peremptorily, "Let me see it, please."

"I am bringing it to you, my dear," Sheila said. " 'Tis from Lord Rande, of course." She proffered the envelope to her brother, who grabbed it from her hand, tearing it open and reading it swiftly.

"Damn and blast him, may he rot in hell," he exclaimed. "I am damned if I will, you can tell that to the messenger."

"What does he say, dear boy?"

It was a moment before Brian could answer. Instead, he took three or four deep breaths and then finally rasped, "He has expressed a . . . a desire to see the estate . . . and the horse. He has asked that I show him *his* property." Tears gleamed in Brian's eyes. "*His* property and . . . and I've yet to see it myself."

"Well," Sir Jasper said regretfully, "I cannot see that you have a choice, Brian, my lad. He's won it fairly."

"Fairly!" Sheila stamped her foot. "There was nothing fair about it. My brother was drunk."

"Alas," Sir Jasper said regretfully, "so are most of the

men who play at Brooks. But enough, I will accompany you, Brian, if you choose."

"And I!" Sheila cried.

Sir Jasper visited a look upon her. "I do not think that would be wise, my dear."

"Why not?" It was Brian who answered him. "I want my sister to come with us."

"Do you?" Sir Jasper asked. "Well, then, of course she must come."

"And I, too, must come," Miss Martyn said staunchly.

"Very good." Brian's laughter was loud and mirthless. "His thieving lordship will have a full house." He turned his eyes on Sheila. "Give that intelligence to the messenger —and say we are at Lord Rande's disposal." His eyes fastened briefly on Sir Jasper's face, and Sheila, on her way toward the door, saw him give a small nod. A little thrill of disquiet went through her. Her brother, angrily and outwardly submissive, must be planning something with Sir Jasper . . . and of a sudden, she was rendered most uneasy. But she could not think about that now. She hurried out of the room to tell the butler to inform the messenger that they would be at his lordship's disposal— whenever he chose to leave for Wiltshire.

Corbett Manor lay some eighty-four miles out of London, in Wiltshire, an area that contained the famed Stonehenge monument as well as other ancient relics. The house and grounds were near enough to the River Avon for it to enliven the view from the windows on the upper floors, her mother had told Sheila. It was also a day and a half's ride. In getting there, they had passed the Avebury Stones and also Oliver's Castle, a fort dating back to the Iron Age. Her mother had also mentioned these with something close to dread.

Moira Corbett had been full of fancies, Sheila recalled. She had been wont to find portents in the weather, in the movements of livestock, in the fluttering of birds; a robin's red breast, she had asserted, was bloodstained because its ancestors had pulled the thorns from the crown that encircled the head of the Savior at his Crucifixion. Consequently, to chase a robin from the house should it fly inside was bad luck, and to kill it meant sure disaster. She was terrified of crows. To see a single crow was to reap sorrow. The hissing of geese presaged a storm and killing a spider meant bad luck also. She had been gentle, credulous, and childish, and Sheila, on the last leg of their journey to Corbett Manor, was comparing herself and Brian to the late Lady Corbett. They had both been too trustful!

Brian had put his trust in Lord Rande and she, much as she would have liked to deny it, had been well on the way to admiring him. She had not blamed him for his anger with Brian, had privately regretted that it would preclude a second meeting. She would never have dreamed that he would have lowered himself to the point of getting even with her brother, and up until she had read the message he sent, she had half-believed that he would relent and send Brian back the note he had insisted on his writing, the note that signed over property and horse to Ivor Damerall, Earl of Rande.

"I have been a fool," she said to Miss Martyn, who sat beside her huddled in her corner on the coach.

Miss Martyn, startled out of a semidoze, looked at her confusedly. "What did you say, my dear?"

"I have been a fool," Sheila repeated vehemently, and then found herself unwilling to elucidate any further. Instead, she turned away and stared gloomily out of the window.

"Perhaps he will relent, after all," Miss Martyn said, surprisingly putting Sheila's fugitive hopes into words. "It does seem so small to take advantage of a young man in his cups."

"Sir Jasper says that is how the earl has acquired his vast fortune," Sheila pointed out.

"Oh, yes, I heard him say so, but I do hope not. 'Twill go very ill with him when he is summoned to his maker."

Sheila released a quavering sigh. "He has quite a while to wait before retribution."

"One never knows," Miss Martyn murmured. "Everyone said that Jeffrey would live longer than Father. Papa was eighty-nine when he died. Then, poor Jeffrey got his feet wet, a quinsy set in, and he was gone in a fortnight."

The coach was slowing down and Sheila, gazing out of the window, said on a note of relief both for the concluding of the journey and for Miss Martyn's talk of mortality, "I think we are near to the manor." She waved as she saw Brian ride past but was not surprised when he failed to return her salutation. They were not on a pleasure trip and he could not be glad that the journey was nearly at an end.

They entered a driveway guarded on either side by stone pillars topped by eager heads. The rendering of those fierce predatory birds had once sent a shudder through Moira Corbett. Sheila remembered her mother describing them. She had seen them first on her wedding trip, spent in the house with her husband's mother, a cantankerous old woman who seemed to loathe the Irish, not excluding her daughter-in-law. In those days, the place had been badly in need of repairs and Moira's dowry had provided them.

Her mother had not liked the house, but now, as the coach rounded a bend in the road, giving her a view of it, rising foursquare in the distance, Sheila thought it very imposing. She had not expected it to be so large, and compared to Dahna, it was not excessively big. Still, she wondered if they had brought enough servants with them to ready the rooms. There was a skeleton staff: old servants of the dowager Lady Corbett, who, surprisingly enough, had survived her daughter-in-law and her son, and had died seven years ago—or almost seven, since it had been in the November of 1809. However, as she was quick to remind herself, they would not be staying long, no more than two or three days at the most, the time it would take to turn the manor over to its new owner.

Looking at it, Sheila was pleased that the original castle had been torn down by the order of Charles II and the present structure was little more than a half-century old.

Of course, its lack of years meant that it would have more modern conveniences. She wondered what Lord Rande would do with it. He had his own estates, but of course, that did not matter. He could entertain friends here in Wiltshire, which was only a county away from Hampshire, where the hunting was said to be tolerably good. The nearer they came to the mansion, the deeper grew an empty feeling in her solar plexus. Her heart was beating near her throat. She feared . . . She did not know quite what she feared, violence, perhaps, on the part of Brian, seeing his inheritance for the first time, appreciating its grounds and stables, its parks and fields, then turning them over to Lord Rande, whom he had wronged and who had avenged himself a hundredfold, even a thousand! Thinking about that, Sheila found herself most reluctant to descend from the carriage and face her brother and Sir Jasper.

She frowned. She would need to act as hostess during the time they were here. Consequently, she would not be able to retire early as she had at the inn last night, mainly to avoid Sir Jasper's unwanted attentions. She had been barely polite to him, but instead of taking umbrage at this treatment, he had actually smiled at her brusque answers to his questions concerning her welfare and her state of mind. He had tacitly excused her rudeness by commiserating with her on the exigencies of coach travel over indifferent roads. He seemed utterly oblivious to the fact that she avoided his society whenever possible. Brian, however, had been quite aware of her state of mind, and cornering her in an alcove not far from her room at the inn, he had protested her treatment of his friend, growing angry when she insisted again that she did not like Sir Jasper.

"And why not?" he had demanded belligerently.

"For reasons you seem to have willfully forgotten," she had retorted. "You yourself agreed that he was not quite a gentleman, and I am of the opinion that he had an ulterior motive in mind when he introduced you to that beastly game."

" 'Twas not he who robbed me," Brian had retorted.

"Nor was it Lord Rande, since 'twas you who wagered estate and horse."

"He goaded me into it, I tell you. He jeered at me when I hesitated, suggesting that I should not be playing cards at Brooks, and with him, if I were afraid to lose. He laughed at me too."

She did not want to believe Brian, but unfortunately, she did. Lord Rande had taken her brother's measure quickly, had known that he could never refuse a challenge, and then had basely acted accordingly.

Never had she been so mistaken about anyone, she reasoned unhappily. She had believed Lord Rande to be above such petty actions. It was petty to revenge himself on a boy who had wrongly, of course, tried to steal his mistress. But poor Brian hardly deserved so cruel a retaliation. Sheila bit her lip as, on gazing out of the window, she saw a tall pine tree. They were supposed to grow to a great age. How long had it stood sentinel on Corbett land, only to be lost at the turn of a card? She blinked furiously at the string of tears but was quite composed by the time the coach stopped and Mickey brought the stairs for her descent.

Brian had ridden straight to the stables and Sir Jasper accompanied him. Dismounting from his horse, he surrendered the reins to a small boy who had run out at his approach. With a bitter look at his companion he said, "All this . . ." and was unable to say more, overcome by his emotions at viewing the great bulk of the mansion and the spread of the stable yard. Added to these was the park, glimpsed as he had ridden up the driveway. Moving away from Sir Jasper, he strode into the stables. Somewhere about would be Tom Toolan, his groom, sent down to care for Actaeon, and now for Sheila's stallion Aldebaran, brought with them in a dray behind the servant's conveyance. Toolan would soon hear the news about Actaeon. He shuddered, not wanting to face his groom,

not wanting to hear him recite Actaeon's lineage—
from the line of the Goldolphon Barb and, as everyone
said, bound to follow in the hoofprints of his famous
forebears Lath and Regulus. Brian swallowed a lump in his
throat and said gratingly, "I'll see him laid in earth before
I give him up—Actaeon, I mean."

"That would be a sad waste of some excellent horseflesh, dear boy. Best see his would-be owner in that
condition," Sir Jasper murmured.

"If only I could . . ."

" 'Tis not impossible," Sir Jasper drawled. "I thought
we'd reached an understanding about that."

Brian avoided his gaze. "I . . . we . . . we said nothing,"
he muttered uneasily.

"Were words necessary?"

Brian lifted his head and stared at Sir Jasper. "What
could we do? I've no wish to end my life at rope's end."

"Nor I. An affair of honor, conducted without the
presence of seconds or a medical man . . . and who knows
what the outcome might be?"

"You'd force a duel on him?"

"Quite so. Rande's not as cool as he appears. He has a
hot temper when his honor's impugned, so I have heard."

"I've heard he's an excellent shot. I am not," Brian said
nervously.

"You're uncommon modest, dear boy. However, I was
not suggesting that yours be the hand that pulls the
trigger."

"You?"

"None other."

"Why would you expose yourself to this danger for
me?"

"Because I loathe injustice. Are you game?"

"I am not sure . . ." Brian said uncertainly.

"As you choose, then." Sir Jasper shrugged and started
toward the driveway.

Brian caught up with him. "Besides, if anything did
happen to him, would not this property revert to his
heirs?"

"He has no heirs, dear boy. He is the last of his line, and I doubt that he's made any changes in his will as yet. I would guess that if he were to die, you'd not be the loser."

"But I signed a note!"

"Which would be rendered null and void."

"Ah, in those circumstances . . ." Brian mused.

"Have I your ear, then?"

"I would like to speak further on the subject."

"Then, come, let us talk out of the stables and into the park, where only the rabbits and the deer can listen."

Contrary to Sheila's expectations, Lord Rande did not appear to claim his winnings that day. He sent a message explaining that he was detained—intelligence that depressed her, giving her more time to explore the house her brother could no longer claim as his own.

Her depression deepened at supper and she was not in the mood for the excellent meal served up by their cook. The dining room was long, and the walls were painted with a fanciful banquet scene: musicians strummed lutes while ladies in peaked hats and veils, garbed in what appeared to be sumptuous silks and velvets, and gentlemen in brief doublets lavishly embroidered in gold, admired a long table groaning under gold and silver dishes filled with all manner of delicacies, including a roast peacock served with its magnificent tail spread to the fullest. Finally, Sheila and Letty, who was not less depressed, left the gentlemen to their port and wandered into the music room, a large chamber, also with painted walls and a ceiling depicting Orpheus playing his lyre for an Arcadian assembly of rapt nymphs and shepherds, gods and satyrs.

Sitting down on a tapestried chair, Letty Martyn sighed. "Oh, dear, that poor, poor boy—to wager all this."

"He did not know what he was doing," Sheila said for perhaps the thousandth time. She moved to a white-and-gold pianoforte and, lifting its cover, found it painted inside with the likeness of medieval musicians. Inconsequentially, she remembered Lord Rande's love of music. Undoubtedly he would value the pianoforte . . . if he did not sell it. A sudden idea came to her. Did he have it in mind to sell the manor? If so, she could buy it from him! She would broach the matter to Brian immediately he came in. No, she decided a split second later, she would have to wait until they had ostensibly retired for the night. For her brother's pride, she could not make such an offer in the presence of Sir Jasper; it would probably send Brian's spirits plummeting even lower at the thought of being rescued from his plight by his sister.

It was near midnight when Sheila knocked on Brian's door and was admitted by his valet, who looked surprised and faintly hostile. Undoubtedly, McDermot, weary and longing for bed, must see her presence as another barrier to that design. "Himself's about his ablutions," he said.

"I will wait, but you need not," she told him.

He regarded her dubiously. "Sir Brian—"

"Will not mind that I have dismissed you," she finished firmly. Moving to the door, she held it open. "Please, McDermot, leave us."

"Yes, Miss Sheila." He bowed and went silently out of the room.

Sheila settled down in a chair and stared about her at the bedroom. A huge chamber with walls paneled in dark wood, it had fine furniture, some made by Chippendale, but a carved chest and a matching cabinet dated, she knew, back to the seventeenth century. There was a huge fireplace with a carved marble mantelpiece over which hung a portrait of her father as a child, a merry little imp who bore a strong likeness to a painting of herself at the same age, she realized reluctantly, decrying, as usual, her English heritage and her resemblance to her father's side of the family.

Her gaze moved to the bed, an immense four-poster in which many Corbetts had been conceived. It was hung with costly silks provided by her mother at the Dowager Lady Corbett's direction or, rather, command. These also hung at the windows. Sheila unleashed a long sigh. Even given her prejudices against her grandmother and her father, the idea of this house—her family's house, no matter how hard she tried to refute the connection—going to a stranger filled her with anger and pain, the latter being even greater because the stranger was not quite a stranger. She was also experiencing shame because she had been warned and had failed to heed those warnings merely because he had been pleasant to her at the opera.

"Fool," she muttered resentfully.

"Sheila, what are you doing here?" Brian, clad in a long white nightshirt, entered from his dressing room. "Where's McDermot?"

"I dismissed him." She rose. "I must speak to you."

"Well?" His attitude was not welcoming but grew more so as she revealed her plan. His reaction, however, surprised and pleased her. It hinted at a maturity she had not known he possessed. "My dearest," he said, giving her one of his increasingly rare hugs. "I'd not think of letting your inheritance go to pay for my folly. Why, Grandfather'd be down—or up, as the case may be—in a trice to haunt me."

"But what will you do?" she cried.

His eyes turned bleak. "I do not know, but perhaps Rande can be persuaded to let me manage the estate for him."

"Manage it for him?" Sheila cried indignantly. "I would see him in hell first!"

His eyes glowed. "Is it possible that the soft spot you had for him is gone, then?"

"I never had a soft spot," she cried.

"Did you not?" He gave her a quizzical look. "You were monstrous pleasant to him at the opera."

"Do you imagine I could ever forgive him for what he's done to you?"

"Could you not?"

"Why do you even ask? I am your sister and my loyalty is with you."

"My lovely Sheila." He kissed her. "Go to bed now . . . perhaps matters are not as black as we believe."

His courageous optimism surprised and touched her. Sheila felt warmed by it, and as she went down the hall to her own chamber, she realized with something of a shock that in her own mind she had been becoming more and more estranged from her brother—or had it been the other way around? She was not sure, but at this moment in time she was buoyed up by the feeling that the Brian she had known before her grandfather's death had finally returned to her.

5

RIDING TOWARD CORBETT Manor, Lord Rande looked up at the sky and found it more vivid blue than he usually perceived in England. A fugitive but potent memory assailed him. He thought of Spain . . . Spain in August and the smells of gunpowder, blood, and manure. There were sounds, too. Cries, shrieks, groans, the wild neighing of startled and wounded horses, the crack of gunfire, the boom of the cannon as he, with the men under his command, approached Madrid. They had entered the beleaguered city on August 13, 1812, four years ago, an anniversary that he had not celebrated. It had been a notable victory, but as was usually the case with victories, it had carried with it an appalling loss of life.

A grim little smile twisted his lips at the futility of his prayers on that day. He had prayed for death. Many of his comrades had perished, but he had survived, to be commended for valor. He had also been sternly chided for his recklessness in plunging headlong into the fray. He had not been reckless, only desperate, wanting to die and join the one he longed to meet again, provided that there was an afterlife. He preferred to believe that there was, because it seemed so wrong, so terrible, so agonizing, that she had been snatched away from him forever—and in the peaceful groves of England—while he survived amid the turmoil of the Peninsular War.

He wondered why he was thinking of Spain and the past. He decided that it was the oppressive heat that had brought it to mind. Of course, it was now another August and he was embarking upon another mission, a rescue mission, too. He would show a foolish young man the extent of his folly and wrest him from the clutches of Sir Jasper Tennant, a man who, to his certain knowledge, had been directly responsible for the death of Guildford Farne: young Gilly, the headstrong, foolish, charming lad who had been the brother of Sir Roger Farne, his comrade-in-arms and one of his best friends. He had known Gilly since the boy was in long clothes.

Lieutenant Roger Farne had died as Wellington's army entered Madrid, and Gilly had inherited Farne Hold. He had subsequently lost it playing cards with an esteemed new friend named Sir Jasper Tennant, something Lord Rande had not told Paxton the other night. Tennant had not cheated the lad; he had only "taught" him how to win, buoying up his confidence with the same tricks he had passed on to Brian, and then he had moved in for the kill. Gilly had subsequently shot himself, leaving his mother and sister penniless. The mother, an invalid, had been unable to sustain the loss of two sons. She had gently drifted into death. Kitty Farne had gone on to become a governess.

All this had happened while he was at Waterloo and, later, in France. Returning, he had been told of the tragedy. He had tried to find Kitty but had been unsuccessful. At length, he learned she had married a footman employed in the same house where she had been working as a governess. They had emigrated to New South Wales. It would be a hard life for one he remembered as a charming, heedless butterfly of a child. Yet, it was not of Kitty Farne that he was thinking as he skirted the village and turned toward the road that, he had been told, led to the manor. It was of Miss Corbett, who, he decided ruefully, must hate him. Undoubtedly she would regard him as he regarded Sir Jasper, a hardened gamester willfully defrauding her brother of his inheritance. He wished that she knew the reason behind actions that must seem totally nefarious to her. She was cut of different cloth than Sir Brian, he knew, and wondered why he was so positive of that.

A single dance at Almack's and a brief conversation at the opera did not ensure knowledge. He paused in his thinking. He had reached the gates with their sculptured eagle-heads, ugly and forbidding. Were this estate his, he would have them replaced. He smiled as he recalled that for the nonce the property did belong to him, the property and the horse.

He was more reluctant to return Actaeon than the manor. He had seen the animal in Ireland. He was a beauty, a proud beauty who never should have been wagered in a card game. It would serve young Brian right if he did decide to keep him, but of course, he had no such intention. He wondered when he should tell Brian that he had played not to win but merely to instruct. At the end of the day, perhaps. He urged his horse forward, banishing the slight smile that had been playing about his lips. He had had some success in amateur theatricals as a boy. He hoped that it would stand him in good stead as he prepared to be the villain of the piece.

Bridget, answering a tap on Sheila's bedroom door, opened it to Kevin, one of the footmen, who frowningly gave her the message she hastily brought to her mistress. "Miss Sheila," she said excitedly, "Kevin told me that his lordship's below."

Sheila, who was sitting at her dressing table, rose immediately. "Brian, I expect, is still out riding with Sir Jasper?"

"I do not know, Miss Sheila."

"Well, if he is, see that someone goes after him and alerts him to his lordship's arrival. Meanwhile, I will see Lord Rande. You may pass that information to Sean, immediately, please. It would not do to keep the new owner of Corbett Manor waiting."

"Oh, Miss Sheila," Bridget groaned. "It is too terrible, that it is."

"I agree, Bridget, but please do as I asked."

"Yes, Miss Sheila." The girl hurried out of the room.

Sheila stared after her and stopped. She did not want to

descend the stairs on the heels of her abigail. Moving back to her dressing table, she sat down and stared into her mirror. She looked pale—not surprising, since she had barely slept the night before. When she had dozed, she had been prey to disturbing dreams which she did not remember but which left a sense of unease in their wake—only natural, considering the circumstances! She also looked angry. She must compose her features. Though she had every right to be angry or, rather, furious, she must maintain her dignity and be a lady, an English lady, cold and statuesque. The English had a low opinion of the Irish. She would not add to it. She would not give vent to the temper that boiled within her. Rising and pivoting before her glass, she decided that she looked tolerably well. In deference to the warm weather, she wore a blue muslin morning dress, one of her London purchases. It was made along the lines of a Grecian tunic, with an embroidered border at the hem and . . . But she must not waste any more time thinking about her appearance. Lord Rande was waiting for her below.

She took a long breath and had difficulty releasing it. She was very tense. She must control herself. She could not leave him cooling his heels down there, though probably he would like that. It would give him an opportunity to survey and appraise his winnings.

On her way down, Sheila found herself more and more reluctant to face Lord Rande. It was not fair, she decided stormily. Her brother had no right to ride out and leave her to deal with his acquisitive lordship. She had half a mind to let him wait in the drawing room alone until Brian returned.

"Good morning, Miss Corbett."

Sheila came to a dead stop and stared down into the hall at Lord Rande, cool, composed, and looking exceptionally handsome in a gray coat, black breeches, and shining Hessians. His tall hat was worn at an angle on his dark waving hair. He was regarding her gravely, and of course, it was too late to turn back. She continued on down the stairs and, reaching him, said frostily, "Good morning, my lord," thinking that it was the absolute antithesis of a "good" morning, but she had promised herself to adhere to the amenities. Mindful of these, she continued, "Did no one show you to the drawing room?"

"They did, but I preferred to wait until you joined me."

There was delicacy in that, she thought reluctantly, but a split second later she had dismissed that supposition. Probably, he had waited because he wanted to emphasize his ownership. She said, "I expect you will want to see the house. I will show it to you. My brother and Sir Jasper have gone riding."

"Sir Jasper?" he questioned with a frown. "He is here?"

His tone of voice surprised Sheila. It reflected the same dislike she felt whenever she thought of the man she held partially responsible for Brian's problems. However, the moment that theory occurred to her, she dismissed it as quickly as she had her first idea concerning him. She was *facing* the man who was entirely responsible for *all* of Brian's present woes. She said coldly, "Yes, Sir Jasper came with us yesterday. He felt my brother needed a friend at this trying time." Annoyance flooded through her. She had not intended to speak so frankly. Yet, it was with some righteous satisfaction that she saw her unwanted visitor wince.

"I am aware that you must be disturbed over this situation," Lord Rande said. "I wish to tell you—"

Sheila raised an imperious hand. "I do not believe we need to discuss the matter, my lord. Obviously, you felt that you had been wronged and that my brother should be taught a lesson."

"A lesson?" he repeated. "Yes, I did think he needed a lesson, Miss Corbett, but—"

"Lord Rande," Sheila interrupted again. "My brother is out riding, not for pleasure, I might add. He is overseeing the property so that he can better discuss it with you. Unfortunately, we have been in London only a brief time and this is the first opportunity he has had to view the inheritance you have won. When he returns, I expect he will be more informed on the subject. Meanwhile, I will show you the rooms on the first and second floors, if you so desire. Do you wish to come with me?''

He hesitated, staring at her; then much to her surprise and anger, he smiled. "Yes, you may show me the rooms, Miss Corbett. Shall we go at once?''

"Certainly!" she snapped, wishing belatedly that she had not responded that way. It was too annoying, she decided bitterly. A rogue ought to look like a rogue. He should not have honest gray eyes that captured the light from his smile. He should not have a face that was not only handsome but strong and manly—and also sensitive, but he could *not* be sensitive! No one with any sensitivity . . . She must not give rein to her thoughts, not at this moment. She went on up the stairs and waited in the hall until he joined her before saying, "Of course, I, in common with my brother, am not as familiar with this house as I should be, since I, too, was reared mainly in Ireland.''

"A beautiful country and much to my liking,'' he commented.

"Yes,'' she said sarcastically, "a great number of Englishmen have been in agreement with you, starting with Henry the Second.''

"Who came in at the invitation of Pope Adrian the Fourth and at the behest of many of Ireland's high kings— to settle a civil war. However, I am not here to argue with you on ancient history.''

"No, you are here to stake your claim,'' she retorted. She managed to swallow a spate of angry words. "I am sorry,'' she continued, "I had promised myself not to refer to your . . . your victory over my brother, who, I understand, is only one of the many youthful unfortunates who have swelled your fortunes. But, please, we will start with the library.'' She continued on down the hall.

"Wait!'' he commanded.

Sheila stopped immediately and turned. "Yes?''

The smile had vanished from his eyes. He looked grim and she noted with some pleasure, angry. Undoubtedly he did not relish references to his machinations. His tone was chill as he inquired, "Might I know where you had your information concerning my other 'victims'?"

"What does it matter?" she countered. "Will you deny it? Will you deny that you have amassed your fortune luring innocents like my poor young brother into gambling hells and fleecing them?"

He stiffened. His gaze, she noted, was even colder than it had been that night in the Green Room. He said, "I cannot see that my denial would carry any weight at this present moment, Miss Corbett. I leave you free to believe as you choose. I hope it will not hinder you from showing me through my house."

Sheila's hands curled into fists. She would have dearly loved to shove both of them into his eyes. Better yet, she would not have minded pushing him down the stairs—if either action would have served to extricate Brian from his predicament. Yet, at the same time, Lord Rande's response to her accusations surprised her. There was anger aplenty, but there was no guilt. Either he was so hardened a gamester or . . . But she would not dwell on his reactions any longer. She said, "Of course. The library lies this way." She moved down the hall, and as luck would have it, the first door she opened proved to be that of the music room. With a slight lessening of her icy composure, she said, "As I explained, I am not very familiar with the plan of this house."

"No matter," he returned. There was a slight gleam of humor in his eyes as he added, " 'Tis said that music hath charms to soothe a savage breast—at least according to the playwright Congreve." His eyes fell on the pianoforte. "Ah"—he moved toward it—"I hope that it is in tune."

"I would not think so," she returned. "Not after so many years." She wished that he had not brought their conversation at the opera to mind again. He played the pianoforte, he had told her. And now he was lifting the fallboard. Sitting down, he ran his long fingers over the ivory keys, playing a scale. "Ah," he commented with real pleasure. "It does seem in tune. A very nice tone. How do you account for that, Miss Corbett?"

"I do not know," she replied. "Unless the housekeeper or one of the servants was entrusted with its care. We arrived only yesterday."

"That must be the answer." Seemingly unmindful of her, he began to play.

The anger that lay just beneath the surface of her mind rose again at this casual invasion—as if the piano belonged to him! It did not . . . or did it? Could he claim everything . . . the furniture, the paintings? The question faded from her consciousness as the music filled her ears. It was unfamiliar but beautiful and powerful. He performed amazingly well. Obviously, he was a fine musician, but he should not have been. Music was an ennobling art, or at least, so she had always believed. And what was he playing? The harmonics of the work had a certain familiarity. The composer made ample use of the keyboard, going up and down it in endless variations.

Beethoven! she thought suddenly. She was not acquainted with that particular selection, but the master's signature was easily recognizable. She opened and closed her mouth on a protest as he suddenly ceased to play. She said coolly, "That was well-performed. It sounded like Beethoven."

He looked surprised and pleased. "You are quite right, Miss Corbett. It was Beethoven—his Sonata in F Minor, the Appassionata, it is called. I take it you are familiar with his music?"

"Yes." She nodded, not willing to tell him that she was not only familiar with the composer's works but that she revered him even more than Mozart. There had been a time when she had longed to travel to Vienna merely to glimpse him. She did not feel impelled to comment, "I hope now that the wars are over, he will come to this country."

"I fear he will not. He's growing very deaf, you know."

"Deaf!" She regarded him in horror. "Beethoven? I pray you will not say so!"

"My uncle studied with him in 1802. His hearing was going even then."

"Oh, dear," she said in real agony. "Such a tragedy!"

"Sheila!" Brian exclaimed.

She turned swiftly to find her brother framed in the doorway, watching her with a mixture of anger and incredulity, for which she could not blame him. He must have heard the piano, and now to find her apparently chatting casually with his worst enemy must have shocked him deeply. She said, "I was showing his lordship through the house," she said.

Lord Rande, dropping the fallboard over the keys, rose, saying, "Good day, Brian."

Brian did not return his greeting. With a poisonous glance at Sheila and another for his unwelcome visitor, he said coldly, "You are here in good time, I see."

"Yes, I came by easy stages," Lord Rande responded. "This is a very pleasant part of the country. I was able to view Stonehenge and the Avebury Stones as well."

"That is very daring of you, my lord," Brian commented. "They are known to be unlucky."

"I cannot believe that stones or other inanimate objects bring luck or ensure the lack of it." Lord Rande shrugged.

"You do not agree that some people are more fortunate than others?" Brian inquired.

"I believe that some are wiser than others."

"Or more skillful." Sir Jasper strolled into the room. "Ah, Rande"—he inclined his head—"you must pardon me for breaking into your conversation but I could not help overhearing you." He paused, then added, "I must, I expect, congratulate you on a game well played."

Lord Rande surveyed him a moment before answering, "I thank you, Sir Jasper. I must appreciate compliments from an expert player such as yourself, I know." His gaze shifted to Sheila. "But you were going to show me the library, Miss Corbett. Should we not be on our way?"

"Of course," she responded uncomfortably. She had been surveying the situation as it must have appeared to Brian coming into the room and finding her in apparently idle conversation with his arch enemy, who, in turn, had been seated at the piano! Not only that, he had actually been playing it, a most provocative action considering the circumstances. She could not blame her brother for his reaction and she knew that this would not be the last of it. She must needs gird her loins for an argument. It was all very unfortunate. And, on top of this, she found Lord Rande's attitude toward Sir Jasper bordering on the insolent. It was quite apparent that he did not like him. She wondered if he might share her feelings regarding the man or . . . But that did not matter. Lord Rande's reactions or the lack of them did not matter! She said, "I suggest we go to the library now, my lord."

"Hold," Brian protested. "I think I must be your guide . . . but should you not like to see your other acquisition? I am referring to Actaeon."

"In good time. I am partial to books. If we might see the library and then, yes, by all means Actaeon. From what I remember, he was a most noble animal."

"Yes." Brian winced. "He is. I raised him from a colt. There's not another like him in all Ireland—at least not to my thinking. In England, neither."

"If you will excuse me . . ." Sheila started for the door.

"My dear, will you not come with us?" Brian asked.

"No, I think not. I have other duties." Her anger with Lord Rande was high and hot again. Could he not see how her brother was suffering? (Sir Jasper understood. He was looking somber and regretful. She guessed that he must blame himself in part for Brian's situation.) She moved into the hall, wanting to go outside, into the fresh air. The house was oppressive. She longed to be at Dahna—anywhere away from Lord Rande, who had no heart, none whatsoever! How could he stand listening to Brian as he spoke about Actaeon and be so absolutely calm, so entirely unmoved! Was he totally oblivious to what Brian must be experiencing? He did not strike her as an insensitive man, and yet . . . She sighed deeply and hurried down the stairs. A moment later, she was walking toward the gardens.

The foliage, she thought, looked dark and a little dusty. It was the tag end of summer. In less than a fortnight it would be September. Where would they be? What would Brian do, now that he was stripped of his fortune, his house, his horse? He had refused her offer, but maybe he would return with her to Dahna, after all. He had managed the estate well—because he had loved it and thought that it would eventually be willed to him.

"Why?" she murmured, thinking of her grandfather's inexplicable decision. Why had he left Dahna to her? She loved the estate but she loved her brother, too, and in that willing, Lord Carlingford had driven a wedge between them. Could he have anticipated what had happened to the manor? How could Brian have been fool enough to wager it when he was already losing?

Again, Rande, damn him, was her answer. Unbidden, she remembered his lean fingers coursing over the keyboard. He loved music, that was evident. He played beautifully, sensitively . . . There it was again! How could she apply the term "sensitive" to him who had robbed her brother of his inheritance? It could not actually be considered a robbery, but he shouldn't have done it.

"He shouldn't have," she whispered. And he was not sensitive, else how could he have come here to establish his claim—so hastily, so ruthlessly, so oblivious to her brother's pain? Tears started to her eyes. She wiped them away but more came. She wept for Brian. She wept for herself. She wept for reasons that had nothing to do with her or Brian—for foolish, foolish reasons!

It might have given Sheila some little satisfaction had she known that Lord Rande was feeling just as uncomfortable as she believed he ought to be. The library was a commodious chamber with tall windows facing the vast lawns in the foreground and, in the distance, a church spire rising over masses of trees. There were high bookcases on three sides of him—two flanked a marble fireplace topped by a huge square mirror set into an ornate metal frame. Over the bookcases hung paintings: two of them he recognized as Titians, another was a small Botticelli, and the fourth was a Rembrandt, so magnificent that he ached to possess it. The books themselves, leather-bound, gold-stamped, looked as if they had been purchased for show rather than perusing, but Lord Rande, glimpsing some familiar and beloved titles, had some difficulty keeping his hands to his sides. If he had been alone, he might have scanned some of them, but not when he was in the company of Brian and Sir Jasper. He particularly resented the latter's presence. If it were not for his own most opportune intervention, he had no doubt that Sir Jasper would be standing in his place, this day, but he would have had no intention of returning the booty.

The very thought of the man had always set his teeth on edge; his proximity was a trial. Furthermore, he was positive that Sir Jasper cherished similar thoughts about himself. He could almost feel his seething rage. Consequently, he said casually, "I am extremely impressed, but I find it passing close in here. I think I would like to see the horse." He had wanted to say "my horse," but in view of the regret and pain that must be racking Brian, he could not bring himself to rub any more salt into that smarting wound.

"Very well." Brian's tones were low and husky. He did not look at him, but instead he faced Sir Jasper, in whose narrowed eyes flickered a commiserating light. "We'll go to the stables. And afterward, perhaps you will want to ride over the property?"

"Afterward, yes," Rande agreed, privately determining to separate Brian from Sir Jasper and tell him the truth, bringing a charade that was becoming more and more uncomfortable to its speedy conclusion. What he particularly resented was that the colors in which he was presenting himself should have been donned by Sir Jasper. It was amazing to him that Brian could not divine the perfidy of his companion, which, to him, was obvious. Brian, however, was young and impressionable. It seemed to him that, rather than the seven years that separated them in age, twice that number intervened. Brian seemed generations younger. Of course, he and his sister had been raised in the country, where they were not likely to encounter the likes of Sir Jasper. Yet, he had the feeling that Miss Corbett did not care for Sir Jasper, either. Of course, she was older than her brother—if not in years, at least in common sense—and so lovely. Her eyes . . .

"Shall we go to the stables, then?" Brian prompted.

Lord Rande started. He had been so sunk in thought that he had actually forgotten where he was. "Yes, do let us go at once, please."

Actaeon was even more beautiful than he remembered—with his dark burnished coat and his small shapely head, a throwback to those steeds bred to race on desert sands, a felicitous blending of bloodlines: a noble animal! More than ever, he was tempted to claim the stallion for his own, but again, that was not his intent. And he must remember that intention, which was still to teach Brian a lesson.

"A beautiful creature," he drawled, approximating, he decided wryly, Sir Jasper's own languid way of speaking. He added, "I shall be honored to have him in my stables."

"Honored?" Sir Jasper repeated. " 'Tis a word that sits ill on your lips."

Rande whirled on him, the anger that Sir Jasper's presence always inspired in his breast mounting. "And what would you be meaning by that?" he demanded.

"Brian, here, is no novice at piquet. 'Twould take a fine player to outwit him."

A short laugh escaped Lord Rande. "Not fine, Sir Jasper, merely experienced."

"Experienced at what, my lord? Cards or sleight of hand?"

"Sir Jasper!" Brian exclaimed. "What would you be suggesting?"

"He is suggesting—and rather broadly, I might add—that I cheated you," Lord Rande explained. The pent-up anger that the proximity of Sir Jasper had been inciting for the last hour was rising to a boiling point. That this out-and-out scoundrel should accuse him of employing his own nefarious tactics was outrageous. That it was also a deliberate attempt to provoke him also occurred to him. Sir Jasper, balked in his scheme to secure Brian's holdings for himself, was trying to force a duel on him. He could respond or he could not respond. Meeting Sir Jasper's eyes, he read calculation rather than anger, and in a second, his gaze had turned evasive. In that same second, Rande reached a decision. His fist shot out, connecting with his enemy's chin.

The baronet staggered and fell heavily. He was on his feet in a trice. "Damn you," he bellowed. "I will have satisfaction."

"Send your seconds!"

"Damn and blast my seconds, we'll settle this now," Sir Jasper exclaimed as he tenderly massaged his chin.

"Very well, now!" Lord Rande agreed.

"Good God!" Brian protested. "You cannot mean a . . . a . . ."

"You have pistols, have you not?" Sir Jasper said to him.

"Yes, but sure you can reach an easier understanding, gentlemen." Brian, his eyes wide, looked from one man to the other.

"Perhaps my Lord Rande can, but not myself," Sir Jasper snapped. "I demand satisfaction!"

"I will be delighted to give it to you," Lord Rande responded coldly.

"But 'tis madness," Brian protested again. "We'll need seconds and a doctor!"

"And a constable, perhaps?" Sir Jasper questioned sarcastically. "Best settle this matter among ourselves!"

"Yes, among ourselves," Lord Rande agreed, feeling . . . He was not sure what he felt, save that he had always longed to send a ball through Sir Jasper, and though this was a flimsy enough pretext, it would more than serve his real purpose. He was an expert shot. However, he had no intention of shooting to kill. A hole in the arm or the shoulder, a hurtful wound by which Sir Jasper would atone in some part for the death of Gilly and for the pain and misery he had inflicted on that whole unfortunate family.

"I beg your indulgence, gentlemen. Can we not forget this incident?" Brian persisted.

"I think not," Lord Rande said.

"No, lad." Sir Jasper nodded. "I do not take kindly to

a blow delivered when a man's off guard any more than I take kindly to canny cardplay."

"Do you not?" Lord Rande asked in some surprise. "I thought 'twas how you'd made the greater part of your fortune."

"You . . ." Sir Jasper's fists clenched. His look was murderous. He turned to Brian. "Fetch the damned pistols and have done!"

Brian frowned. "I do not like this. I will have Paddy in attendance. He's very knowledgeable about medicine." Turning, he hurried out of the stables.

Lord Rande, seeing no reason to remain in the company of his glowering opponent, strolled out into the stable courtyard. The redheaded little lad who had put his horse away was tossing a ball against the wall. Evidently, he had been informed of his identity, for he received a lowering look. Directly after the duel when, hopefully, he had put Sir Jasper out of action for a month or so, he would tell Brian the truth and advise him to eschew gambling.

Brian was back with the flat box containing the dueling pistols rather sooner than Lord Rande had anticipated. He brought a short, grizzled man with him. The latter had bright blue eyes and features that had a faint simian cast. He addressed the boy. "Get along wi' ye, Mickey," he ordered. "Sure'n yer mother's waitin' dinner for ye."

"I am sorry to interrupt your meal, Paddy," Brian said. "I'll have cook give you something later."

"Aye." The coachman's mien was grim and disapproving.

"Where's Sir Jasper?" Brian's question fell between Paddy and Lord Rande, as if he were unwilling to address his unwanted guest.

"He's in the stables, still," Lord Rande answered equably.

"Fetch him, Mickey," Paddy ordered, glaring at the boy as he, in turn, gazed interestedly at the pistol case. Mickey hurried into the stables and a moment later returned with Sir Jasper.

Brian looked from Sir Jasper to Lord Rande. "Paddy, here, will be calling out the paces."

"Unless one or another o' ye wishes to change his mind." The coachman frowned.

Circular wrinkles over his eyes enhanced his resemblance to a wise monkey, Lord Rande thought. He said. "I have no intention of withdrawing from this duel."

"Nor I," Sir Jasper agreed. "Where will we go?"

"There's a stretch of land by the woods, a clearing, where no one is liable to come," Brian spoke reluctantly. "But I must ask again if this quarrel cannot be settled less . . . bloodily."

"Not by me," Sir Jasper said sharply.

"Nor me," Lord Rande agreed. His initial anger had not cooled. The image of Kitty Farne fluttered through his mind, and Gilly, whom Sir Jasper had so cruelly cozened. They cried out for vengeance, and Brian, unknowingly, demanded protection, too. The Sir Jaspers of this world needed to be removed from it, but he would not kill him. That was a purely selfish consideration. He was not minded to go abroad. Yet, he would not need to go abroad, for there was none to know that the affair had ever taken place. Still, he shrank from slaying his opponent. He had killed too many already—on the battle-field where such action was expected. He had not liked it then, and even if men such as Sir Jasper deserved such a fate, it was not for him to assume the role of executioner. Perhaps, he decided with a grim smile, he would be able to put his opponent's arm out of commission and that would certainly hinder his expertise at cards.

By the time they had reached the aforementioned strip of land, Lord Rande was experiencing a deep sense of unreality. It was such a beautiful day; the place to which they had come was bordered by tall verdant trees, their tops seemingly brushing the sky, the vivid blue sky which, he remembered thinking, duplicated the cerulean hues of Spain. The grass beneath his feet was clipped. It reminded him of a bowling green rather than a dueling ground. He had not come to Corbett Manor to duel, he had wanted only . . . But he could not dwell on that now. He must concentrate on the matter at hand. He heard a rustling among the bushes that rose beneath the trees. He cast a look over his shoulder and saw a gleam of red, the vivid red locks of Paddy's young son, he knew. The lad had been ordered home by his father, but instead he had crept down here to watch. He ought to alert Paddy to his presence, but that would earn the lad a beating. He decided against it.

Paddy said, "Are you both still of the same mind?"

It was a question usually asked by seconds. It was the seconds who examined the pistols. That had been left to Brian; he had found them in order, but had given them to Paddy to examine, too.

Paddy, instructed by Brian, said, "You will walk to my count, ten paces. On the count of ten, you will turn and fire."

Sir Jasper had buttoned up his coat and Lord Rande did the same. His sense of unreality persisted as the numbers rang out: "One . . . two . . . three . . . four . . . five . . . six . . . seven . . . eight . . . nine . . ."

Lord Rande was turning as the redhaired boy screamed out something, startling him and causing him to step back slightly, looking in that direction. At that same moment, he felt a blow to his shoulder, and as the number ten rang out, he raised his hand and, much to his surprise, found he could not lift the pistol. He was feeling very strange. He tried again and then fell to the ground. Looking up, he saw the bright-blue sky. He heard but dimly a scream and also an angry yell.

"Ye shot too soon," that was Paddy. Lord Rande could not place the scream.

Paddy's simian face was close to his own. He glared down at him. Standing nearby were Brian and Sir Jasper. There was no mistaking the look of satisfaction Lord Rande read on the latter's face; he knew what had happened now. Brian looked frightened. Rande had misjudged Sir Jasper, fatally misjudged him—once a cheat, always a cheat—but oddly enough Rande could summon

up no anger toward him. Elsie would be waiting for
him . . . Elsie of the blue eyes and the dark curling hair.
Rande frowned slightly. Elsie had golden hair, had she
not? Hair of the hue of Marie's . . . Marie, who was
Marie? he wondered, and could not place her. He was
faintly puzzled by his increasing confusion and by the
aureoles of gold around the two men, but these were
fading and everything was dimming . . . Darkness came
swiftly in Spain, he recalled.

Sheila, seated in the rose-garden, heard the shot. A
poacher in the woods, she reasoned. Keepers . . . were
there keepers to apprehend him? She actually hoped there
were not. Probably the poor man needed the food. She had
heard a scream, too. Had it come before or after the shot?
After, probably. The scream of a wounded rabbit or a
stoat. Did deer scream? No, she thought suddenly, and
paled. It had sounded human. Had somebody been hurt?
She jumped up and hurried to the path that led toward the
woods—at least she thought it must. She was not sure
about anything here, nor was she likely to be. Where had
Lord Rande gone and Sir Jasper and Brian? Had they
heard the shot? She walked on farther, telling herself it was
futile to try to find out what had happened. It had been a
distance away, probably deep in the woods—woods she
had never entered. She came to a sudden stop, hearing
panting and sobbing. She tensed as she saw Mickey
running toward her.

"Child, what's amiss?" Sheila stepped in front of him,
blocking his way so that he ran against her, nearly
knocking her off her feet. She clutched him, steadying
herself.

"Oh, M-miss S-sheila!" He looked up at her fearfully.

"Mickey"—she stared into the tearful eyes and put a
gentle hand on his shoulder—"tell me what's amiss, my
child."

"He . . . he hadn't ought to've shot so . . . so soon.
'Twasn't on the c-count of t-ten . . . 'twas before'n . . ."

"What is it? What has happened?" Sheila's heart was

close to her throat, its pounding seemed to be in her ears as well. "Tell me," she ordered.

She listened to his account. His brogue was thick, so thick she could scarcely understand him, especially since his voice was choked with tears. She had to ask him to repeat himself several times, but finally she understood what had happened and how Sir Jasper had not waited. She did not understand why the duel had taken place because Mickey did not understand it either. Striving for calm, Sheila asked him to guide her to the place. He was unwilling. He was in trouble already for yelling so loudly, but she was Miss Sheila and he would do anything she wanted.

"It's this way," he sobbed, and started off, running.

Sheila ran too. She was breathless by the time she arrived at the clearing—to find Lord Rande lying on the ground, his face drained and white, blood staining his gray coat—the left side of his gray coat, near the heart, she thought with a shudder. Paddy was kneeling at his side. Brian stood staring down at him and Sir Jasper was standing a few paces away. Paddy knew a great deal about medicine, she remembered, but looking at the fallen man, she wondered if that knowledge would be needed.

"It was the exigency of the moment," Brian explained. "Rande was the aggressor." He spoke loudly, assertively, but his voice was trembling still.

"If he dies, it will be murder." Sheila glared at him, moving away from the door of the chamber where, at her orders, Paddy and Kevin, one of the footmen, had borne the wounded man, Brian being in deep confusion and seemingly incapable of issuing even the simplest instruction.

Her brother raised a hand. "Only we know that," he said warningly.

"*He* must know."

"Paddy has told you . . ."

Sheila's teeth clenched. She felt . . . She was not sure of her feelings, they were chaotic. No, one was separate from the rest, and that was anger. It colored her tone as she said,

"It seems to me that you actually desire his death. That is not very intelligent. Lord Rande is still breathing. Paddy is getting ready to extract the bullet. He thinks there's a chance."

"A very small chance," Brian said. "The wound's close to his heart. If little Mickey'd not screamed out and startled him, causing him to turn aside, he'd be a dead man now."

"And was that what you hoped would happen?" Sheila demanded contemptuously.

"Of course it was not what I hoped would happen. I was speaking about the position of the bullet," Brian retorted.

"It is closer to the shoulder bone than to the heart. Paddy told you that as well as me. I think you'd prefer to believe that he'll die."

"I'd be a hypocrite if I said I was praying for his recovery," Brian growled. "If he lives, I will be dispossessed."

"Brian!" Her hand crept to her throat. "You . . . you wouldn't want . . . you wouldn't connive to—"

"Connive!" he interrupted, glaring at her. "What are you suggesting?" Before she could respond, he continued roughly, "I did not want this. I did not instigate the quarrel. It came about quite naturally, out of Sir Jasper's concern for me and his righteous anger at Rande. But sure you cannot blame me if I cannot cast my shawl over my shoulders, as it were, and fall a-keening for his plight, which he brought on himself."

"You should have forbidden the duel," she flashed.

"I tried. They'd not heed me."

"You furnished the pistols."

"I had no choice. They were primed to fight." Brian glared at her. "Lord, Sheila, Rande accused Sir Jasper of cheating and knocked him down. You saw the bruise on his chin."

"For which he was very well avenged," she snapped. "And does that excuse him for having shot before the count of ten?"

"No, it cannot excuse him," Brian returned. "I have told you what I thought of that. He took it ill—I thought that he might challenge me as well. He will be leaving soon, I assure you."

"At your request, I hope."

" 'Twas his decision."

"And if Lord Rande should not survive, I expect he will make a second decision that will see him in France?"

"That need not concern us," Brian growled.

"Need it not?" Sheila took a restive turn around the hall. "Lord Rande is not without friends, you know. They will make inquiries. What will be your answer?"

Brian paled. "He's not dead yet."

Sheila nodded. "And you'd best pray that he remains alive, dear brother," she said sharply.

His face grew even paler. "They could not hold me accountable for this quarrel. I tell you that Rande brought it on himself by impugning Sir Jasper's honor and attacking him."

"And whose idea was it that they should settle their differences upon the spot and without any of the formalities usually attendant upon a duel?"

"It was their decision!" Brian cried.

"You should have refused to countenance the match. You had that right."

"Miss Sheila . . ."

Sheila whirled, seeing Paddy at the chamber door. "Yes?"

"You'd best come. I'm ready."

"Yes, at once." She hurried after him.

Lord Rande, divested of his coat and shirt, looked incredibly pale against the pillows. The contrast between him and the strong attractive young man who had ridden out to claim his winnings this morning was well-nigh overwhelming. Given the fact that he had obviously provoked the altercation that had laid him low, she should have felt that he had received his just deserts, but as she joined Paddy at Lord Rande's bedside, Sheila was experiencing emotions that teetered on the edge of anguish. Though she cherished many doubts concerning the efficacy of prayer, she prayed for him in the moments before Paddy, knife in hand, prepared to extract the bullet.

6

HE HAD THE feeling that he had been on a ship, a vessel racked by storms, buffeted about by high, shrieking winds. He, good sailor that he always was, had been vilely seasick. His body felt drained and empty. There had been pain when a spar had evidently fallen across his shoulder, but that had abated, mainly because he had put it out of his mind. He could not think of pain when Elsie was with him, her presence so real that he had expected to find her with him . . . When he opened his eyes he was in an unfamiliar place, not the small cabin he had expected to find but a huge room with walls paneled in a light oak and green draperies at tall windows bright with early sunshine. He closed his eyes against the glare.

He was extremely confused. It was also odd to feel so very weak. Yet, he had the distinct impression that he was alive. He had not expected to be alive, because something had happened. He frowned, trying to recollect what it had been, and in his mind a vision coupled with a sound: someone acting improperly, someone screaming loudly. He had moved back, had turned aside, and then something had hit him in the shoulder—not a spar, because he had not been on shipboard. He remembered grass and trees, neither of which grew in the ocean, nor on a ship.

He tried to sit up, but a gentle hand pushed him back. He must resist that determined action. He could think better if he were sitting up, but he felt so ridiculously weak. He lay back on the pillow.

"That's better," a woman said.

"Elsie . . ." he murmured, trying to turn toward her,

but turning was difficult, a part of him hurt and throbbed. A groan escaped him. Then, cool hands on his brow began to stroke his hair.

"Lie still, my lord." The voice was as gentle as the touch. He seemed to know it. Elsie's voice? It could not be her voice, he reasoned. She was dust and ashes these four years past. If it were Elsie, he was no longer living. He gazed around him and knew he could not be in heaven. Heaven would be filled with clouds and stars and blue skies —not light oak paneling and green draperies. And Elsie never would have called him "my lord." She would have said, "Ivor, Ivor, my dearest love."

"That is what she would have said," he spoke out loud or, rather, tried to speak. His tones were so low, mere threads of sound.

"Shhhh, you must not try to talk. You must lie still and rest. You are better, you know."

"You are . . . not . . . not Elsie," he said effortfully. "I thought you were . . . but she could not be here . . . I thought she . . . she was. That . . . is very strange."

"I am sorry, but you were dreaming."

That sounded reasonable. He was in the habit of dreaming, but not as much as recently. There had been many, many dreams recently. "I could have been . . ." he told the voice. "It's been four years." He decided that did not make much sense. "It has been . . . four years since she . . . died. "

"I am sorry for that," the voice said. "But try to sleep now. You need all the rest you can get."

He made another effort to turn his head and see the speaker, but he could not. His eyelids felt heavy. He fought against sleep because he wanted to see the female— Female? Yes, there was a woman sitting beside his bed, whose voice he had confused with Elsie's. It was similarly soft, similarly beautiful, but deeper. Who was she? His eyelids drooped—and darkness, waging a battle with sunlight, triumphed.

Since it was so early in the morning and she was alone in the chamber allotted to his lordship, Sheila brushed back her patient's dark locks with a gentle hand. Tired as she was, she felt like dancing for the sheer joy of Lord Rande being awake and conscious at last—well, semiconscious. Some confusion did remain, but the worst was over, she was sure of it. No longer would he toss and turn on his bed calling out to comrades dead or dying in Spain, would not beg them to take him, too, and rail against the cruel God that had let him live when his Elsie was dead, four years dead, as he had said a moment ago. She shuddered. He had very nearly had his wish.

Thought Paddy had extracted the bullet with less trouble than he had feared, it had been a deep wound and fever had set in. It had lasted nearly a fortnight, and during that period there had been times when Paddy had shaken his head and told her gloomily that it was touch and go. The crisis had come last night. Sheila and Letty as well had wept when Paddy had emerged from the sickroom looking almost as exhausted as his patient. They had feared the worst until he had told them exultantly that his lordship was finally sleeping peacefully.

She would have to write to Brian. Sheila clicked her tongue in disapproval. Her brother had gone away shortly after Rande had been shot. He had returned to London and a week later he had written her a long letter—the gist of which was that Brian had *forgiven* Sir Jasper for his dastardly conduct in the duel.

He had stated that the baronet had come to him full of abject apologies and had sworn on his honor that he had believed he heard Paddy call out ten. Brian had readily credited the tale. Sheila had answered his letter with a stinging, sarcastic reply, suggesting that he wanted to believe Sir Jasper's careful lies and in the honor he did not possess. She had not heard from him since.

Sheila was sorry about that. Evidently, she had temporarily alienated Brian, who would turn more and more to Sir Jasper. If only Rande were well enough to prosecute him, but he was not. It would be at least another month before he was on his feet. Paddy predicted six weeks. Sir Jasper would have the better part of two months to continue his dubious practices in London, and more specifically, to favor Brian with his doubtful company. She grimaced. If Brian was able to see into her head, he would be most resentful. He would accuse her of actually defending Lord Rande's reprehensible actions. And if she were to be absolutely truthful with herself, she did consider him more victim than villain.

"Elsie . . ." he murmured.

Sheila tensed. Had he drifted into delirium again? She put her hand on his forehead but found it cool. He must only be dreaming. On other mornings, other nights, he had thrashed about, calling on Elsie, chiding her for leaving him, begging her to come back and take him with her.

Letty, who had also spent long hours at his bedside, had wept over those anguished pleas, as she had, too. While Sheila had been angry with Brian for leaving, she was glad he was not there to see her tears. Looking at the man on the bed now, she blinked back more tears. He was so very pale. His skin was almost transparent. It looked even whiter by reason of the dark beard that had sprouted on chin and cheeks. Yet, oddly enough, he seemed even more handsome than he had when he had ridden here. In fact, his features could almost be called beautiful. His hair waved naturally, his eyelashes were long and curling. The sleeping Orpheus, she thought, who with his music could charm the very snakes from their holes. It was strange— also embarrassing to admit, even to herself—that the image of Ivor at the piano was something she could not erase from her mind. And she had no right to call him Ivor. They did not know each other that well, would never know each other that well. She had to remember him in relation to her brother. She had to remember Marie, whom he had not mentioned during those fever-ridden days and nights. There was another image she must keep in mind: Lord Rande going off with Marie that night, protecting her from Brian's importunities, guarding his preserves. Yet, on the other hand, it was ridiculous to maintain that she did not know him, that she had not held him in the night and been Elsie when he had cried out for her in his fevered fantasies.

"Yes, my love, I am here," she had said on more than one occasion.

"Will you take me with you, Elsie, please, Elsie? I miss you so dreadfully."

"That I cannot do, Ivor."

"Please, my love, please . . ."

"I cannot take you, Ivor. 'Tis not your time."

He had clung to her weakly, his face against her breasts, and though she must forget those moments, that memory, intrusive and vivid, returned. She had smoothed his sweat-soaked locks back from his burning forehead, murmuring comforting little words to him as if he were a sick child. She could not understand the feelings that came to her in those hours. He was so needful and in such pain that when she would leave him to the care of Letty or Paddy or Bridget, she would lie wakeful and weeping in her own room, wanting to be with him again, thinking no one else would know how to care for him. His agony seemed to envelop her, the more so since she was unable—and Brian refused—to turn the man who had hurt him so cruelly over to the magistrate.

"I hate him," she mouthed. "He should be hanged."

"It was an error." That was Brian's voice echoing through the corridors of her mind.

"I do not believe you, Brian. More specifically I cannot believe Sir Jasper."

The action must have been deliberate, she reasoned. Deliberate and cowardly. Sir Jasper had undoubtedly feared an exchange of fire! Yet, if he had feared it, why had he deliberately provoked a duel? She shuddered away from the only logical explanation: murder. Why? A friendly gesture for Brian's sake. No! She did not believe that, did not believe in their friendship. Sir Jasper was no one's friend, and Brian was a blind fool for imagining that he could be. He had his own purposes in acting as he had. She was sure of that, too. Brian was mad to have cultivated

him and to have sided with him once the crime—for it had
been a crime—was committed.

A soft tap on the door interrupted her uneasy reflec-
tions. Sheila rose hastily, went quietly across the floor, and
opened the door that led into the sitting room.

Miss Letty was standing there, her small face tense.
"How is he?" she whispered.

"He's on the mend, thank the good Lord," Sheila said.

"Oh." Miss Letty clasped her hands, pressing them
against her thin chest. "Do you mean he's no longer
confused?"

"A little, perhaps, but he does know that Elsie's dead.
'It's been four years,' he told me. He's not sure of my
identity. He spoke only briefly and then he dropped off to
sleep again, but 'tis a peaceful sleep."

Astonishingly—or perhaps not so astonishingly—tears
appeared in Miss Letty's faded brown eyes. "Oh, I am
thankful. There is something about him." She paused,
adding timorously, "I hope you'll not be angry with me
when I say he is . . . or seems . . . Well, it is difficult to
imagine that he would want to cheat or hurt Brian, he
himself having been so unhappy, poor young man."

"I know." Sheila nodded. "One must feel sorry for him
. . . despite his actions."

"So sorry . . . so very sorry," Miss Letty agreed,
clasping her hands together so tightly that the knuckles
turned yellow.

Sheila said, "I must fetch Paddy. He'll want to look at
him. You sit with him, Letty, if you do not mind."

"Oh, no." Miss Letty's face was brightened by a smile.
"I do not mind." She hurried past Sheila and disappeared
into the bedchamber.

Paddy, arriving shortly thereafter, ordered Miss Letty
out of the room while he examined his patient. She joined
Sheila in the outer hall. "He does look better," she
murmured.

"Yes, he does."

"Paddy will have to shave him. I am sure he'll not want
that beard."

"I am sure he's in no condition to give it a single thought." Sheila bit down a giggle.

She was wrong about that.

On the night of the day he recovered his senses, Lord Rande was well enough to take some light nourishment. It was brought to him by Miss Letty, who came back to tell Sheila, not without a note of triumph in her voice, that he had asked if he might see Miss Corbett and that he had also complained because he was sure he must look a "hairy monster."

"I will tell him that Paddy will shave him." Sheila laughed. "And I'd best see him."

"But not alone, my love," Miss Letty warned. "Now that he's on the mend, we must consider the proprieties."

"I'd not dream of flouting them," Sheila assured her anxious little cousin, valiantly ignoring an inner compulsion to dispense with her company.

Coming into the room where she had spent so many long hours watching over him, Sheila, with Miss Letty behind her, was glad that the sun was nearly down, for her cheeks were warm and she did not think that the flame from the single candle on the nightstand would give off enough light to reveal any change of color. Now, as she moved to the foot of the bed, she did not dwell on that. She wondered what he must be thinking. He had lost a fortnight from his life. He had been grievously wounded and must still be in pain. Paddy had told them that it was diminished. "Or," he had said in disbelieving tones, "so his lordship assures me. It should be lessened a bit . . . especially since he'll not be tossin' about so much, poor lad."

It was unusual for Paddy to express sympathy for a Britisher, particularly one who had wronged his young master. Evidently, Lord Rande's stoicism when he had awakened when Paddy was removing the bullet had impressed him.

The bullet. It seemed terrible that this unfortunate occurrence had taken place on their grounds. Then, she dare not forget the reason it had taken place here. It had grown out of his own reprehensible actions: coming out here, bold as you please, to inspect the property he had won from her brother in a card game.

However, it was difficult to work up much indignation on that count. She ought to be indignant. To have encouraged Brian to wager everything on the turn of a card was dreadful. Still . . . She was confused. She was not usually so confused. She had always been considered to have a very level head. She must collect herself. She would have to face him now and must concentrate on the proper attitude with which to confront him. She would be cool, but not too cool, polite but not icy. Even given the reasons that had brought him to the manor, she must exhibit a certain amount of sympathy, but there would also have to be restraint in her manner. Sheila stepped forward and leaned on the footboard. Then, everything was resolved— at least for the time being because Lord Rande had fallen asleep again. Gratefully, Sheila, followed by Miss Letty, tiptoed from the room.

Holding a copy of Defoe's *Moll Flanders,* Sheila left the library and went down the hall toward Lord Rande's chamber. She hoped the volume would keep him entertained for at least two days. If she were reading it, she would not be finished in twenty times that period, but his lordship, she had learned, had an insatiable appetite for books. In less than a week he had read both Defoe's *Journal of the Plague Year* and *Robinson Crusoe.* He had begged Miss Letty for *Moll Flanders,* but she, while approving of plague-struck London and shipwrecked mariners, did not hold with tales of kept women and had been reluctant to procure it for him.

"It might heat his blood, poor lamb. And he's been doing so well this past week. I do not think he should be given *Tom Jones,* either. My brother would not have any of Mr. Fielding's works in the house."

Miss Letty being out in the garden, Sheila had decided to procure the proscribed volume for him. Though he was much better, he still had some pain and Paddy had ordered that he must remain in bed. That, she guessed, must be very difficult for so active a man.

Coming into the sitting room, she tapped on his bedroom door.

"Come in," he called, and as she appeared on the threshold of his bedchamber, he added with real pleasure, "Miss Corbett . . . and alone!"

Sheila reddened. "I came to bring you *Moll Flanders.*" She gave him a conspiratorial smile. "But you must promise to put it beneath the covers when Miss Letty's about. She has strong objections to its contents."

"I know." He nodded. "I have heard them. I do thank you and I shall do as you ask, of course."

Sheila put the volume on the nightstand. "I hope you will enjoy it," she said, adding, "Paddy tells me that you are mending very rapidly. I am so glad of that. I cannot think it will be overlong before you are up and about again."

"I am told 'twill be another three weeks. But be that as it may, I have something I must discuss with you. Will you not sit down?"

Sheila hesitated. "You put me in jeopardy of a scolding from Cousin Letty, who is a stickler for the proprieties."

He looked at her pleadingly. "I cannot think that they will be flouted. And I must speak to you regarding a matter that has been preying on my mind. I would prefer to unburden myself to you, alone."

She was not proof against that request from one who had been touchingly grateful for every service performed for him and who had, as yet, made no reference to the circumstances that had brought him to this pass. Sheila experienced an interior quaver. Now was probably the time when he would mention them. She said, "I will not summon Cousin Letty, my lord."

"I do thank you. Will you not sit down?"

She pulled a chair closer to the bed and settled herself in it. "I must warn you that before you unburden yourself of whatever you wish to say, you must not speak too long. You are still not completely recovered and Paddy has given us strict orders that you are not to tire yourself too much by either talking or reading."

"I promise you that I'll not give any speeches." He smiled at her. "Paddy's a remarkable fellow. Where did he learn so much about medicine?"

"He is friends with a surgeon from County Wicklow who instructed him in treating horses. Paddy went with him on his calls to his human patients as well and I expect he picked it up that way. 'Twas the opinion of my grandfather, whose coachman he used to be when he was a very young lad."

"I understand, and I am most grateful to him. As I am sure his horses must be, too. It is of Actaeon and this house that I wish to speak." He hesitated and flushed. "I am by way of being punished, Miss Corbett."

"Punished, my lord?" she repeated in some confusion. "I do not understand."

"I am being punished for my sins, which are many, not the least of these being arrogance. I set myself up as a teacher, an instructor of foolhardy young men—my pupil being your brother, who seemed bent on meeting perdition in gambling hells. I had a liking for the lad . . . this in spite of various matters that, at the time, annoyed me. I did not want to see him in the maw of a known shark and set out to wean him away from the tables. I thought that if he became truly aware of what could happen to a green lad such as himself when matched with a superior player—"

Sheila leaned forward. "You," she interrupted. "You are telling me 'twas all playacting on your part."

He nodded. "Yes, Miss Corbett. By egging him on to bet so extravagantly, I hoped to cure him by providing him with an example of what could happen were he to continue mixing with—"

"Sharks!" she finished, her eyes glowing. "Oh, that was a splendid notion."

"So it appeared to me. There were, however, some aspects of the situation that I could not like. Chief among these was the playacting to which I was forced to resort when I came here." A rueful smile twisted his lips. "However, from your reaction, I think I was most convincing."

"You were," she said. "But it was a great surprise, for

though I'd been warned you were a rake . . ." She paused and glanced down quickly. "I mean . . ."

Amusement sparked his tone. "My dear Miss Corbett, I know that my reputation is entirely malodorous in some circles. Nor can I argue that 'tis not unearned. But please continue. You admitted being surprised by my actions in regards to your brother. Why?"

"I . . ." She raised her eyes. "It appeared to me that despite what you describe as your 'well-earned reputation,' you seemed to have a great deal of integrity. I could not imagine that you, of all people, would wreak so paltry a revenge on Brian because of his clumsy and ill-advised pursuit of your friend."

"That, I admit, angered me; it seemed a poor return for all I had tried to do for him."

"It was," Sheila agreed. "I cannot excuse it either, but Brian has suffered a severe disappointment in this last year and is not entirely accountable for his actions."

"A disappointment of the heart?"

"In a sense, but it does not involve a female." Sheila told him about her grandfather's will.

He listened intently, frowning slightly. "But," he said as she concluded her account, "you did agree to share the property with him."

"It is not the same thing."

"No, I expect not . . ." Another rueful smile curled his lips. "And then I seemed to rob him of his own inheritance." He sighed. "I wish I'd known, but I can tell him the truth once he returns. Where is he?"

Sheila said reluctantly, "He is in London . . . with Sir Jasper, who ought to be in prison."

His gray eyes turned glacial. He nodded. "Yes, in prison," he agreed. "He tried to kill me, which is carrying friendship a mite too far." A mirthless smile twisted his lips.

"Friendship?" she questioned.

"Brian's friendship, I expect. He was trying to save his lands—at least that would have been his excuse if questioned by your brother."

"But you believe there was another motive?" she probed.

"I do, Miss Corbett. I think 'twas his intention to restore your brother's fortune so that he himself might claim it. I do not base this theory on mere supposition. Sir Jasper has accumulated a tidy fortune by fleecing youngsters new arrived in town and anxious to cut a dash and taste of its fleshpots."

Sheila clapped her hands. "I knew it. I guessed as much myself. The moment I laid eyes on him, I disliked him!"

"You are most discerning, ma'am. And when was that moment?"

"We met him on the boat coming over from Ireland. Oh, I do pray you'll prosecute him. He should be hanged, or at the very least . . . transported."

"We would need witnesses for such a charge."

"There's Brian."

"Who yet seems to favor Sir Jasper."

"If you return his lands he will not."

"*When* I return them," he emphasized. "But I think we must let the other matter drop until I can see to it myself."

There was a grimness in his tone that chilled Sheila. "You will issue another challenge, then? No! I beg you'll not consider it!"

His eyes, which had been hard, softened. "I am unable to put my mind to it as yet. Come, do not look so distressed, Miss Corbett."

"He does not merit a challenge," she insisted. She looked at him and found his face slightly flushed. "Oh, dear, I think we have talked far too long," she said apologetically. "You must rest."

"I am in no mood for resting. If you go, I shall have to read. *Moll Flanders* is a poor substitute for your company."

"My cousin . . ." Sheila began.

"Is not here, and if she were, she would not prevent an act of kindness, who is all kindness herself."

"An act of kindness . . ." she murmured. Distress seeped into her tones. "Look what resulted from your efforts in that direction—and it was uncommonly kind. Nothing I could say by way of thanks could ever be enough.''

''I would consider it more than enough if you'd stay with me a little longer. Rake or not, I am quite harmless. My wings or rather *wing* is clipped—so that I cannot fly. I am a caged bird who wants only a few more grains of your time.'' The look in his eyes was beseeching.

She laughed at his whimsy, but she could not ignore that look or the pleading note in his voice, did not want to ignore it. ''Very well,'' she relented. ''I will risk dear Cousin Letty's displeasure.''

''She is a very gentle little dragon, I'm thinking,'' he murmured.

''She is that,'' Sheila said fondly.

There was a slight pause while he studied her face. He said finally, ''I think she tended me, did she not?''

''She did. Has she not told you so?''

''I've not questioned her on it.'' His gray eyes had the sheen of silver again as he added, ''But I think she was not the only one who sat beside me.''

''There was Bridget, too.'' Sheila was very conscious of his fixed stare, which remained on her face as if he would peer beyond it into the very convolutions of her brain.

''There was one other,'' he persisted. ''I have a memory of a soft gentle voice and firm young arms that held me.''

''Fevers are mightily conducive to dreams.'' Sheila's gaze dropped to her fingers. Obviously, there had been moments when he had been less feverish than she had imagined. She did not like the direction the conversation was taking. She wished that she had not agreed to remain. If he ever found out the truth, it would be extremely embarrassing, not to say intimidating. However, if driven to the wall and forced to admit the imposture, it, too, could be called an act of kindness. She hoped he would regard it in that light.

''Were they dreams?'' he probed.

"My cousin tells me that there were nights when you were very restless. Bridget, too, has described how you called out a name."

"What name?" His eyes were compelling her to look at him.

"Elsie," she said too promptly, adding hastily, "or so my cousin and Bridget have said."

"I dreamed that Elsie held me and spoke to me, too. Though it did not seem to be her voice."

"You were often confused."

"Yet, that particular dream seemed so very real to me, as real as the arms that held me . . . 'Twas as though she were in this very room. But, of course, she has been dead four years."

"So you said."

"When?"

"Letty told me you'd said so."

"I see . . . Letty."

She wanted to ask the identity of Elsie, but she had already said too much. His eyes still roamed over her face making her feel self-conscious and embarrassed. She wanted to leave, ought to leave. Propriety demanded it— she never should have yielded to his begging. Yet, he was bored and lonely and she did feel sorry for him; and his eyes, framed in those lengthy lashes, compelled her, silver eyes, holding her there while he talked of a dead girl he must have loved, had loved enough to want to follow her into the dark realms of death. The words were forced from her almost before she knew it. "Who was Elsie?"

Had she spoken aloud? She blushed. The name hung in the air between them, the name he might not want to remember in his waking hours, but he had spoken it, too.

"Elsie Trefusis," he said. "I met her in the Assembly Rooms at Bath on a summer when I was home on leave from the Peninsula. She was a slim little girl, as graceful as a fairy. She had quantities of golden hair that curled around her face. She was quicksilver in her movements. I asked her to dance. She consulted her card, she had only one country dance left. She gave it to me. As I looked at her, danced with her, it seemed to me that I had been waiting for her all my life. I was half in the clouds, half in despair." He smiled wryly. "Naturally, I was not the only one of her suitors . . . and I had come late to the ball, as it were. Furthermore, it was near the end of my leave. I asked if I might see her again, and her mother, who was also her chaperone, said I might and gave me their direction.

"I found that she lived in a moldering old castle, some distance from Bath. She was the youngest of four sisters, the others were wed. However, I saw their likenesses in the family portrait gallery. They were much alike, slim, delicate, lovely . . . but none was as enchanting as Elsie, who wove a spell around me. Her mother liked me. Her father was more reserved, she being the last of the brood. However, I did not have the reputation I possess now, and since, to my utter delight, Elsie returned my regard and shyly confessed that she had responded to me as I to her at that ball, we resolved to be wed upon my next leave. I went back to the wars. I wrote every day and she wrote, too. Her letters were often delayed. But I learned that her mother had died of an old complaint. I thought of her in black. It seemed too impossible to imagine Elsie in mourning garb.

"Yet, despite her grief, she wrote that she would wed me as soon as I came back to her. That letter was written two months before I received it. I replied at once, but before another batch of mail came to us, I was granted my leave. My commanding officer, a good friend, knew of my attachment and gave me a longer time than usual. I was full of plans for our honeymoon . . . we'd go to the Isle of Man. She had never seen it and had told me there were supposed to be fairies there. I had told her that she would be the only one, the queen of all the fairies. I had also bought a ring for her, a ruby. It seemed too gaudy for her, but she had told me she had a fondness for them. I could not wait to get to Bath.

"When I arrived at the castle, the old butler answered my knock and burst into tears directly he saw me. I gave him my condolences for his mistress's death . . . and then

Elsie's father came into the hall. I asked after my darling, expecting foolishly that she must come running down the stairs, immediately she heard my voice, as if she could hear it up so long and winding a flight! Her father brought me into his library and gently told me that Elsie had died three months after her mother. He had written me on it, but of course, I had not received his letter.''

"Oh, dear." Sheila blinked tears from her eyes. "How did she die?"

"Of the consumption inherent on her mother's side of the family. That fairylike slimness, that delicacy. Elsie was not strong. She caught the disease they call 'galloping consumption' from her mother and had not the strength to resist it.''

"Oh," Sheila said again, envisioning the eager young man he had been and the terrible shock he must have experienced. "I am sorry," she murmured. "I hope it has not hurt you to speak to me about it."

"No, it has not," he replied, staring at her perplexedly. "In a sense, it has been a relief. I've not talked about it before. I could not, until now. I do thank you for bearing with me."

"You must not thank me," she said gently. "I am glad if the telling of it helped in some part to ease your mind."

"It has—greatly," he said.

He looked weary, she thought. She rose. "I think you must rest now, my lord," she said firmly.

"I will, on one condition."

She saw that he was smiling and was pleased. "The patient is not allowed to make conditions," she said with mock sternness.

"Not even one?"

"Tell me what it is?"

"Your brother mentioned that you could sing. Might I not hear you. Now?"

She shook her head. "I will sing for you when you are able to play the accompaniment. And you will not be able until your shoulder heals—and it will not heal unless you have more rest."

"Is that a promise?"

"It is, my lord."

"I will see that you honor it, Miss Corbett."

"I hope you will, my lord," Sheila said meaningfully, and moved toward the door.

"I thank you, Miss Corbett," he murmured. "You have a very pleasant speaking voice . . . I can imagine your singing voice must be very lovely."

"I hope I will not disappoint you, my lord," she said demurely, but with a gleam of humor in her eyes.

"You could never do that," he said.

He watched her walk across the room. She moved swiftly but gracefully. She was tall—a head taller than Elsie, more than that, he guessed. She was on eye level with him, he remembered, such lovely eyes, too. They were a dark blue. Sapphires would become her. Her hair was black, blue-black, an Irish beauty but with English blood as well. She was warmer than most Englishwomen. That was the Irish part of her, he decided, and remembered a moment when the clouds of fever in his head had parted briefly and he had felt her arms around him, her deep beautiful voice in his ears telling him he must not seek death—and caught by her plea, his agony had dissipated. He had wanted to stay, wanted to live so that he might see her again.

"Arthur Bellmore."

The name suddenly arose in his brain. Why had he thought of him—of Major Bellmore to be exact?

He knew why and tried to discard the memory, but it remained as a warning. Arthur, a brave and daring soldier, had been grievously wounded in hand-to-hand combat as they had marched into Madrid. He had been tended by a Mrs. Higgins, the widow of Sergeant Higgins, killed in that same fray. Ordinarily she would have been sent back to England, but she proved to have had some experience in nursing wounded men. Arthur had been only one of her charges.

She was a comely little creature, he remembered. She had been sixteen when she married Sergeant Higgins, or

'Iggins, as she had pronounced the name. She had turned eighteen by the time they were in the vicinity of Madrid and she had paid special attention to Arthur. He, weakened by his illness, had fallen madly in love with his charming little nurse. Though dissuaded by the colonel of his regiment and by his friends as well, Arthur insisted on wedding her. And once he was recovered enough to make the journey, he took his bride home with him—home being a hoary ancestral pile in the North of England.

He had lost sight of Arthur until he rejoined his regiment in Belgium. He had encountered him on the eve of Waterloo and hardly recognized the once-gallant major. Arthur's face had a bitter, almost a hangdog expression. He had not appeared to be in the best physical condition, either. His leg had been cut in Spain and he still limped badly.

"Well, old man," Rande remembered saying, "I thought you'd settled down at home."

"Home?" Arthur had echoed bitterly. "I have no home. We've been living in London. My wife did not appeal to my parents, and nor did they appeal to her. 'Too stuffy by 'alf, Artie,' " he quoted in her cockney whine. "As it happened, we did not agree either. My lady wife has flown with a baker named Jones."

"I am sorry to hear that, Arthur," he had responded mendaciously, privately believing that his friend was much better off.

"Do not be," he was assured immediately. "It should have happened sooner, before I had the ill fortune to meet her. If had not been in a weakened condition, I would have known her for the conniving little trull she turned out to be. And, my dear fellow, if I should be wounded in this present conflict, let us pray that I am nursed by some pockmarked orderly with a squint!" His laugh had not been quite successful.

As it happened, he learned that Arthur had been slain in the first hours of the battle.

Rande frowned. Certainly, he could not, not by any possible stretch of the imagination, couple Sheila with the

Widow Higgins. The idea was ludicrous and preposterous. All they had in common was their gender. However, he did remember the widow as a sweet armful and very pretty. She was also a most attentive nurse, and consequently, the situation had been fraught with danger from the very outset.

A man was not at his best when he was ill and dependent, especially when he was dependent on someone as incredibly beautiful as Sheila Corbett. His defenses were down. He reasoned with his emotions rather than with his brain. Her voice, her fluid grace, her incredible loveliness, coupled with her gentle reserve, her intelligence, and her obvious good breeding were as lethal a combination as any he had ever encountered. Much as he rejoiced in her company and longed to see her when she was not present, he must not encourage her to remain in the room without the leavening presence of Miss Letty Martyn. He must not let the clouds of illness obscure the fact that she was twenty, not an undesirable age for a man of thirty to marry—but he did not want to marry. He was perfectly satisfied with the life he was leading at present.

He enjoyed gambling, horse racing, yachting, amusing conversation with his cronies, light flirtations with the wanton beauties of the *ton,* and Marie. He grimaced. At this juncture, he could hardly remember what Marie looked like. Furthermore, she must be wondering what had happened to him. He could scarcely send a message to her from here, and consequently, by the time he was on his feet again, it was more than likely that she would have flounced off into the arms of another protector. There were a great many men who courted and coveted her. When they quarreled, she would throw up the names of Lord Such-and-So or the Marquess of Whatever and be furious when he laughed and advised her to seek them out or let them seek her out. And how would he feel if he learned that she had?

"Free," he muttered, and liked the sound of the word. His eyelids drooped, and sliding down in the bed, he glimpsed the volume of *Moll Flanders*. "You're woman enough for me, my love," he muttered with a touch of defiance and straightaway fell deeply asleep.

Sheila, coming out of Lord Rande's chamber, walked slowly down the hall, down the stairs, and out into the garden without really being aware of where she was headed until she heard the plashing of water and saw that she was near a charming little grotto in which a stone flounder sent up a stream of water that fell over its scaly body into a marble basin. There was a wooden bench nearby. She sank down upon it and released a long sigh. She had the sense of having escaped from an extremely dangerous situation.

His eyes were in her mind, his glance varying from the inscrutable to the frank, and either way, it was attractive, more attractive now because he had dropped his wolf's mask. Yet, even if he could no longer be considered in the light of a predator, it was dangerous to remain overlong in his company. Unfortunately, she found that same company extremely stimulating and she could not help but like him.

Sheila gazed back at the bulk of the house rising over the garden. Years ago, it had been put in order by her mother's dowry. Had her mother come to this fountain in agitation of spirit comparable to her own—though stemming from a different cause, her husband's neglect, his frequent absences in London to visit his mistress?

Lord Rande had a mistress named Marie, Lord Rande was a crony of the Prince, as her father had been twenty years earlier. Lord Rande would eventually marry for an heir—and would his wife ever see him? Probably not, for in addition to his mistress in London, there was a dead love enshrined in his heart. And what difference did any of this make to her, who had vowed never to marry?

"I meant it," she muttered defiantly, and saw the trees about her aureoled with an iridescent glow occasioned by the sudden moisture in her eyes. Fiercely she blinked her tears away and, rising, went toward the rose gardens in search of her Cousin Letty.

7

SHEILA STOOD AT the window, one hand holding back the draperies. Her eyes were fixed on the driveway winding down to the road. Cloud shadows were sun-cast on its dusty length, and looking upward, she found the clouds themselves edged with gray. The size of them suggested that they must soon mass together and moisten the land. Generally she did not mind the rain. It would refresh the asters, the chrysanthemums, and the dahlias as well as the late roses, but it would also muddy the roads.

Brian had sent word that finally he was coming down to the manor. It was high time, she thought resentfully. He should not have remained away for a month, lacking only three days. Even given his natural embarrassment over the duel and its ramifications, he ought to have arrived sooner . . . much sooner. That he had not was, unfortunately, typical. He had no way of reading Lord Rande's mind and Brian was always wary of confrontations, especially when he might hold himself partially to blame for the duel. He could have stopped it, should have stopped it, had not *wanted* to stop it, hoping, undoubtedly, that Sir Jasper would put an end to the man who had appeared in the light of an enemy. That was the truth, and an ugly truth, indeed. She had arrived at this conclusion some time ago, which was the reason that, in her letters to her brother, she had neglected to mention Lord Rande's stratagem. Better to let him stew in his own juice until he gathered enough courage to return.

She wondered what Brian's reaction would be, once she informed him of the truth. She hoped that he would be properly ashamed of himself. Of course, there was the possibility he might resent a ruse that had engendered so much anguish. Yet, he must agree that it was an exceptionally generous gesture, one that he had not deserved, especially after the episode with Marie. However, soon the tangled skein of circumstances would be combed out, and then, hopefully, their friendship could be renewed. It would be wonderful if her brother were once more back in Lord Rande's good graces, and then . . .

Then, what?

Then, nothing! Very probably, Lord Rande would be out of their lives as soon as he was well, and he was already better—much better. His health was improving. His shoulder was giving him much less discomfort, and though he still spent a great deal of time in his chamber, resting, he had been able to go down to the library on occasion. She and Miss Letty, of course, fetched the books he wanted to read, but yesterday, her cousin had told her, he had been able to reach one for himself with only minimal discomfort. In another month, he would be well enough to return to London, and very likely they would meet only upon occasion. They did move within the same circles, but there were circles within circles, and if her brother continued to cultivate Sir Jasper, she could not imagine that they would see much of Lord Rande. There were other reasons why they would not see him. He was in the Prince Regent's set and probably he was eager to get back to it, eager to meet with his friends. Though he never complained, she could not imagine that he was happy, confined here in a country house with no one but herself and her cousin in attendance. He would be wanting to see his mistress, too.

She wondered if there were other women besides Marie in his life. She did not want to dwell on that. There was no sense telling herself over and over that she had no feeling for him and that the thought of Marie and the many other ladies he must know was not anathema to her. She did care for him. She could not deny that. Unfortunately, as sure as she was of her own feelings, she was equally sure of his. He liked her and that was all. He was charming, pleasant, and always glad to see her, but in the three weeks that had passed since she had brought him *Moll Flanders,* they had never again achieved the intimacy they had shared during that one conversation.

That, of course, might be due to the fact that she never entered his apartments unless accompanied by her cousin. Yet she sensed a withdrawal in him, as if, indeed, he had regretted his confidences of that day.

She guessed that he was a man who did not like to reveal his feelings to strangers, and in a sense, they were strangers, brought together by a situation that was hardly conducive to a sustained relationship—and she ought not to desire one! Only . . . Sheila leaned forward. A horseman had suddenly appeared at the end of the road. Brian! She dropped the drapery and hurried into the hall, dashing downstairs and out into the driveway to meet him.

"Sheila!" he called, and spurred his horse forward, leaping down to embrace her.

"Oh, I am so pleased that you were able to get here ahead of the rain," she cried.

"The rain?" Brian squinted into the sky. "It looks like a fair day to me."

Sheila glanced upward and laughed. The clouds had drifted away. There was something prophetic in that, she thought, but on facing her brother, her laughter died. He did not look well. There were dark circles under his eyes and his face was puffy, as if he had been drinking too much. She stifled a burgeoning sigh. Brian ought not to drink. Liquor, even light wines, had a disastrous effect on his temperament, turning him belligerent and unruly. He said sarcastically, "And how fares our honored guest or, rather, host?"

"As I told you in my last letter, he's improving rapidly. Of course, his shoulder still pains him. It was a very deep wound."

"Has he been about much?"

"Oh, yes, he's been down to the first floor. He has been

spending some little time in the library. He enjoys reading. I am glad of that, else his period of recuperation would be sadly tedious for the poor man."

"The poor man?" he repeated. "It seems to me that you could save your sympathy for a worthier object."

"As it happens, you are wrong. And once I tell you the truth, you will share my opinion, I think."

He clutched her arm in a hard grip. "I do not understand you. What is this truth you mention?"

"Brian." She held her gaze with her own. "Lord Rande had absolutely no intention of taking this property for his own."

"What nonsense is this?"

"It's not nonsense. Listen to me." As Sheila told him of Lord Rande's intentions, a variety of expressions crossed her brother's face. He looked surprised, then skeptical, then vaguely alarmed, and ultimately thunderstruck.

"You are saying that 'twas all pretense on his part? You are saying that he never intended to keep it?"

"Yes, yes, yes," Sheila cried. "He thought to save you from plunging into deep play with the many unscrupulous rogues who haunt the gambling hells. Men like your dear friend Sir Jasper, who has the reputation you were so eager to affix to Lord Rande. And for this act of kindness, he came near to . . . to losing his life." Sheila's voice broke.

"Good God!" Brian had turned pale. "I . . . I can scarce credit it."

"It's the truth," she answered him. "I do not blame you for being surprised, especially after your actions with little Marie."

"M-Marie," he rasped. "What do you mean?"

"You cannot have forgotten so soon . . . that night at the opera?"

"That night at the opera," he repeated dully. "No, I've not forgotten."

"And in spite of that, he wanted to help you, Brian. He is so good, so patient, so brave"—bitterness crept into her tone as she continued—"even though you could have halted the duel had you been so inclined, and do not tell me 'twas out of your hands! You could have stopped it, but in spite of that, he told me that he covets neither house nor horse nor property. As far as he is concerned, that card game never took place. You are indeed fortunate, Brian. I cannot believe you'd have been treated with such consideration had you been playing with anyone else.''

He regarded her narrowly. "You seem . . . uncommonly fond of his lordship."

"I admire him as must anyone confronted with such a display of selfless generosity."

"It appears to me that you more than admire him," Brian mused.

"I do not love him," she said coldly, "if that is what you are suggesting, but that is aside from the point. 'Tis time and past that you returned, and now that you have, I suggest you come and express your gratitude."

"I will in due course, but not at this precise moment. I must get back to the inn."

"The inn?"

"You did not imagine that I would stop here in a house no longer my own?"

" 'Twas hardly necessary to put up at an inn."

"I thought it was, not being aware of his lordship's munificence. Now that I am, I will fetch my luggage."

"Will you not come and see him first?"

"The inn's not far from here. I will return quickly." Brian leapt on his horse, and before she could protest further, he was gone in a cloud of dust.

"Tell me the whole of it," Sir Jasper ordered as Brian paced back and forth across the small private parlor of the King's Head Tavern on the outskirts of the village.

"There's no more to say," Brian rasped. " 'Twas all a trick to frighten me from the tables, as it were." His voice rose to a bleat. "And now what am I to do with that damned French witch?"

"Pack her off to France, dear lad."

" 'Twill not serve and you know it. There are letters. There are packets to carry her thither and packets to bring her back. And what a tale she'll have to pour into his ears."

"You should not have treated her so roughly, my boy. I know you blamed her for his revenge, as it were, but was it not enough to have possessed her without blacking her eyes and splitting her lip?"

"If she had not screamed and nearly alerted the watch, I'd have done neither," Brian growled.

"Nonsense, my lad. You were primed to make someone pay for your losses," Sir Jasper said. "Besides, did you not tell me that she was most amenable afterward? 'Twould seem to prove the truth of that old saw: a woman, a spaniel, and a chestnut tree, the better you beat 'em, the better they be."

"Yes, she seemed content enough when I left her, but I'll bet you a monkey she'll be all over him when he gets back to London. Then, we'll see how generous he will be to me. He'll keep the lot and kill me in the bargain."

"You may be right, dear boy. Rande is very chivalrous to women." Sir Jasper sighed. "At least when it suits him to be."

"Is that all you can say?" Brian demanded furiously.

"Not quite all, lad. You mentioned a trick and I would like to mention another being played, perhaps, on your sister."

"My sister?" Brian glowered. "What about her?"

"Rande is thirty. He'll be thirty-one in another two months. I know that for a fact because we have a mutual friend who was with him at Madrid four years ago when he said he'd celebrate his twenty-sixth birthday with his marriage."

"His marriage, but he's not—"

"No, I understand that the girl died. Since that time, he has had mistresses and cozy little liaisons among the *ton,* but as the last of his line, he must settle down and produce an heir if he does not want that line to die out. Now, dear boy, he has had some four weeks of your sister's company, and from what you have told me, she is not indifferent to him. Consequently, it might be in his mind—in fact, it might have been there all along—to ingratiate himself with her by this seeming sacrifice of his winnings. In that way, he'll secure himself not only a lovely bride but Dahna as well.''

"No, I'll not allow it," Brian thundered. "Dahna is mine. 'Twas stolen from me!''

"Your grandfather's will—''

" 'Twas Sheila managed it. I'm sure of it. She was forever in his company. He said she reminded him of our mother and how she played up to him. 'Tis my belief that she knew the contents of that will before it was read, blast her, for all she pretended that she was as surprised as myself. In fact, I am of the opinion that she might have dictated it—the conniving little wench!''

"I hope you never let her see how much you dislike her, dear boy."

Brian breathed deeply. "I try not to, but how would you feel if a sister played you such a scurvy trick?''

"I would respond with a few of my own.''

"Would you?" Brian gave him a long, penetrating look. "And what would they be?''

Sir Jasper regarded Brian with a kindly eye. "You've said you are her guardian?''

"Only until her twenty-first birthday, which will take place on March the fifteenth.''

"Only until March? But 'twill not be October until Friday, dear boy. March is a half-year into the future. Now, though I'm neither an astrologer nor a fortune-teller, I predict that many changes will take place in the next six months . . . especially in regards to when and whom your sister will wed.''

"She has told me that she has no intention of marrying.''

"I have a distinct feeling that was before Lord Rande appeared on the scene.''

"Damme, why isn't he dead? He ought to be dead. If only that wretched little urchin'd not screamed out and startled him . . .''

"It was a most unfortunate turn of events, but we

cannot change the past, dear boy, only the future."

"Change it?" Brian's eyes narrowed. "How?"

"You are not very imaginative this day. Perhaps 'tis your choler keeps you from that clarity of thought that is so desirable at this moment."

Staring into Sir Jasper's bland face and reading nothing, Brian barked, "Be more explicit, please."

"I suggest that by anticipating my lord Rande's moves, you might move first and find a suitable bridegroom for your sister, one who would be cooperative when it comes to dowries, who would, in fact, cede Dahna to you."

"I know of none who'd make that sacrifice."

"You know of one," Sir Jasper said gently. "Myself."

"You!" Brian regarded him with a kindling eye. "She does not like you," he said bluntly.

"I am quite aware of her feelings in regard to myself. She does not scruple to hide them. However, I, on the other hand, find her adorable—a Persian kitten rather than the tiger cat she aspires to emulate. She is all fire, but beneath those flames she is gentle. In common with many females, she wants only to be tamed."

"She'll not be tamed by you," Brian retorted. "She would fight you every inch of the way."

"Did you ever imagine that little Marie would yield so readily to your persuasions, lad?"

"But I used—"

"Your fists. Precisely. Let them know who's master and—"

"Sheila'd never acknowledge you as her master," Brian said insistently.

"You seem mighty sure of that, dear boy. Do you speak for your sister or for yourself?" Sir Jasper regarded him through narrowed eyes.

"I speak for her, of course. I'd quite like to see you wed to her. And if you could tame her, as you say, all the better. She's too headstrong by half. Of course"—Brian's glance was equally narrow—"all of this is contingent upon Dahna."

"If you will countenance the match, dear boy, Dahna will be yours immediately the bridal register is signed."

"I'd have that in writing before anything is signed," Brian retorted.

"You do not trust me?" Sir Jasper's eyes glittered.

"I do not trust anyone," Brian said succinctly.

"Very well, dear boy, I will not argue with you. You will have the writ."

"But"—Brian frowned—"I do not see Sheila ever agreeing."

"We'll not need her agreement. You are her guardian, and if that does not suffice, I will see that she capitulates."

"How?"

"A woman, a spaniel . . ."

"No!" Brian protested.

"Your brotherly concern does you justice, but there are diverse ways to persuade her to this match. Still, 'tis early to discuss these. The plans must be drawn up and the time established. I think it must be after Rande departs for London. You'll soon be seeing him. You can advise me as to his state of health."

"God, if only he'd not turned aside . . ."

"I make it a point never to cry over spilt milk. I pour myself another cup and often I find it even more nourishing than the first," Sir Jasper said gently.

"But supposing Rande proposes before he leaves?"

"He'll not wed her on the spot, dear lad. He'll have to return to his London house so that he can set his affairs in order, not the least of these being little Marie, who will have left him a note to the effect that she has found another protector."

"She'd never write such a note and . . . Oh, God," Brian groaned and ran a hand through his hair. "What am I going to do about her?"

"I have a very acceptable solution, dear boy."

"Tell me," Brian exclaimed eagerly.

"Among my friends is a most accommodating lady, one Mrs. Fisher, who keeps an establishment euphemistically called the Aviary. Are you acquainted with it?"

"No, I've not heard of it," Brian said.

"I expect 'tis because you have not been in town long enough. 'Tis very popular with some members of the *ton*. It boasts a number of charmingly furnished rooms on the third floor. There customers can repair and be entertained by any one of a bevy of pretty females."

"Cyprians?" Brian demanded.

"Quite so, and, er, apprenticed to the lady of the house so that before their indentures are at an end, they must needs remain in her employ and on the premises."

"Would she take Marie?"

"She will do anything that I ask. We are old friends, and as I think I have said, she is most accommodating."

"If Marie were to escape . . ."

"That would be quite impossible, dear boy. The only drawback's that you would have to share her charms with . . . other patrons."

"I will leave those charms to the others." Brian shrugged. "I've had my fill of her . . . she's a temperamental little thing, you know. But those patrons, might she not tell them that she was decoyed there against her will?"

"I am sure she will." Sir Jasper smiled broadly. "The fair residents of that bagnio all have similar tales to tell, dear boy. They can be quite heartrending on the subject. Innocence betrayed and so forth . . . but those customers who visit Mrs. Fisher's, er, birdhouse are in no mood to listen, not at the fees she extracts for services rendered."

"Oh, then it's all right and tight," Brian said blithely. "But how will I get her there?"

"You may leave that to me. You have but to give her a bauble of some sorts and provide a bottle of wine. I'll lace it with a substance that will send her off to sleep. When she awakens, 'twill be in the establishment of my good friend."

"But will they not wonder where she is gone? I am talking about the theater."

"They are used to these sudden disappearances, my lad."

"Ah." Brian clapped Sir Jasper on the back. "You are a friend in need. How can I ever thank you?"

"I thought we'd already agreed on the nature of that, er, thanks, dear boy."

"We have, indeed!" Brian held out his hand, which was warmly grasped by Sir Jasper.

"Miss Corbett."

Sheila, on her way down the hall, came to a sudden stop as she saw the tall, slender figure of Lord Rande descending the stairs. For the fourth morning in a row, he was fully dressed, his arms in both sleeves of his coat. His cravat was beautifully tied, his own handiwork, since he had not sent for his valet. It was a further reminder that, during this fifth week of his stay at the manor, most of the stiffness had left his shoulder. She could hardly believe that so many weeks had passed since his ill-fated arrival. In that time, her anger had given way to respect and respect to . . . That was one progression she preferred not to pursue.

"Good morning, my lord."

"Good morning." He moved to her side. "Are you going anywhere in particular, Miss Corbett?"

She had been, but his appearance had swept all memory of that destination from her mind. "Not really," she responded.

He smiled and then held out his hands, fingers spread apart. "You made me a promise, Miss Corbett. 'Twas contingent upon my cooperation, the which I am now ready to provide." He flexed his fingers. "You see . . . both hands."

"I am delighted . . . but the promise, I am not sure—"

"Do you not remember, then? Well, let me remind you. I am in the mood to play the accompaniment if you will sing for me."

"Oh, I did promise that, did I not?"

"I am delighted that, after all, you do remember. May I hold you to that promise? 'Tis a long time since I have heard music, and I miss it."

"I, too," she responded. "Though I would much rather hear you play than spoil it with my indifferent singing."

"Come, you are too modest."

"You have not heard me, my lord."

"And 'tis high time to rectify that omission, I'm thinking. Consequently, Miss Corbett, I am in hopes that you will fulfill your obligation." He regarded her quizzically. "I have seen very little of you in the past week. Miss Letty tells me that you are much involved with household affairs, and since I will be leaving very soon—"

"Will you?" she broke in.

"Have I not been your inadvertent guest long enough?" he inquired.

"Paddy has said that you'd not be fully recovered for at least six weeks."

"Did he indeed? Besides being an excellent physician, he is also a prophet."

"You've been here only five weeks, my lord."

He shook his head. "I fear you are no mathematician, Miss Corbett. I came here during the third week in August. It is now the seventh of October."

"Is it?" She felt a throbbing in her throat. "Gracious, I have lost track of time."

"I am sure that your brother has not. Undoubtedly, he must be most anxious that I leave. And you have been burdened with an invalid's care long enough."

"It has been no burden," she assured him. "Though, of course, I am glad to see you on your feet." Anger tinged her tones as she continued, "It is a shame that you were made to suffer so cruelly and so needlessly."

"My suffering is at an end, or will be when you sing for me," he said insistently. "Please, Miss Corbett."

"Very well, my lord," she agreed with a tiny sigh. "A promise is a promise. Come." She turned down the hall, going in the direction of the music room. He had caught her off guard, she thought wryly. Remembering his skill as a musician, she felt ill at ease and regretful. No, the regret stemmed from another source: from the fact that soon he would be leaving for London.

The door to the music room stood open, and Sheila, going inside, said, "I hope you'll keep in mind that while I have studied singing, I am yet an amateur."

"We will be on an equal footing, Miss Corbett."

"I cannot believe that, my lord, since I have heard you play. I, on the other hand, have not been practicing of late."

"Enough of procrastination," he ordered. Sitting down at the pianoforte, he ran his hands lightly over the keys and then began to play some finger exercises. "There," he said after a few moments, "I have taken some of the stiffness from my hands. Do you need to sing some scales?"

"No, I would rather not," she said self-consciously.

"As you choose." He looked at the pile of music on a table near the instrument. "What will you sing for me?"

Sheila was silent a moment, mentally running over her repertory. "I believe I would like to sing 'Dove sono,'" she said finally.

"Ah, from *The Marriage of Figaro*. Capital! 'Tis one of my favorite arias."

"Oh, dear." She regarded him ruefully. "Perhaps I should choose another selection."

"No . . . this one." He played the opening chords.

"You know it, then."

"I am fond of the music. Will you need the score?"

She shook her head. "No, I have it in my memory."

"Good." He played the opening chords again and much in the manner of her teacher waved his hand at her, ordering her to begin. It was an aria, she realized, that suited her mood exactly—with its underlying sadness, its emphasis on past joys and lost love. She began to sing and, as usual, forgot everything save that compelling music, magnificently played by her accompanist. When the last chord had been sounded, she was still lost in the reminiscences of Rosina, the unhappy countess whose husband's eyes were straying in the direction of her maid-servant.

There was a brief silence after she stopped singing and

then he said in a low voice, "Oh, Miss Corbett! What a tragedy!"

She felt as if he had thrown a bucket of cold water over her. "Was it so bad?" she whispered, adding defensively, "Mozart is not easy. I should not have—"

"Miss Corbett!" Springing to his feet and taking her hands in his warm grasp, he said earnestly, "I only wish Mozart might have heard you. You mistook my words . . . the tragedy is neither yours nor mine but that of those who'll never hear you perform upon the operatic stage." Releasing her, he moved back, saying, "You should be heard."

Her hands tingled from his touch. She said, "I fear you wax extravagant, my lord. I am not nearly good enough to sing in public."

"My dear Miss Corbett, you are mistaken. You could take your place with anyone performing at the King's Theater today! It is a voice of quality and faultlessly produced. I am sure that your teacher told you so."

"He wept," she said, and flushed. She had not meant to tell him of what Brian considered Signor Mancini's excesses. Her brother, while admiring her voice, had been wont to imitate the teacher's gestures and accent. Mancini, overhearing him, had left in a huff, something she still regretted.

"When you are in town again, we must arrange a musicale so that the bushel will only shut out a part of your light."

"Oh, no," she protested, laughing now. "I should die of fright, and besides, my brother would not hear of it."

"Surely, you'll not let his opinion sway you."

"I have no choice, not until the fifteenth of March, at least."

"Why not until then?"

"He's my guardian until my twenty-first birthday."

"Your guardian!" He regarded her amazedly but said merely, "I'd have thought you'd have had someone a little older and more settled, no offense against Brian, but—"

"I do understand, but you see, there's only my great-aunt, who is eighty-eight and needs care herself. Brian, of course, does not exercise his prerogatives. He was as astonished as yourself when he heard the will read. Actually, I think it may have been Grandfather's way of imbuing him with a sense of responsibility for someone besides himself." She looked down, adding self-consciously, "I . . . I do not mean to criticize Brian, but he is impulsive as you have learned. There was another reason, too. Since Grandfather left Dahna to me, he wanted Brian to have an excuse for managing it."

"I cannot see what any of this has to do with your singing."

"Brian feels the onus of being Irish . . . half-Irish, rather, in a society that believes we fall into two categories: entertainers and insurgents."

"Nonsense!" Rande said explosively.

" 'Tis not nonsense, my lord. And I do agree with him. I would feel most uncomfortable being on display, as it were."

" 'Twas Brian told me you had a fine singing voice," he persisted. "Are you sure?"

"I could not," she said firmly. She added, "You are a splendid musician. Do you ever appear in public?"

"Not in public—I would not want you to appear in public, Miss Corbett, but I have played in special programs. I belong to a small musical society. All of us have an avocation for the art; some are violinists, some pianists like myself, and others perform various wind instruments. I imagine that, as a musician, you must be aware of the small groups of interested amateurs who meet at various private homes in Vienna to perform chamber music?"

"Yes, my teacher told me about them."

"Our society began with similar aims, but on occasion we have been asked to play at the homes of friends or friends of friends. We have also been bidden to Carlton House." His eyes gleamed. "That would be an admirable setting for you—in the ballroom or—"

"No, no, no," she protested laughingly. "I beg you will put it out of your mind."

"Having heard you, Miss Corbett, I do not believe I will ever be able to put it out of my mind. I am a very persistent man—"

"And I," she said firmly, "am a very stubborn female."

"Perhaps you will change your mind when you hear one of our concerts," he said. "Directly I return to London, I shall certainly tell our members of my discovery. And I will send you and your brother an invitation. I hope that you will accept."

"Of course, I know we would both enjoy it," she said, aware of a sinking feeling. There had been something extremely impersonal in that suggestion. He had not asked her to come as his guest. However, that was hardly surprising. They were friendly, but they were not really friends. In fact, this was only the second time they had been alone together, and however much she might long for the intimacy they had achieved during the first week of his enforced stay, she had to remember his condition at the time, had to remember, too, that he had not achieved his reputation as a rake by his circumspect behavior. That she had seen another side of the man was due to his wound and resulting illness. No doubt, he must be chafing at this enforced idleness, and that he had not attempted to wile away his time by commencing a flirtation with her was certainly to his credit. However, it was also an indication that he was not attracted to her. True, he had seized her hands and held them warmly, but only as an admirer of her art. She had seen others equally moved by her singing but similarly impersonal in their approach.

She said, "When will you return to London?"

"I have decided to abide by your physician's advice. By Friday, I will have been here over six weeks. I think that I can safely consider a return, do you not agree?"

"Are you sure?" she asked quickly—too quickly, she sensed. Still, without giving him a chance to respond, she added, "I hope you will make your journey in easy stages."

"Most assuredly," he responded. "I will go by post chaise. I have written to my staff advising my coachman to be here by noon on Saturday."

"Saturday," she echoed. "But that is only four days off. I hope you will be as fit as you seem to believe." She could not conceal the anxiety that crept into her tone.

"I assume that I am. I could never have had better care than I have received from yourself and your cousin . . . or company, either."

"It was the least we could do," she burst out. "With you so hurt and here on our land."

"My dear Miss Corbett"—he put an arm around her—"I cannot blame you for that." His arm tightened. "You've been most kind." Releasing her, he moved away quickly. "And when will you be returning to the city? Soon, I hope."

"It depends on Brian. He will want to enjoy the estate a little longer, I expect. I wish he'd remained, but I expect that he felt uncomfortable in your presence."

"He should not. 'Tis not his fault what happened." He suddenly looked very grim.

Seeing that change of expression, Sheila moved toward him and impulsively put her hand on his arm, looking up at him beseechingly. "I pray you'll not do anything foolish, my lord."

"Foolish?"

"Sir Jasper," she said nervously. "I hope you will not consider issuing another challenge."

The grim look remained. "I shall bide my time, of course."

"You'd be far better off to have him arrested. He's no better than a common criminal. He'd have killed you and could very well try the same thing again."

"Here, I must disagree with you, Miss Corbett. He'll not have a second chance at that."

"Not unless you provide it for him, by issuing your challenge," she said in some distress.

He regarded her with a slight frown. "My honor demands—"

"Damn your honor," Sheila cried with a stamp of her foot. "What good will your honor do you if you are dead and he remains alive?" Much to her embarrassment, tears filled her eyes. She looked away quickly.

He was silent a moment, then he said softly, "My dear Miss . . . Sheila, I—"

"Ah, here you are," Miss Letty said from the doorway. "I have been looking for you, Sheila. You had promised you would join me in the gardens. And you, my lord, surely you should be resting?"

He moved away from Sheila. "My resting days are at an end, Miss Letty." He had a fond smile for her. "Just as your days of tending a tiresome invalid."

"You were never tiresome, my lord. My brother . . . But I'll not refine upon that." She blushed. "Let me but say that *you* were as good as gold."

"I have not enough encomiums for my treatment here," he responded gently. "It has been a pleasure, a very great pleasure to know you, Miss Letty. I hope that I will see you in London."

"I hope so, too, but you must not think of London as yet. You need at least another fortnight of rest."

"Lord Rande has decided to leave us this Saturday," Sheila explained.

Miss Letty raised shocked eyes. "So soon, surely not! You should wait until Monday or Tuesday at the earliest."

"No, I am very well. 'Tis not my first encounter with a bullet, you know. I have been a soldier, ma'am."

"Oh, dear, I do know, and I am so glad that horrid Boney's off on an island where he cannot harm anyone. My brother never liked me to refer to him in that disrespectful way, but I can see no harm in it, can you?"

"None whatsoever, Miss Letty." He smiled. "I can assure you that we had even more disrespectful names for him."

"Oh, did you? What did you call him? But I expect you'd best not tell me." She reddened. "I know that gentlemen often use expressions that could not pass muster in a drawing room . . . and where he is concerned, I cannot blame them. It is so comforting to know that all the wars are at an end—even that horrid American conflict last year, though we did not show to such advantage in that, I fear."

"I expect we did not," he allowed, and smiled at her. "And now, I think I must follow your excellent advice after all—and rest."

"Oh, you should," she agreed, "especially if you are set on such a long journey at the week's end. Is there nothing we can say to dissuade you?"

"Lord Rande has commitments in town," Sheila said. "I think his mind's made up."

"Is it? I do think—" Miss Letty began.

"I think I must go," he interposed. He bowed over her hand. "Until later," he said with a smile at Sheila.

"Such a fine young man," Miss Letty enthused as the door closed behind his lordship. "And he does seem so very taken with you, my dear."

"Good heavens, Letty!" Sheila essayed a slight laugh. "I cannot imagine why you would think so."

"It seems very obvious to me, my dear," Miss Letty persisted.

"Not to me," Sheila retorted, wondering what he might have said had her cousin not chosen that particular moment to enter the room. He had seemed . . . But it was useless to indulge in speculations that would only prove disturbing and frustrating and, furthermore, had no basis in reality. He would have uttered a few comforting words, nothing more, even if he had called her "Sheila." She doubted that she meant anything more to him than Letty, and that was just as well because he was amply supplied with female friends.

Probably, his determination to leave on Saturday was partially based on the six long weeks he had been separated from his mistress! A gentleman had certain needs. Her grandfather had been her informant on that subject—and she was very grateful to him for knowledge that, he had told her, most females would be the better for sharing. She was in total agreement with him on that score. It might sweep away some of the aura of mystery and romance that surrounded courtship, but at least she was not as ignorant as poor little Letty. With that comforting thought in mind, she murmured an apology, and removing herself from her cousin's presence, she hurried into the gardens, where, sinking down in her favorite grotto, she began to weep while telling herself that she was being utterly ridiculous and that there was no reason for tears, none whatever!

8

LORD RANDE HAD promised Sheila and Miss Letty that he would journey back to London in easy stages and in his post chaise. He had not been on the road half a morning before he realized the truth of what they had both told him. He should have waited another day or two . . . or five. He should never have left the manor so soon. He had not wanted to leave, on the one hand; on the other, he had been eager to return, or so he had told himself. He had half a mind to go back, but with a stubbornness that was characteristic, he kept to his original decision. However, once back in his London house, he was unable to deny himself another week of rest.

At the end of that period, he felt in shape again. Yet, if he had recovered physically, there was a lingering depression of spirit he was unwilling to examine too closely. Instead, he met with friends at Brooks or Boodles, Whites or Watiers and countered their probing questions with an excuse concerning a plague of poachers on his estate. He found himself the recipient of much unmerited sympathy as well as gratuitous advice on how to deal with the miscreants. Most of the men with whom he associated were landowners, and all of them had had more than a little trouble with poachers.

Of course, he could not offer the same excuse to his valet or to the rest of his staff. Fortunately, they had been with him and in the service of his family so long that he knew they would not talk from the other side of their mouths concerning his pallor, which did not suggest a sojourn in the country or about the new and still tender scar on his shoulder. Nor would they mention the several times he had awakened from uneasy dreams with a cry that echoed through his chamber and brought his valet hurrying in from the small room adjoining his own.

The dreams indicated a state of mind he could ignore, at least in his waking hours. Unfortunately, in sleep his mind, unfettered by the restraints imposed by will, roamed freely, and invariably it was full of uncomfortable imagery. He would be back in the country, specifically in the wide four-poster he had occupied at Corbett Manor. Sheila would be sitting beside him while he lay with closed eyes, surreptitiously surveying her through his lashes, noting the tender curve of her cheek, the fullness of her lovely mouth, the dark fall of her hair, the perfection of her bosom. His imagination would range on further. In his dreams, little Miss Letty was mercifully absent, and Sheila, rising from her chair, lay beside him rapturously responding to kisses that trailed from lips to breasts. There were other visions even more explicit that left him angry and frustrated upon awakening. He had to see her again. That was a constant and nagging thought. He missed her, could miss her all the day and every waking hour, if it were not for the iron control that he kept on his thoughts.

By the second week of his return, Rande could no longer deny the fact that he was in love or that this emotion was infinitely deeper and more powerful than anything he had ever experienced before. He had loved Elsie, true enough, but she had not haunted his thoughts or troubled his dreams to this extent. Indeed, before the vibrant image of Sheila, Elsie dwindled like the dying flame of a spent candle. His love for Sheila was a brightly burning torch, and thinking of her, he was positive that she felt something for him.

In his dreams he often returned to the music room, hearing her glorious voice soaring to the rafters. He had wanted to take her in his arms then. It had required more strength than he had known he possessed to keep from embracing her, to keep from lifting her in his arms and carrying her . . . Fortunately, he had been able to subdue those impulses. Caution and the memory of the late Arthur Bellmore, embracing cold steel on the battlefield rather than live with the memory of Mrs. 'Iggins, had aided him. Yet there was no possible analogy. To even think of Sheila in tandem with that lady was an abomination! She was not fit to occupy the same world with Sheila—Sheila with eyes as blue as the Lakes of Cobbenara and dark hair waving above the perfect oval of her face and gathered into a Psyche knot, the thickness of which made him long to see those locks unbound and flowing over her white shoulders and her small, rose-touched breasts . . . He fought against more specific imagery, and then from the sublime, he would think of Marie, whom he must see again, if she were there after nearly two months.

Probably, she would have wondered about him, but not for long. She craved companionship, and if she did not find it with one, she would, like the charming butterfly she resembled, flutter into the arms of another.

There was also the matter of going on a much less felicitous errand: Sir Jasper. The man could not be allowed to escape the consequences of his action. Rande was glad that the bullet had lodged in his left shoulder. His arm was still a little stiff and his wound ached from time to time, but his right hand could hold pistol or sword with ease—a bullet to the heart, a sword point sliding between Tennant's ribs. That excrescence must not be allowed to live!

Consequently, there were two pressing appointments upon an engagement calendar that, judging from the piles of invitations he had not even opened, would be full indeed. Those could wait indefinitely—he had only these two matters to claim his attention before he returned.

Returned where?

Sheila, Sheila, Sheila beckoned him, and he could not close his ears to her siren's song. He would have to attend to what he grimly dubbed his "chores" and then he would go back to Corbett Manor and demand . . . no, he would beg that she marry him!

Lord Rande was close to rejoicing when he could not

find Marie, either at the little house in Chelsea that he had hired for her or at the theater, which she had quit weeks ago, the stage manager explained huffily. "Left us wi'out so much as a word . . . 'ere today, gone tomorrow wi' the fine young gallant as was courtin' 'er."

That she had left the ballet did surprise him. Marie had always been devoted to her art. Love came and love went, but she remained in the theater. Consequently, she must have fallen prey to a greater passion than he had believed her capable of experiencing. He wished her well and mentally dismissed her. His next stop would be the clubs. He could as easily visit Brian, but by this time he was probably back in the country with his sister.

Consequently, he determined to seek out Sir Jasper. He would begin, he decided, at Brooks. He arrived at the club shortly before eleven, but he was not able to begin his careful questioning as to the possible whereabouts of his quarry. Immediately upon crossing the threshold, he was surrounded by numerous friends and acquaintances, all demanding to know where he had been and also anxious to fill him in on the latest *on-dit*. Someone had seen Brummel in Calais, and did he know about . . . Never had gossip been less welcome to his ears. Once, he recalled, he had had a certain interest in it, but never had it been all-abiding and now it rattled in his head like a pair of discarded dice. He contented himself with smiling and nodding, the while his impatience mounted as he waited for a break in his infernally light, inconsequential chatter.

Then, Major Eric Johnstone, a comrade in arms from Spain, joined the group, lingering at its outer limits until Rande's noncommittal answers and obviously flagging attention proved discouraging enough to disperse the gathering.

"Ivor." Johnstone stepped to his side.

Rande turned quickly. "Eric! Good to see you, my friend."

The major favored him with a brief, cold smile, quite unlike his usually warm greeting. "Am I to understand that you have been out of town?" he inquired.

"Yes, for six weeks. I returned a fortnight ago."

"Ah, that might explain it. I hope that it does," Johnstone said repressively.

"What needs an explanation, Eric?" Rande frowned, finding his manner strange.

"Might we talk privately?" Johnstone pointed to a pair of chairs against the wall.

"Of course," Rande responded. Once they were seated, he turned an inquiring glance on the major. "Well, tell me what is troubling you? I see that something is."

"That little ladybird of yours, the dancer . . ."

Rande raised an eyebrow. "What of her?" he demanded in tones that were equally as chill as those of his friend.

"I take it you've not seen her in quite some time?"

To say that he was surprised by these queries was an understatement. It was unlike the major to pry into his private affairs. "I have not. I have been in the country, but I must say that I fail to see—"

"Do not get your back up, Ivor," the major said quickly. "I can see that you know nothing about her present whereabouts."

"I do not," Rande admitted. "I have been looking for her. She's not at her house in Chelsea, nor is she at the theater. I had the impression she'd found another protector. You see, I was rather ill while I was away and I could not get in touch with her. I take it that you have seen her?"

"Yes," Johnstone replied harshly. "I have seen her. I do not like to tell you when and how. 'Tis something that does not reflect well on me. The other evening, I drank too much and was invited to make one of a party bound for Mrs. Moll Fisher's, er, Aviary."

"That foul brothel," Rande exclaimed incredulously.

"The very same. I was two parts foxed, else I never would have consented, but suffice to say I did go and upon arriving found the cage full of poor little captive birds, sitting about in diaphanous gowns . . . you know."

"I do not know," Rande exclaimed. "I do not frequent such establishments." His eyes narrowed. "You'd not be telling me that Marie—"

"Yes, Ivor, that is what I am telling you. She was there, and recognizing her, I asked for her, not for sport, I assure you. Poor girl, you should have seen her expression when she was summoned to attend me—a blend of terror and hopelessness. You could see that she did not want to stir from her chair, but that vicious old harpy, Moll Fisher, dragged her to her feet. Then she had her . . . I expect you'd call him a porter or majordomo show me to a room up on the third floor. The old witch told me, by the way, that Marie was a bit shy but that she would give me a good time. It was all I could do not to strike her across her fat face. However, I managed to keep my temper and followed the majordomo upstairs to a private room. Then, a minute later, Marie came. Poor child, she was shivering but she started to remove her gown, which, I assure you, hid none of her charms. I stopped her and gave her my cloak. That also seemed to frighten her, but eventually I convinced her that I wanted to help her. I asked her how she happened to be there and she told me that you were dead."

"Dead!" Rande echoed.

"Yes. She wept over that. And then—"

"Hold," Rande said sharply. "Who was it told her that I was dead?"

"Her so-called protector, a young man, so I gather. Corbett's his name. Sir Brian Corbett. I went looking for him. They gave me his direction here, but the house is closed. The caretaker did not seem to know where he had gone. He'd not take money from me."

"I imagine I know where," Rande snapped. "Tell me the rest."

"He'd been seeing her, she told me. She'd been wild with grief and he had been kind, comforting her. She knew him to be an acquaintance of yours. She told me that he'd pursued her before and had appeared to be very much in love with her. Poor child, how she wept. She was ashamed that she had agreed to go with him so quickly, but she was miserable and had needed comforting. I take it they were together for about a fortnight. I am not sure of the time because she spoke very quickly. Her English is heavily overlaid with French. At any rate, he went out of town. He returned about a week later. He seemed edgy and nervous, she said, but he had brought her a gold bangle and a bottle of wine. He wanted her to join him in a toast to their . . . connection. The last thing she remembered was drinking the wine. She woke up in Mrs. Fisher's establishment, her clothes and jewels gone. All she had was that transparent shift. She was brought before Moll and told that she was employed there. It was not easy for her to understand, but she gathered that there had been some manner of transaction between Sir Brian and La Fisher. She was horrified. She begged them to let her go, but the old woman only beat her. She's been beaten often. I imagine it's when she begs Mrs. Fisher's clients to take her away."

"Could you not have helped her to get out?" Rande demanded harshly.

"I tried," the major said regretfully. "But I could not afford the asking price. She's indentured there, it seems."

"Indentured!" Rande exploded.

"Aye, like any bond servant. The asking price is five hundred pounds. Either she earns it, or someone pays. I could not. It's damnable, Ivor. I had the impression that that old trull Moll Fisher would take it out of her hide for my having made the offer. The witch looked mad as fire."

"How long has she been there?" Rande asked. His fury was mounting, and coupled with it was horror. He did not love Marie, but he was fond of her, very fond. And to think of her in such a place set him shuddering.

"She's been there . . . Let me think. 'Twas upward of a fortnight when I saw her." Major Johnstone counted on his fingers. "That was some twelve days ago."

"The better part of a month in that cesspool! God in heaven, I must get her out. At once," Rande cried.

"Yes, yes, you must. You did not abandon her, then?"

"Abandon her?" Rande glared at him. "You think I'd leave her without a word, a girl who's been with me nearly two years, and let someone tell her I was dead?" He drew a long breath and then another, endeavoring to calm a rage that was close to murderous. "I was hurt, Eric. Wounded in the shoulder. I'll tell you about it on the way to the Aviary. We'll go there at once, unless you'd rather not accompany me."

"Of course, I'll accompany you." Johnstone rose swiftly. "I've been unable to erase the sight of the poor girl from my mind. She was such a taking little thing when first I saw her."

"God," Rande groaned. "Poor child . . . poor child . . ." Mentally he counted up the days of her servitude. He himself had been at Corbett Manor a month before Brian arrived. He could guess what had happened. Indeed, he could see it as clearly as if it were written in white letters on a dark wall directly in front of him. Brian, seething over his losses had, by way of revenge, taken his mistress. Then, having learned that he, Rande, had no intention of retaining his winnings, had needed to find some way to dispose of the girl so that she would not tell him what had happened. Someone had suggested the Aviary. He did not doubt that that someone was Brian's mentor, Sir Jasper Tennant. Brian had not been around London long enough to know of the existence of that hole. "Let's go," Rande said between his teeth.

Ironically enough, the Aviary lay hard by the King's Theater, one of many similar establishments in that pleasure-seeking area. Rande, descending from his post chaise and bidding his coachman wait, followed the major into a narrow passageway to a house that, from the outside, looked no different from other sagging old buildings that lined the alley, which seemed in imminent danger of toppling forward against each other. He judged that most had been there since the days of Queen Anne if not Charles II.

Coming inside to a hall lighted only by a pair of guttering candles in a battered brass sconce, he heard the tinkling of a pianoforte and muted laughter coming from overhead. A graceful, curving staircase, relic of an earlier day, was directly in front of them. As they started toward it, a large man in a dark-maroon livery lavishly trimmed with gold stepped out of the shadows. Rande, looking at bulbous features in a far-from-prepossessing countenance, guessed that he was the majordomo mentioned by Johnstone. He was powerfully built and very tall. Though Rande was over six feet in height and Major Johnstone an inch or two taller, the latter towered over them. He planted himself squarely in front of them.

"Might I hinquire wot ye'd be wantin'?" he demanded in a low, threatening tone of voice.

"To see the lil' doves in their cages." Major Johnstone's tones were slurred, as if were the worse for drink.

"Doves, tha's it." Rande nodded solemnly several times, following the major's lead.

"Ah, ye bird-fanciers, then?"

"Aye, doves . . ." Major Johnstone agreed.

"Ye gotta 'ave lots o' birdseed to feed them birds wot're 'ere."

"We have a bit o' the ready." Rande laughed drunkenly. "More'n bit. Gold."

"Gold is it? H'I'd like to see the color o' that gold."

Rande produced a sovereign from his purse and pressed it into the giant's huge palm. "There's more where that came from. I wanna see the lil' doves."

"Ah," the man bit into it. "Come this way," he grinned broadly. "Ye'll 'ave yer doves'n cockatoos'n swallows'n robins, if you likes."

They followed him up the stairs and into a dark corridor. A few paces away, light seeped through the cracks of a door and the music was louder. He opened the door and bowed them into a small anteroom. Its walls were painted a garish pink and emblazoned on one of them was a bird cage in which lolled a naked girl, her head topped with an ornate headdress of plumes. One painted hand stretched through the bars of the cage pointing in the direction of an archway curtained in a bright-pink satin. The floor of the anteroom was covered with a carpet in a matching pink emblazoned with huge golden roses. Drunken laughter mingling with the music reached them.

Their guide swept the curtains aside and beckoned them to follow him, saying jovially, "Come in, come in, gentlemen."

They entered a huge octagonal room. Its walls were also painted pink and there were other depictions of naked girls in cages. Sitting on couches and chairs around the room were girls, most of them very young. They were heavily made up, and ostrich feathers, dyed variously orange, pink, yellow, scarlet, and purple, were affixed to beaded bands on their heads. They wore transparent chiffon shifts and their feet were bare. Some were laughing loudly as they were cuddled by men, most of whom were middle-aged or older. Servants passed among them with bottles of wine and near the pianoforte a slender girl, clad in a mere wisp of a chiffon tunic, was pivoting. A little group of men watched her, grinning and whispering. Rande tensed as he caught sight of her garishly rouged face and eyes heavily lined with kohl. With a muttered curse, he started forward, only to be caught by the major.

"It's Marie," Rande muttered furiously.

"Aye, but you must be calm, Ivor," the major said between his teeth. "We're outnumbered here. Wait until we get to a room."

In that moment, Marie stumbled, and a man standing near the pianoforte caught her and pressed a long kiss on her lips. She stood passively, making no response. In another second, he frowned and released her, giving her a push. The pianist, who had stopped playing, began to pound out another tune and she began to pivot again, tiredly, dispiritedly.

Rande had always thought of Marie as the very spirit of the dance—Terpsichore herself. She had moved with such grace and delicacy, the epitome of joyous youth was another analogy that had often occurred to him. The change in her shocked and horrified him. She moved so stiffly, and with her nodding ostrich plumes and her weary painted face, she looked, he thought, not unlike a puppet pulled by wires. She had aged too. She looked a good deal older than when he had last seen her. It was as much as he could do not to stride to her and, lifting her in his arms, bear her out of this horror.

"There's Moll Fisher," Johnstone muttered, moving his head to the right.

Looking in that direction, Rande saw a monstrously fat woman waddling toward them. She was clad or, rather, upholstered into a pink velvet gown stitched with brilliants. A huge pearl necklace was clasped about her thick neck, and clamped on her brawny arms were several diamond and ruby bracelets. Pearl earrings hung almost to her massive shoulders. She had a seaman's walk, rolling from side to side. She was accompanied by the brawny porter, who seemed no more than an inch or two taller than herself. As she neared them, she favored the major with a brief glance and then turned her attention upon himself. Her eyes, small and embedded in her fleshy face like currants in a plum pudding, Rande thought, were narrow, calculating, and suspicious.

"Yer new 'ere," she commented. Waving a fat, short-fingered hand at the couches, she produced a grin that failed to elicit a corresponding gleam in her eyes. "See anythin' 'ere that meets yer fancy? There be more upstairs, but ye'll 'ave to wait if ye wants to see 'em."

It was with some difficulty that Rande kept his hands from knotting into fists. He said, in his slurred tone, "I like dancers. That little creature over there by the pianoforte is much to my taste." He indicated Marie.

"'Er?" The woman sneered, "Ah, whadya want wi' 'er. She won't gi' ye a good time, ain't worth 'er keep, she ain't. We uses 'er to dance . . . usta be a dancer afore she come 'ere, but she ain't much good at that either."

"All the same, she pleases me," Rande insisted. "I understan' you've got rooms here. I'd like to hire one for the lil' dove . . . brought to me."

"Yer sure you want 'er?" Mrs. Fisher demanded.

"I'm sure . . . Pay good for her, I will." Rande looked at her owlishly.

"As ye choose," she said in disgruntled tones. "Bert 'ere will show ye upstairs'n if she starts blabbin', which she might, gi' er a taste o' yer fives. That'll shut 'er up. I warn ye, she'll not gi' ye much o' a time, an' since I warned ye, I want the fee in advance."

"You'll have it. I want the lil' dove," Rande promised with a wide grin.

"An' ye"—Moll Fisher visited a glowering look on the major—"wot d'ye want?"

"I will go with my friend," he said, not without a blush.

"Ah, 'e'll share 'er wi' ye. The two o' ye wi' 'er, an' there's scarcely more'n a bite to that chicken'n the two o' ye'll 'ave 'er . . ." She laughed deep in her throat. "Tha's rich, that is. Ten pounds each'll do it."

Rande counted out the money, and at a sign from the proprietress, Bert lumbered over to them and grunted, "Ye c'n follow me."

He led them back into the anteroom and thence to the hall. They went up another flight of stairs and emerged in a dimly lighted corridor also lined by doors.

"Come," he muttered, leading them toward the far end of the hall. As they followed him, Rande, aware of smothered laughter and, on occasion, moans and wails of protest, was caught between white-hot fury and pity at these all-too-revealing sounds. And Marie, his delicate and fastidious little mistress, had been in this hell a month! Rage was a lump in his throat and a swelling in his chest. He longed to throttle the porter, and as for Mrs. Moll Fisher, he would have liked to roast her over a slow fire. He strove for calm and achieved it by telling himself that neither of these animals were responsible for her presence here: that lay at the door of another!

" 'Ere we are," Bert said, ushering them into a room lighted only by a candle on a plain deal table. In the uncertain light, they made out the bulk of a large canopied four-poster. Then, as Bert struck a flame from his tinderbox and lighted six more tapers on a large candelabrum, they saw that the bed, piled high with pink satin pillows, was draped in pink brocade and with satin sheets of the same hue.

"This be 'er room," he said. "She'll show ye a good time, she will, wi' a little urgin'. She gets a bit above 'erself, but ye let 'er know wot's wot'n she'll be eatin' outa yer 'and. She—"

"That's enough," Rande interrupted. "I do not need any advice from you."

Bert glowered at him, but meeting Rande's coldly furious glare, he looked down. "Just tryin' to be 'elpful. This one's an 'andful, leastways she can be. She be a frog, ye understand. A Frenchie." He lumbered out, slamming the door behind him.

"God, oh, God." Rande smote his fist against his palm. "Did you see her face . . . Marie, I mean? That woman . . . that creature from the depths. God, I could have strangled her."

"As I could have myself," the major said gloomily. "Lord, I wish I could have taken her out, Ivor. She looks—"

"Yes." Rande gave him a glance that blended fury with anguish. "As if she'd been living in torment. Poor child, poor, poor child. God knows what she's been forced to endure." He took a turn around the room. "And why? Revenge, Eric, revenge. I will show him revenge, I . . ." He paused as the door was thrust open and Marie pushed inside.

She stood a few feet away from the door, her eyes wide and expressionless. She was no longer clad in the short tunic. Her gown was longer but equally transparent. She was still wearing the ridiculous headdress of ostrich plumes. Though she stared straight in front of her, she did not appear to see either of the two men.

"My name is Marie," she said in a dull, expressionless voice. "What do you wish of me?"

"Marie, love, do you not know me?" Rande strode forward.

She tensed, and gazing up at him, her mouth fell open

and a long thin scream emerged from her. "No, noooooo, you're dead. He told me you were d-dead . . . dead and b-buried . . . killed . . ."

"He lied, my dearest." He moved a little closer. "Sir Brian Corbett . . . he lied in his teeth."

Marie shrank back against the door. "*Nom de nom,* you c-come not n-near me. *Tu es mort* . . . he tells me . . . he tells me dead . . . dead. You."

"Love, he lied to you. I am here. I am solid, my own." He reached out, trying to clasp her arm, but she put it behind her looking at him with wide, horror-filled eyes.

"*Non,* you mus' not touch me. Ivor?" She stared at him, unbelievingly. "Ivor?" she repeated. "Oh, my love, I do not dream. I have dreamed so often, *et puis c'est toi, n'est-ce pas?*"

"*Oui, c'est moi,* my very dearest," he said huskily. " 'Tis no dream. Your eyes do not deceive you, my poor darling."

Dry sobs escaped her. "You go, you not come back. I am afraid, I think, and he me tells that you are dead. And I, I too wish to die, but I am afraid."

"I was hurt—*blessé,* my love, but not killed. I am here. *Regardez,* Marie, I have come to take you away from this place, now!" He reached for her a second time.

She moved against the door as if she would press herself into it. "No, I pray you. I cannot be with you." Tears filled her eyes and rolled down her cheeks. "I am finish. There 'ave been so many. I do not wish it. I beg them—no, no, no—but they do not listen. She beats me often and I 'ave fear. Oh, Ivor, 'elp me to die. I pray each night for death, that it come to me soon, soon. I am finish, I am old and ugly . . ."

"No, no, no, you are not old or ugly, my dearest. And you must not speak of death."

"I am ready. I wish the death. I wish it, but you . . . you are alive. Ahhh, Ivor . . ." She suddenly crumpled and lay on the floor at his feet.

A groan escaped him as he quickly knelt beside her,

looking into her white drained face. Then, taking her in his arms, he lifted her and carried her to the bed.

"Poor child, poor child," Major Johnstone said.

"Yes." Rande's tone was harsh, his face grim.

"I wish I had a vinaigrette," Johnstone said. He touched Marie's feathered headdress. "Burnt feathers will suffice."

"No, we'll not revive her yet," Rande said. "First we'll take her out of here." Angrily, he wrenched off the headdress and threw it down. As he bent over her, he saw that there were bruises on her upper arms, and remembering what she had said about the woman beating her, he gently turned her over and then gasped as he found more welts scoring her back and buttocks. She had been beaten severely—and often, from the look of it. Between his teeth he said, "I will right this wrong, and soon."

"It's horrible," the major said in low furious tones. "I would like to shoot that harridan between the eyes."

"We'll shoot no one here, not unless it's necessary," Rande cautioned. "We'll go down the stairs." He took a pistol from his coat pocket and handed it to the major. "Take this."

"I have my own."

"And now you have mine," Rande said. "If anyone attempts to halt us on the way out, you'll shoot above their heads and suggest that the next, er, Good Samaritan who approaches us will receive a bullet rather farther down."

The major regarded him with some concern. "Had I not better carry the girl, Ivor? Your shoulder . . ."

"Damn my shoulder," Rande said explosively. "If she should wake, she'll want to be with me."

"You're right, I expect." The major accepted the gun. "When do we make the attempt?"

"Now." Taking off his cloak, Rande wrapped it gently around the girl, and lifting her again, he added, "You will go ahead of us."

He half-expected to find the giant porter lurking in the hall outside, but as they emerged from the room, they found the corridor empty. It was not until they were halfway down the stairs that the man suddenly appeared on the next landing, staring upward, his face heavy with menace, a knotted fist resting on the newel post.

" 'Ere. Wot're ye about?" he demanded.

"You can see," the major rasped.

The porter started up the stairs. "Ye'll go nowhere—"

"Now," Rande whispered.

The major nodded. "Keep back," he ordered, producing the pistol and aiming at the man's head.

The porter did not stop in his rush until the shot rang out, reverberating through the hall. With a cry, the man staggered and, stumbling, rolled down the stairs. He was on his feet in a trice and dashing toward the anteroom while the major, reaching the landing, hesitated.

Rande joined him. "Go on down, man," he breathed, and at that same time the door to the anteroom was flung open. In the spill of light, he saw the porter with Moll Fisher behind him.

"Stop, damn ye, stop," she bellowed, surging forward, her fists clenched.

"Now," Rande ordered.

The major discharged the second pistol, aiming once more for a spot just above their heads. There was a howl from Moll Fisher as Rande, not wasting any time, made for the second flight of stairs. The major remained behind for the second it took him to order, "Do not move. Another step and you'll have the next ball through your damned eye." Then, he too hurried down the stairs.

In another few seconds, they were out of the house and at the waiting post chaise. The major clambered inside, and taking the still-swooning Marie from Rande, he placed her gently on the seat, holding her against him as Rande sprang after him. He barked an order to his coachman and the equipage started up immediately.

"We'll take her to my house," he panted.

"You should have let me carry her," the major chided. "Your wound . . ."

"No matter," Rande assured him. "I felt nothing." His

shoulder burned and throbbed, but he ignored it, ignored, too, the white-hot flame of his rage and the agony of his grief, both directed at the same young rogue whose sister he could never claim, could never see again—not after he had slain her brother, as he fully intended to do once he had seen to poor Marie's future. If, indeed, she had a future . . .

9

SHEILA, RISING EARLY, went to her window and looked out at woods turned yellow, red, pink, and gold. Some of the trees were already bare. Others still bore leaves that were shaking and dancing in the winds that had battered at the house most of the night and that still moaned around the corners of the building, rattling the panes and sending showers of elm leaves to the ground in a golden rain. She shivered, and then, without ringing for Bridget, she washed her face in the icy water remaining in the basin and put on her riding habit, a London purchase made from pelisse cloth and warm enough to brave the morning's chill. She had to be outside and on horseback. Her mood demanded it.

" 'Tis the restlessness come upon ye, mavourneen."

That was what old Peggy, her former nurse, had been wont to say, adding, "Yer a creature o' moods, right enough."

She would have found considerable corroboration in that opinion this morning. In fact, during all the days, close on three weeks give him a day or so, since Lord Rande had left for London, she had been edgy and ill-tempered or happy and lighthearted by turns. The latter mood earlier on when, she thought dismally, she still had hopes. These were diminishing swiftly. She had not expected to hear from him at once. He had not told her he would write, but somehow she had expected . . .

It did no good to dwell on expectations. Once he was back in London, he would have much to keep him busy. He had been away for quite a while. His friends would have wondered about him, and there was Marie, the beautiful little dancer who had been his constant companion before they met. She did not like to think of Marie, who must still have a place in his heart and in his life. Would he give her up if he were to marry? Her father had not abandoned his mistress, but the situation was entirely different. He had been forced to marry an heiress to replenish his fortunes. Undoubtedly, he had loved the woman who died with him. In her new knowledge of the heart she could even feel sorry for him, who had needed to marry where he did not love for the sake of his family as well as himself—for the sake of this house, which he must also have loved. Yet, he could have been kinder to the loving childish girl her mother had been.

Rande, however, was wealthy in his own right. He did not need to wed a fortune . . . Why was she thinking of marriage so constantly, who had vowed never to enter the state, who had all but promised her grandfather that she would not even contemplate so dangerous a move? It was easy enough to make promises when one was seventeen and ignorant of the tricks the heart could play upon the head, she thought regretfully. Her grandfather could not have anticipated those or, perhaps, he had suffered a disappointment that had turned him against love. She had never known her grandmother. Lady Carlingford had died young, but from her portrait that hung in the gallery at Dahna, she had been a beautiful girl, much like her own mother. Why was she dwelling upon all this ancient history?

Minutes later, Sheila crept down the stairs and out into the windblown morning, making her way to the stables. There was no one astir yet, but she could saddle the mare she proposed to ride. She had just reached the stall when Terry, one of the stable lads, climbed down from the loft, straws in his curly black hair and his eyes still bleary from sleep. These widened as he saw her.

" 'Tis early ye are, Miss Sheila."

"I am that," she responded, "but 'tis a fine morning for a gallop."

"Shall I be saddlin' Albebaran for ye?"

"No, I've a mind to take Saba."

"She's usually in a contrary mood, come morning, Miss Sheila."

"No matter, I can manage her. Will you saddle her, please?"

Saba, named after the mysterious beloved of the legendary Finn, leader of the Fianna, was a skittish little chestnut, dainty and temperamental. She was extremely contrary this morning, shying at wind-tossed tree branches and even at the fall of leaves. However, once they were on the forest path, she settled down to a steady trot.

Sheila envied her. Her own mood was far from steady. Rande occupied her thoughts and she kept remembering those unsettling moments when, caught in her arms, he had called on his lost love. Elsie, however, was forever beyond him and often he had seemed on the verge of saying something to her. She knew he found her beautiful. Most men did, and that was not being conceited. It was stupid to be humble about her looks, but what good were they if they did not attract the one man she could love? She did love him and missed him to the point that sometimes she went to the room he had occupied and sat there trying to envision him still in the great four-poster, needing her ministrations, needing her.

It was a miserable way to feel, especially since he said nothing, and when he might have said *something*, had looked as if it were on the very tip of his tongue, Letty had come in! Damn Letty! If only . . . But there was no use in following that line of thought. She had come in and had interrupted whatever he meant to say. It might have been nothing. Yet, from the way he had pronounced her name, using her given name for the very first time, from the way he had looked at her. But she was refining too much upon very little.

The wind was rising. It was very cool. It would be warmer in London, where there were not so many open spaces. He had spoken about coming to see her in London.

It was time to return, past time. She was waiting on Brian, but she did not need to wait. He could follow her to London. Sheila's eyes brightened. She would go! She would go at the week's end, and that was only two days away. Brian could meet her there.

She turned Saba around and rode back the way she had come. As she came upon the road leading to the stables, she heard the sound of pounding hooves. Looking over her shoulder, she stopped breathing for a moment. It was a solitary horseman sitting tall in the saddle. Had Rande been party to her thoughts, to her longing? Was it he? In another moment, she had recognized him. It was Brian, of course, come at this moment when she most needed to see him. They could go back to London together. That would make everything much, much easier!

Yet, even before Brian joined her, doubt set in. Rande would not want to see her. She would have heard from him, but he *had* said he would call on her when she returned. Did he wonder why she had not yet returned? Could she hope that he was missing her too?

"Sheila." Brian came up to her side. "You're out early."

"I wanted to exercise Saba," she said, looking at him concernedly. His face was pale and there were dark pouches under his eyes, as if he had very little sleep.

He corroborated that assumption after they had dismounted and were walking toward the house. "I've ridden most of the night," he said gruffly.

"Why? Were you in such a hurry to get here? Has London been that dull?"

"Lord, how you do shoot the questions at a man," he complained. "Yes, to your last. London's been monstrous dull. I am sick of the place."

To her surprise, he seemed actually to shudder. "What's the matter, Brian?" she demanded. "Is something amiss?"

"Amiss?" he repeated edgily. "Why do you ask?"

"You seem extremely tense."

"And so would you, riding over these damned dark roads and never knowing what you'll find or what will find you around some bend."

" 'Tis amazing that nothing did," she commented. "Travelers are warned not to brave the roads at night. Why were you in such haste?"

" 'Twas time to put London behind me." He stared at the ground. "Past time."

"What happened there?"

"Nothing!" he barked. "Why should you imagine anything happened?"

She tried to catch his eye and failed. He still continued to stare at the ground. "Something must have happened," she retorted. "At any rate, whether it did or not, I will be sorry not to have your company upon my return to London this Saturday."

"No!" he cried, glaring at her now and actually shaking his fist. "You cannot. 'Tis impossible."

"Oh?" She regarded him in consternation. "Why is it impossible, if nothing has happened?" Her eyes narrowed. "There's something you're not telling me, Brian. What is it?"

"You cannot go back," he said sulkily. "I've other plans for you."

"For me?" Her consternation was coupled with annoyance. "*My* plans," she emphasized coldly, "entail returning to London. It is high time. If you'll remember, we came here only because we thought Lord Rande meant to annex the estate."

"Which he may yet do," Brian said bitterly.

"Nonsense! He swore he would not, and in your presence. He—"

"Enough!" Brian commanded. "I do not want to talk about Rande. We are going to Ireland."

"Ireland?" she repeated. "When we've hired that house for the Season?"

"We have it no longer," he retorted. "I've turned it back to the agent. I have had our garments and other belongings packed and they'll be sent on to Dahna."

"You . . . you've done all this without a word to me?" Sheila glared at him. "How dared you?"

He glared back at her. "Why need I consult you, my dearest sister? Have you forgotten that I am yet your appointed guardian?"

"My guardian?" Sheila echoed, and laughed contemptuously. "Sure you must be funning, Brian."

He gave her a sulky, resentful look. "It was so stipulated in our grandfather's will. Until you reach—"

"The age of twenty-one," she finished, "which I shall be doing in no more than five months. Sure you are not taking that absurd clause seriously? I am positive grandfather meant to change it. You agreed, if I'm not mistaken."

"If he meant to change it, he did not. And consequently, it stands."

"Brian," Sheila said tartly, "if you are going to talk such arrant nonsense, I'll not listen to you. You might be my 'guardian' on paper, but nowhere else. Now, why did you close the house?"

"Because I hate London and have no wish to remain there," he exclaimed with a bitter look at her.

"Well, I do not," she retorted. "And if I cannot stay at the house, I will put up at Grillons!"

"Why are you so set on returning to that ugly, miserable city?" he rasped.

"Because I want my London Season!"

"Or is it Lord Rande that you want?" Brian demanded. She was taken aback by a question that bordered on accusation, and at the same time she was surprised by his perspicacity. To add to her annoyance, she felt warmth in her cheeks and guessed that she was blushing, something she hoped he would not notice. However, she did manage to say evenly, "Why should you think that?"

"Why?" He uttered a short, unpleasant bark of a laugh. "You are red as a beet, for one thing, but you'd better get him out of your head. He's betrothed."

"Betrothed?" she whispered, feeling as if he had struck her.

"Yes, my dear sister," he said tauntingly. "But I doubt that the banns will be posted at Saint Martin in the Fields or some equally fashionable church. Nor do I believe that the announcement will be sent to *The Morning Post*. His family, if he had a family, would probably be attending the ceremony in funeral garb."

"What are you saying?" she asked.

"I am saying, my sweetest Sheila, that he has done the unthinkable and the unimaginable. The noble Earl of Rande will marry his mistress."

"The dancer?"

"Aye, the dancer." Brian laughed harshly. "Your rival in his affections, my dear. Now, are you so anxious to go back to London and perhaps attend his wedding? Or would you rather marry someone of my choosing, who is madly in love with you?"

She was so stunned and shocked by what he had told her that she was hardly attending. "But he did not call her name, not once," she said stupidly.

"What?" Brian demanded. "What are you babbling about?"

"He spoke only of her, of Elsie," Sheila murmured half to herself.

"Elsie? What can you mean?"

"It does not matter," she said dully.

"No, you are right, it does not," Brian agreed. "What matters is that I've received an offer for your hand, my dear."

"An offer?" she repeated, staring at him blankly and wondering why she should feel so sharp a pain in her chest —or was it in her heart? She was not sure of its location. She had often read that people who suffered great disappointments in love felt actual pain, but she had always believed this to be a figment of the novelist's imagination. Evidently, she had been mistaken. The pain was *real* and it was persisting. Her brother, she recalled, had been speaking to her. What had he said? Something about an offer. "An offer?" she said again. "Who has offered for me?"

"A man who has adored you ever since he first set eyes on you, my dear, for all you've given him no encouragement. I am speaking of my good friend Sir Jasper Tennant."

Sheila felt as if he had thrown cold water in her face. She said unbelievingly, "Sir Jasper Tennant!"

"Yes, my dear." There was a note of triumph in his tone, and his eyes actually glowed with satisfaction. "Sir Jasper has offered and I have given my consent."

Shock left her completely speechless for a moment. Then, she said furiously, "You may take your damned consent back. I would as soon marry an ape. Sooner!"

"Sheila, as I am your guardian, it is my right to decide whom you should marry."

"Your right. Damn your right," she exclaimed. "If I had ten thousand guardians and all of them ordered me to marry that rascal, that knave, my answer would be the same. No, no, no! How could you, my own brother, have the effrontery to try to couple me with that villain, that murderer who shoots before the signal is given and shoots to kill!"

"You mistake him," Brian retorted sharply. " 'Twas not true!"

"You yourself agreed that it was true," she cried. "I would die before I would marry that wretch. You may tell him that. Oh, 'tis outside of enough! I'll not waste my time speaking to you on this subject, and I warn you, do not mention it to me again, not ever!" Turning on her heel, Sheila ran into the house and headed for the stairs, hoping to get to her room before the threatening tears could emerge.

"Sheila, love, where have you been?" Miss Letty, standing on the first landing, looked down at Sheila in dismay. "And what's amiss, pray?"

"Oh, Letty, he's betrothed," Sheila moaned.

"Who, my darling?"

"Lord Rande, he will marry his mistress." She reached the landing.

"His mistress!" her cousin exclaimed. "But gentlemen

do not, do they?'' Her hand flew to her mouth. ''I mean, I have heard dear Jeffrey say as much. It's very odd. I could have sworn that he and you—''

''You were wrong,'' Sheila said stonily. Regret surged through her. She had not meant to mention Lord Rande's forthcoming nuptials, nor had she meant to betray an agony she should have kept to herself. She could not rectify that wrong, but she could remove herself from her cousin's presence. ''I must go to my room, Letty. Oh, yes, I meant to tell you that Brian's home. If he should ask where I am, explain that I have gone to bed.''

''Of course, my dear. Oh, my love, I am so shocked. I thought that surely Lord Rande and yourself . . . 'Tis all very, very surprising.''

Sheila nodded and hurried down the hall to her room, startling Bridget, who was mending some of her garments. The abigail jumped up. ''Ye look all done in, Miss Sheila,'' she said worriedly.

'' 'Tis nothing, Bridget, but I would rest.''

''I'll help you out of yer clothes, shall I?''

''Very well.'' Sheila stood passively while Bridget began to remove her garments.

'' 'Tis early yet,'' the girl commented. ''I'd not expected to find ye out so soon.''

''I went riding.''

''I can see ye did. Are ye feelin' poorly, Miss Sheila?''

''I do not know. Perhaps,'' she spoke vaguely, wanting Bridget to go away, wanting to be alone, and wondering at the same time how she was going to pass the minutes, the hours, the days, the years that stretched in front of her, now that hope had fled from her life. She saw Bridget look at her strangely and guessed that the abigail had never seen her in so despondent a mood before. Undoubtedly, she was curious. Servants were always curious. She would be sharing that curiosity with the rest of the staff in the servant's dining hall on the far side of the kitchen. Perhaps some of the older ones would conjure up memories of Moira O'Neill Corbett, who had been very unhappy in this house. Or would she be remembered at all?

"Would ye be wanting anything more, Miss Sheila?" Bridget asked.

Sheila looked down and found that she was in her night-shift. She had not even been aware of having her gown removed. "No, nothing, Bridget. I have a headache. I think that I will try to sleep."

"Would you like me to rub your temples for you, Miss Sheila? It might make you feel better."

"No, Bridget, thank you. You may go."

"Very well, Miss Sheila. But you'll ring if you want anything, please."

"I will."

Once the door had closed on the abigail, Sheila lay down on her bed. She tried to sleep, but to no avail. Each time she closed her eyes, they seemed to open of their own accord and leave her gazing steadily at the underside of the lacy canopy that stretched over her four-poster. However, they also brought pictures to the back of her eyes and invariably they showed Lord Rande in the wide bed down the hall or at the pianoforte, smiling at her. Now he was going to marry the little blond girl she had met in the Green Room. She wished that she did not remember her so well, but unfortunately, she could picture her froth of golden curls, her white skin, her graceful body, her great eyes adoringly fixed on Lord Rande.

"But she's a ballet girl, an *opera* dancer," Sheila murmured.

They had many lovers. Did he not mind the fact that he must have shared her with others? Obviously he did not. He had not called out to her in his delirium, either. Why did she keep thinking of that? If he had loved her so devotedly, devotedly enough to risk the condemnation of the *ton*, why had he not mentioned her name as well as that of his lost Elsie?

She could imagine him going back to his house to find Marie waiting for him, repulsed and ignored by his snobbish servants but insisting and being admitted to the hall, where, curled on a chair, she would remain until he returned.

Of course, it would not have happened that way. He would have gone to the theater, open now for the fall performances, or he would have gone to her house, the house he had probably purchased for her. She would run to him and wrap her white arms around his neck, her delicate little face upturned for his kisses. She was so dainty, so tiny—half his height. He probably liked that. It undoubtedly made him feel powerful and protective. To dwell on her or him was useless as it was to tell herself that she did not care, that her life was not ruined. To keep her vow would be very easy now. She would never marry, for she had given her heart to Lord Rande, and though he had rejected the gift, she could not take it back.

Sir Jasper. Sheila shuddered. Surely, Brian was half-demented to suggest so repugnant a union! He knew her mind. What was the matter with him?

Marie.

It could be that the news concerning Rande's forth-coming marriage had hit her brother as badly as herself. He had been extremely attracted to that blond chit, that little vixen.

Sheila released a long sigh. It did no good to vilify her fortunate rival. Her pain and anger were not alleviated. Marie still reigned supreme. She would not be the first dancer who had claimed a noble husband, and she would not be the last. There was something infinitely beguiling about those slender creatures who looked not unlike the fairies of her childhood imagining. They were always dancing, too. Fairy rings. She could remember a morning when she and Brian had gone in search of one and had been soundly chastised because they had disappeared for half a day. Her grandfather had laughed and said, "I thought you spirited away by the fairies, to their underground caves."

Spirited away. That had been the fate of Lord Rande, and to an underground cavern! He would be living under-ground, at least as far as the *ton* was concerned. No, *he* would not be living there, but his bride would until she was recognized. Sheila moved restlessly, not liking what she was thinking or envisioning. Once more she tried to sleep and finally she succeeded.

She awakened to a tentative knock on the door and sat up in bed surprised to find that the sun was setting. Amazingly, she had slept most of the day. She heard a second knock and called, "Yes?"

"Sheila." Brian opened the door a few inches. "I hope you'll be coming down to dinner."

There was a contrite, almost a humble note in his voice, which she chose to ignore as memory came flooding back and, with it, his mad suggestion concerning Sir Jasper. "Go away," she ordered. "We have nothing to say to each other."

Of course he did not obey her. Instead he came in and stood by one of the high posts at the foot of the bed. "I wanted to beg your pardon, my dear," he said.

"You did?" Her response was as much an exclamation as a question. Brian rarely made apologies. "Why?" she added suspiciously.

"Because I have come to my senses. I've been doing a great deal of thinking, and while I like and respect Sir Jasper, I cannot expect you to share my opinion. Also, I must beg your pardon for mentioning that foolish clause in the will." He said in comically stentorian tones, "Let it be known that I, Brian Corbett, Baronet, being of sound mind and, hopefully, body, hereby renounce my guardianship of my sister, Miss Sheila Corbett, who could easily be my guardian since she has far more than an equal share of common sense." Moving to the side of the bed, he bent down and reached for her hand, holding it tightly. "Am I forgiven?" he asked softly.

"Oh, of course you are." She found to her surprise that she could actually smile.

"And will you come down to dinner? Cousin Letty's extremely concerned, first by your early-morning ride and then by your long sleep, the which I hope has refreshed you."

"It has," she discovered. "I do feel much better, now that you are not demanding that I bestow my hand upon Sir Jasper."

"I would never force you to marry anyone you did not respect, even if it were in my power to do so," he assured her. He bent to kiss her hand. "Shall I send Bridget to you, my love? She's just outside in the hall and looking anxious."

"Please do," she smiled, much cheered by his surprising change of mood and his tacit admission that he was in no position to force her to marry anyone at all.

Bridget was still looking anxious when she entered. "Lor, I thought you was goin' to sleep the night away," she said with a concerned glance at her mistress.

"I feel much better," Sheila assured her untruthfully. With complete wakefulness had come memories of the shocking confidence that had sent her to bed in the first place. Lord Rande and Marie Hiver. In French, she remembered, Hiver meant winter. A winter of the heart. She dared not dwell on that. "I think I will wear the blue lutestring. No, that is not right for dinner. Silk . . . I believe I'll wear the new ruby silk, which I like because it is not blue. Fancy, I am tired of blue, Bridget."

" 'Tis a most becoming color to you, ma'am. Yer eyes bein' so blue'n all."

"No matter. 'Twill be the ruby, which will add color to my cheeks if not my eyes."

"As you choose, ma'am."

She was looking well, she decided as she stood staring into her glass while Bridget fastened the row of tiny buttons at the back of her neck. The color was becoming and so was the cut, low but not too low across the bosom and with long sleeves puffed at the shoulder but fitting closely all the way down the arm to the wrist—almost a medieval look. Silken floss edged the bottom of the skirt and embroidered on the front panel was a fanciful golden tree. Bridget had clasped her gold necklace, one of her father's bride presents to her mother. She had never liked that particular necklace. It was set with three opals and her old nurse had said the stones had brought bad luck to her poor little mother. However, it did complement the gown, and only the ignorant, superstitious peasants believed in jewelry bringing bad luck or the lack of it. Her hair was caught up in its usual Psyche knot but with a gold butterfly perched to one side, its wings sparkling with tiny gems, an inexpensive but pretty trifle.

Dispassionately surveying her reflection once more, Sheila thought she was dressed far too regally for a simple dinner at home, but at the same time, if Brian persisted in his intention to leave for Ireland, she would have few chances to shine at Carlton House or Almack's or the opera. She swallowed a lump in her throat, as her mind automatically attached the word "dancer" to "opera."

She could not see Lord Rande with that pretty girl. She looked so fragile, too fragile to bear him the sons he needed to carry on the line. It did not do to dwell on it. Marie was the reason he had been so anxious to return to London that he had not even waited until he was well enough to make the journey! And the announcement might not be inserted into *The Morning Post,* but her name would be inscribed on a marriage license along with that of her bridegroom, and that was all that was needed! Sheila turned away from the mirror and went swiftly out of the room.

"My dearest, how very well you are looking! The rest did you good," Miss Letty exclaimed as Sheila entered the drawing room.

"Does she not?" Brian rose and, coming to his sister, bowed over her hand.

"Such gallantry," Sheila teased. "And you are looking very well yourself. That evening suit is new?"

"Yes, I had it made a fortnight ago."

The coat was embroidered with gold scrolls on either side. He was wearing a brocade vest patterned with fanciful flowers and there was a fall of lace at his throat. Evidently, when he had purchased it, he had had no thought of returning to Ireland so soon—but Marie was getting married. She felt sorry for him, who must be

suffering as much as she was suffering. Also, she felt more
in sympathy with him than she had at any time recently,
she realized with a little pang. Once more she regretted her
grandfather's will, questioning, as usual, the peculiar
decision with its stipulation forbidding the transfer of that
same property to her brother should she so desire. It was as
if her grandfather had early disliked him—something that
had never been revealed until the reading of the will.

"A penny for your thoughts, my dear?" he said.

Sheila started and essayed a laugh, adding a bit self-
consciously, "They are not worth so much as a goat,
Brian, my love."

"Shall we go into dinner, my dears?" Miss Letty asked.

"Dinner, not supper? We are fashionable," Sheila
commented.

"What could we do when you were locked in sleep like
Briar Rose in her thorn-covered castle?" Brian demanded.

"Wait dinner for me, of course!" Sheila's laugh, though
still forced, was more successful this time.

The table looked festive, Sheila thought, with its snowy
linen and the fine old silver gleaming under the soft multi-
colored glow from a crystal chandelier adorned with fruits
and flowers of blown glass bought in Venice during the
grand tour of their Great-Uncle Ralph. She wondered
about her father's kin. Were they all as heedless as her
father and Brian? She ought to know more about them, an
old family whose only heir smiled at her across the length
of the table.

She was really very ignorant about her father's family.
She might have found out more about them by examining
the records in the library. There was a family tree. She had
glanced at it when they first arrived, but then Lord Rande
had come. Her preoccupation with him had precluded such
studies, and later, when he departed, she had wasted long
hours thinking about him, dwelling upon the few pitiful
scraps of seeming encouragement he had given her,
building on them like a silly schoolgirl. Now, when she
might have done some delving into their past, Brian was

determined on leaving for Ireland. She was nothing loathe. England had lost its appeal for her.

The lights in the chandelier and in the silver candelabra on the table blurred. Sheila sipped her wine, telling herself that she must not give into grief. Was it really grief? Yes, grief coupled with agony. She could not disguise these twin feelings from herself, and then, on top of dealing that harsh blow to her heart, her brother had had the temerity to tell her that Sir Jasper, that sleek, serpentine creature, cared for her, had offered for her, and he, as her *guardian,* had accepted! Guardian! That he should even refer to that ridiculous stipulation amazed her, but even more amazing was his mention of marriage with a man whom she had not only seldom seen but whom she had cordially disliked even upon first meeting. She downed her wine. She must not dwell on these things now. Brian had apologized and it was up to her to be pleasant, if only for dear Letty's sake.

It took considerable effort and concentration for Sheila to pretend that she was enjoying the dinner and to exchange small talk with Brian and Cousin Letty, but she managed it, managed, too, to eat a good portion of what was put before her, though she did not taste any of it, or of the wines served with each course for that matter. She was greatly relieved when dessert came, for then she could leave Brian to his port and escape once more to her room. She wondered when the pain she was experiencing would be at an end: a day, a month, a year, ten years? Ridiculous to love someone so desperately when he cared nothing, nothing, nothing for her!

"My dear," Brian said loudly, "I do not think you heard me, Sheila."

She looked at him. "I beg your pardon?"

"I thought you hadn't." He nodded. "You are wool-gathering, my love. I said I had a wine from France, bought in London. It has a supreme bouquet and I wanted you to try some of it."

"A wine from France," Letty murmured. "I thought most wines were from France . . . or Italy, of course."

176 ────────────────────────────────── *Ellen Fitzgerald*

"This is a rare vintage, Cousin Letty. It dates back to 1776."

"So old. Why, 'twas before the Revolution and the dear queen still alive—and the poor little dauphin," Letty sighed.

"That's so, Cousin Letty." Brian set a half-filled bottle on the table. "You can see that it's been broached—the bottle. 'Twas so rare a taste that I would have bought a whole case. Unfortunately, I was told that this was the only one left. Give me your glass, Sheila, and yours, too, Cousin Letty."

"Oh, no, dear boy." Miss Letty shook her head. "I have had too much wine already—my head for liquor's not strong."

"As you choose, but you'll join me in a toast to Ireland, Sheila?"

"I dare not refuse." Sheila forced a smile, thinking that tonight Brian was even more like his old self then when she had seen him earlier. She watched while he filled the glass with a golden liquid, and as she did, a curious thought drifted into her mind. She had the feeling that her brother was pouring out some of the waters of Lethe, that dark river where the souls of the dead drank to forget all that passed on earth.

"To you, Sheila." Brian raised his glass. "And to Ireland!"

"To you, Brian, to Ireland, and to Lethe," she added in a whisper and drank deep. The wine had a pungent taste but it was good. Sheila drained her glass and in that same moment heard an exclamation from her brother.

"Oh, dear," Letty cried. "The lovely old crystal!"

"It did not break," Brian said.

Sheila looked about her. "What happened?"

"I dropped my glass," Brian explained. He sighed. "All that good old wine's gone to water the carpet."

"Oh, dear," she said sympathetically. "It was good." She giggled suddenly. "Brian, you do look so . . . so strange."

"Strange?" he questioned, looking at her in a puzzled way. "How strange, my dear?"

"Your f-face, 'tis growing longer and going all sideways."

"Sheila, my love, what's amiss?" Letty cried.

"Oh, Lord," Sheila heard Brian say. "I think she's had too much to drink."

"Haven't . . . not too mush, jus' a few glasses." Sheila was having trouble articulating.

"The poor child. She's so very unhappy," Letty observed.

"Not unhappy, Cousin Letty," Sheila endeavored to speak distinctly. "Le' 'im marry wi' anyone he likes, do not care." She rose from the table and then grabbed at the top of her chair. She was feeling extremely dizzy. She stared vaguely around her and was startled by the odd look in her brother's eyes. It was very, very odd, almost gloating. It filled her with alarm. She turned toward Letty, but as she started to speak, a great darkness rolled over her and the floor reared up to receive her . . . or had she fallen? She did not know. "The waters o' Lethe," she mumbled, and lapsed into unconsciousness.

"Sheila, love!" Miss Letty rose from her chair and ran to bend over the girl. "Child, what's amiss?" She threw a distracted glance at Brian, who had also come to his sister's side. "Fetch the smelling salts, or feather, burnt feathers might do."

"I do not think either would serve, Cousin Letty." Brian stared down at his sister's unconscious face. "I never should have given her that damned wine."

"Wine! It could not have been the wine," Miss Letty exclaimed distractedly.

"I fear it might have been," Brian insisted. " 'Tis very potent and she had too much to drink at dinner." Apologetically, he added, "I'd not taken that into account. I'd best carry her to her room and have her abigail put her to bed."

"She looks so pale," Letty cried.

"She'll be better in the morning," Brian said consolingly. "She needs only to sleep it off."

"You cannot be suggesting that she's inebriated!" Miss Letty regarded him with horror.

"I fear she must be," Brian replied.

"Oh, dear, how dreadful. She did have a mite too much to drink," Miss Letty said mournfully. "But I did not think 'twas enough to make her intoxicated."

"It was my fault," Brian sighed. "As I told you, I should not have given her that wine, but 'tis delicious and . . . But no matter, I will carry her to her room."

"Oh, yes, do. And I will summon Bridget. She's probably with the other servants at dinner."

"Please do." Brian lifted Sheila in his arms and bore her toward the stairs.

"Oh, Miss Letty, wake up, do wake up, Miss Letty!"

"Gracious!" Miss Letty opened her eyes and blinked at Rose, her abigail, who was actually shaking her awake.

She stared at the girl, half-surprised, half-indignant. She was an early riser, but this was too much. It was not even light outside. In fact, Rose was holding a candle in one hand. Miss Letty blinked against the wavering flame. "What o'clock is it?" she demanded crossly.

" 'Tis six in the morning . . . and they're gone. Bridget and Miss Sheila and Sir Brian, an' Terry says as 'ow Miss Sheila were sleepin' when 'e carried 'er into the post chaise. Terry, 'e were in the stable loft'n they didn't know as 'ow he's taken to sleepin' up there."

"Who is they?" Miss Letty sat up and ran a trembling hand through her hair.

"Sir Brian'n that Sir Jasper."

"Sir Jasper here? Sure, you must be mistaken," Miss Letty exclaimed. "He'd not come here."

" 'E were 'ere, Miss Letty'n Terry 'eard 'em say they was takin' Miss Sheila to Dahna, where they'd 'ave a gold ring on 'er third finger left 'and afore she were much older. Sir Brian said that an' Sir Jasper, 'e 'ushed 'im up'n said about there maybe bein' ears about."

"Oh, God." With this uncharacteristic exclamation, Miss Letty threw back the covers on her bed. "What can we do?" She stared helplessly at Rose.

"Beggin' yer pardon, Miss Letty, but I don't like that Sir Jasper." The girl's eyes grew big with indignation. "Last time 'e were 'ere, 'e tried to grab me in the 'all, but I fetched 'im a blow to the cheek."

"That was very good, Rose, very good indeed," Miss Letty murmured distractedly. "Oh, dear, oh, dear." She slipped out of bed. "What are we to do? We ought to go after her. Brian. I do not understand him. Bad blood will tell! Dear Jeffrey used to say that his father . . . But no matter, we must go."

"But what can we do, ma'am?" Rose demanded. "They'll 'ave been ridin' all the night. I be sure o' that'n by now—"

Miss Letty raised a small hand. "Yes, you are quite right, Rose, dear. 'Twould be no use to attempt to follow them. We'll go to him. Perhaps he's not wed yet, and even if he *is*, I am sure he will want to help her. Pack a portmanteau, Rose. Have Terence ready the coach. I would have preferred the post chaise, but they've taken it, you say?"

"Yes, Miss Letty." Rose stared at her wonderingly. "But if we're not followin' them, where would we be goin', please?"

"To London," Miss Letty said decisively.

10

SHEILA WAS AWARE of a great pitching and tossing. She felt vilely ill and heard groans beside her. Opening her eyes, she looked about her but saw only darkness. She tried to lift her head but could not—it felt so heavy. A strange smell was in her nostrils. Tar . . . that was it, but of course it could not be. She must be mistaken! She made another effort to rise but found she was unable to move, and she was feeling so ill. She moaned and now it seemed she was sinking, as if her whole bed were sinking. She retched and coughed and, closing her eyes, knew nothing more.

The next time she became aware of anything, she was being jounced about. Someone was whimpering at her side—no, not at her side but overhead. She opened her eyes and gazed about her, blinking against the onslaught of sunshine. She was lying on the floor of a very small compartment. A coach? She wanted to sit up, but something was holding her down. She glimpsed feet, feet in neat black shoes with worsted stockings. She made an effort to raise her head but she could not. The whimpering, the sobbing continued. She did not understand. She felt very ill and could not seem to think properly. She had to make the effort.

"Where . . . where . . ." she mumbled. Her tongue felt thick and fuzzy.

"Oh, Miss Sheila!"

She knew that voice. "Bri . . . Bri . . ." She could not seem to form the whole name.

"Oh, Miss Sheila," the abigail repeated, and wept.

"When? Wha'?" Sheila muttered, and gagged. The

sickness was upon her again. She did not understand. "Feel so . . . so . . . ."

"I know," Bridget said. " 'Tis wicked, wicked."

Sheila did not understand. "Why?"

The vehicle was drawing to a stop. She was glad of that. She did not feel so ill now that the jouncing had ceased. The door to the coach was opened. She was being lifted out. She tried to see who was carrying her, and . . . Why was she here? She heard voices but could not distinguish words. She did not understand, could not remember; she tried to move but felt so weak, too weak to speak. She closed her eyes again against the glow of the sun and felt an all-pervading darkness descending. It blotted out light and thought together.

She had had such strange nightmares, Sheila thought as she opened her eyes to the brightness of the morning sun. She could not remember being taken to bed and she knew the reason for that: she had drunk too much wine. She never would again! It had given her a night of dreams wilder than any she ever remembered having experienced! And some of them had seemed so very real.

She felt very empty inside. She had a memory of nausea. She must have been sick after dinner. She flushed. Letty would be shocked. She herself hardly touched wine. Half a glass usually sufficed. She had had several glasses and, at the last, the wine from France which Brian had given her. That had proved to be the coup de grace! It had certainly been potent stuff! She stared up at the canopy and her eyes widened. Instead of the lacy cover she was accustomed to viewing, she was looking at the blue silk that covered her bed at Dahna! She must still be dreaming. She pinched her arm and knew she was not dreaming.

She sat up and her head swam unpleasantly. Air bubbles formed in her throat. She was dizzy, had been dizzy before, she recalled. She was feeling very weak, too. She ran her hands through her hair and found it tangled and matted. That was strange, very strange. Bridget always brushed it, a hundred strokes each morning, each night as well, when she did not undertake that task herself, which she often did if she wanted to think. She had to think now, had to think.

Her eyes widened. She was staring straight in front of her and she was looking at a fireplace edged with white and blue tiles, imported from Holland during the last century, her grandfather had told her . . . But what did her grandfather, who had refused to go there, know about Corbett Manor?

It was not Corbett Manor, could not be Corbett Manor. She looked to her left and found windows, bright with sunlight; if she were to rise and look out, they would provide her with a view of a roadway she had known all her life. It was bordered by tall trees and wound up from a pair of huge wooden gates, thick wood, scored but not old, dating back only some 160 years, a replacement for the pair of gates that had been knocked down by Cromwell's man . . . But that was long ago and she would not dwell on the misery and carnage of those years. She had to understand why she was at Dahna!

She slipped out of bed and for a moment everything went black. She clutched at a bedpost to steady herself and in another moment she was all right, or at least she was no longer dizzy, but she was not all right either. She was totally confused! Why was she here at Dahna when all she could remember was having dinner at Corbett Manor last night? But it had not been last night, had it? A memory of sickness came to her. Seasickness. She was never seasick. And she had not been on the sea! But she must have been on the sea if she were at Dahna! Unless she were still dreaming. She did remember chaotic dreams, but it was ridiculous. She knew she was not dreaming. She had already pinched her arm. Besides, other impressions were flowing into her mind.

She crawled back into bed and lay staring up at the familiar unfamiliar canopy. How had she come to be here—at Dahna? Who had brought her here? And why? Brian? Of course, it had to have been Brian. He had said . . . What had he said? It was still difficult to think clearly, to find a pathway out of this confusion! Her head was full of odd fragments, images that were vivid but ill assorted. Darkness, the smell of the sea, the legs of someone walking across a slippery deck . . . Had it been a deck? Yes, she was sure of that, and why had she seen legs and not a face? She had no memory of a face. She had seen only part of a person. A rough something against her cheek . . . a rough jacket and against her cheek? That meant that she had been carried. But she would have had to have been carried because she had no memory of going anywhere of her own volition.

Had she been ill, feverish, and for how long? Long enough to make the journey to Liverpool and across the Irish Sea to Dublin and thence to Galway . . . the better part of a week, and to remember nothing of it? She must have been very ill indeed. A fever? She did feel odd— empty. Yes, she was empty and hungry. How long had it been since she had had anything to eat? She might not have had any sustenance since that dinner at the manor.

She had a sudden vivid image of that table, all gleaming with silver on fine linen. At the head of the table, Brian had sat. She grimaced. He had talked of Sir Jasper and Rande. She groaned aloud. Rande, she remembered now that Rande was betrothed to Marie, his mistress. Tears blurred her vision. She blinked them away, but more came and rolled down her cheeks. If she had not felt so very weak . . . Why was she thinking about Rande when she ought to be concentrating on why she was here? She rose again, went to the armoire, and opening it, found no garments inside. Bridget had not yet unpacked.

She found that strangely unsettling, but no more unsettling than everything else. What had happened to her? Why had she been brought here? There was no one to provide answers to her multitudinous questions, and it was so hard to think, to concentrate. Her eyelids were becoming heavy. She could not sleep, ought not to sleep, but she was so very drowsy. She could not fight against it. She went back to bed and, lying down, fell deeply asleep almost immediately.

Something aroused Sheila, the opening or the closing of a door, she was not sure which. She opened her eyes to find the room in shadow. She glanced toward the windows. The sky was a pale rose, which could mean either dawn or sunset. She looked up and found Brian standing at the foot of the bed. The expression on his face was not pleasant. He was smiling, but it was a gloating, almost a triumphantly gloating smile.

She sat up, glad that her head was no longer whirling. "Brian, why? What happened?" She was surprised by the weakness of her voice. "Why am I here?" Before he could respond, she had suddenly realized something else. "Why did you bring me here?" she demanded, too shocked to be angry.

"I thought it was time we returned to Dahna," he said casually. "You did not weather the journey very well. I expect that was partially because of the drugs."

"The drugs," she whispered in horror. "I was drugged? *You* drugged me?"

"Yes, my dear." His smile broadened. "In your wine, of course, and dear Cousin Letty never suspected a thing. She thought you were tipsy. You did drink quite a bit of wine at dinner, you know."

His admission had an element of pride in it and even a touch of mischief, horridly akin to that of a small boy having stolen a march on his elder sister. Despite the difference in their ages, he had always seemed younger rather than older than herself, never more than now. Caught between shock and confusion, she said, "I do not understand you. You drugged me? Why?"

"Because I could see you were primed to be stubborn. And quite truthfully, I was weary of your arguments, my dear, and in no mood to indulge you."

"To indulge me? I do not understand you."

'I see that you do not, my dear, and I cannot fault you for that. I'd best tell you what I have in mind for you."

"What you have in mind for me?" she repeated. "I do not understand."

"For the second time in as many minutes. Well, I cannot

blame you for being confused. Best be silent and let me give you a proper explanation. I am sure you must want that."

Her anger rose. As she had already noticed, he was gloating. More than that, he looked sickeningly complacent. She had a memory of Brian as a child, winning a race against Dermot O'Rourke, a village lad. He had worn a similar expression as he had bragged about it to their nurse: "And I was never so fleet as he, Mary."

"And so you waited until he'd worked wi' his father in the fields all the day and was weary. And then you challenged him to a race," she had commented caustically.

Odd that this old memory should return to her now. Brian had been much miffed by Mary's remark and five-year-old Sheila had flown to his defense. She could not think about that now. She said coldly, "Very well. Let me have this proper explanation."

"It concerns your marriage, my dear."

"My marriage!"

"Will you parrot my every word?" he demanded edgily. "But of course, you still do not understand, do you? Poor Sheila, that must be very difficult for you, difficult not to understand, difficult not to be in command of every situation that concerns the two of us. 'Tis I who am in command here, my dear. Dahna is mine."

"Yours!" she exclaimed angrily.

"Mine," he repeated. "Mine to administer until you come of age—that sop to Cerberus handed me our grandfather. And you are my ward, my dear, subservient to my wishes until you do reach your twenty-first year. None can argue with that!"

She sat up straight. "You are back to that again, are you? You know that Grandfather did not mean for you to abide by that clause. Why will you keep throwing it at me?"

"I cannot believe that he did, either. I am sure he did not mean for me to abide by it. I am sure he would rather have made a will in which I was subservient to you, but he did not. And since he did not, you and Dahna are mine until the fifteenth of March, my love, a fatal day for Caesar, if you recall your Plutarch.''

If she had been better, she would have laughed in his face as she always had when he mentioned that clause. But whatever vile substance he had given her had weakened her, and she was also hungry, "famished" would be the better term. More than that, she was frightened. She had never seen this side of Brian. He seemed an entirely different person than the lighthearted young man she had known most of her life. In a tone that she had to strive to keep steady, she said, "And how do you plan to exercise this . . . this guardianship?"

"Ah," he said approvingly, "I see that you have decided to recognize my authority in this matter. That is good, that is very good indeed, Sheila.''

She had made a mistake, she realized too late. She had implied that she did recognize that spurious claim. "I meant—" she began.

"It does not matter what you meant, my sweetest Sheila," he said. "Whether you meant it or did not mean it, I am in authority here, and any court in the land would recognize my jurisdiction in this matter. As your guardian, I have arranged a marriage. The bridegroom's here, and most eager to claim his bride.''

Cold fear gripped Sheila, but she must not show him that she was frightened—and she ought not to be frightened, even though she now knew what he intended. He would never be able to make her obey him, never! She said gratingly, "I will not marry Sir Jasper Tennant, if that is what you are suggesting.''

"Oh, yes, you will," he said sharply. "He is my choice for you, and marry him you will!''

"I will not! Why would you have me coupled with a would-be murderer?''

"He is no murderer!''

"He is nothing else. His actions with Lord Rande deserve no other description.''

"His actions with Rande were those of a dear friend who

hoped to extricate me from the clutches of a cheat," Brian thundered. "He was a cheat, else he never would have won so easily."

"You are a fool," Sheila cried. "He won because he was the better player—and you a lamb waiting to be fleeced. Furthermore, he's promised to return those winnings."

"I've yet to receive the note I signed," Brian retorted.

"I find that hard to believe. He told me he'd return it the minute he was back in London."

"He did not. Quite to the contrary, my dearest Sheila, he has changed his mind. He's sent me word on it."

"You're lying," she said contemptuously.

"I am not lying. 'Tis my belief he's taken a fancy to the place. Perhaps he'd like to bring his bride there." A mocking smile played about his mouth. "I know you are in love with Rande. What a pity that he preferred the opera dancer to the, er, bucolic beauty."

There was a pain in her heart so fierce that it took all her strength not to cry out. Between stiff lips she said, "I am not in love with Lord Rande. I am in love with no one, and all that is beside the point. How dared you drug me and bring me here? I could hand you over to the magistrates."

"You could do nothing of the sort, my dear. I am within my legal rights. You are my ward and were proving stubborn and recalcitrant to my wishes, which are that you marry a respectable man of my choosing."

"A respectable man of your choosing and out-and-out villain." Sheila glared at him. "I will never marry him, never! You can drag me to the altar and I will spit in his face."

"You have a choice," Brian said.

She stared at him suspiciously. That horrid gloating smile had returned. It transformed his features, she thought, turning him from an attractive young man into someone quite as repellent as Sir Jasper. "A choice?" she questioned dubiously.

"Dahna."

"Dahna?"

"You can deed me the estate. If you'll sign it over to me, I'll not insist that you wed Sir Jasper."

"I cannot deed you the estate. As you know full well, the will precludes it."

"Yes, I do know it. I just wanted to remind you that though you undoubtedly thought you'd fixed up matters all right and tight for yourself, you erred grievously."

"I fixed? I do not understand you."

"No matter." He gave her a sulky look. "Since there is no alternative, you will wed Sir Jasper."

"I do not understand you," Sheila said slowly. "What can it profit you if I wed him?"

"I need not give you reasons. Suffice to say that you will wed him, and that is final."

"I will not."

"We'll see what you have to say in another few days. I presume you are hungry. You've not eaten these last four days. Let's see what you have to say tomorrow or the day after that or the day after that."

Sheila swallowed a groan. She managed to say steadily, "You mean to starve me into submission? I will die of starvation rather than wed him."

"Brave words, my dear. Perhaps by the end of the week you'll be wiser. Until you are, 'tis bread and water for you, twice a day and no more."

"You are a monster," she whispered.

"And you, my most beloved sister, are a conniving witch, who got around our grandfather with your coaxing ways and managed to deprive me of my rightful inheritance. Dahna should have been mine."

"I said nothing to him. I wanted you to have it. I did not write his will. I knew nothing of it," she cried.

"Liar. I know what you did, and 'tis high time you were punished for it."

"You are mad."

He only smiled and strode out. A second later, she heard the key turn in the lock.

* * *

Lord Rande stood in his chamber, his riding whip in hand. He had decided against challenging Sir Brian to a duel, for now that his fury had died down to some degree, he no longer wanted to kill him and run the risk of having to spend a year or so in France. Instead, he would horsewhip him like the dog he was.

His eyes fell on the bed where Marie had lain for the three days that had passed after he brought her home from the Aviary. In his mind's eye, he could still see her and watch her shrinking from him, from any man who had entered the room, his valet and the physician included.

He had tried to impress upon her that she was safe and that no one, least of all himself, would make any demands on her. He had also tried to cheer her up by telling her how much she was missed at the King's Theater, the manager having been given a laundered version of what had taken place.

"They want you back as soon as you are well," he had said to her, speaking in French, because in her confused state she seemed to understand nothing else.

"I will not be able to dance, Ivor," she had whispered.

"When you are better, my dearest, it will be different, I am sure."

"When I am better, Ivor, but"—she had shivered—"they will be there, watching."

"They? Whom can you mean, my love?"

"There were so many who knew me, who p-possessed me." Tears had welled up in her eyes. "They will p-point at me and jeer, and it may be that they will lie in wait and try again to—"

"My poor child, that is not true. And if they were to lie and wait, as you say, they'd have me to deal with." He had knelt at her bedside and put a gentle hand on her shoulder, only to have her shrink away from him and shudder at his touch. He had moved back hastily. "You have not to be afraid of me, Marie. I mean you no harm."

She had reached for his hand then and held it against her cheek. "I am not afraid of you, Ivor, who are everything that is good, but I cannot be with you. I hurt inside. I wish not to . . . to be with any man, not ever again. I wish only to go home to my mother."

"To your mother, my love? Where is she? In Paris?"

"No, she lives in Calais. She, too, was a dancer. Before the Revolution, she danced for the Opéra, like me, but always in Paris. But she was born in Calais and she has there a house."

"Then I shall take you to your mother, my dearest."

A faint light had shone in her dull eyes. "Ah, truly?"

"Of course, my own. I will take you there as soon as you wish to leave."

"I wish to go now." For the first time, she had smiled. "Is that possible? Could we leave this very day?"

"You must give me a chance to make arrangements, my dearest. However, I can assure you that we will leave tomorrow morning."

He had had the impression that she had not quite believed him until the moment he had carried her out to the post chaise. They had covered forty-two of the seventy-two miles from London to Dover that first day, stopping at the King's Head Inn in Kent, when he realized that she was very weary. He winced, remembering her obvious fear when he had bespoken a private parlor. She had not wanted him to be with her and he had had considerable trouble soothing her and assuring her that she would have a bedchamber all to herself.

Her gratitude, the following morning, had been pitiful. It had been very hard for him to connect this pale, shrinking, self-effacing creature with his teasing, contrary, and delightful little Marie.

They had reached Dover in good time and caught the night boat to Calais, spending the rest of that evening in another inn. The next morning, he had driven her to a house on the outskirts of the city. At her earnest request, he had not accompanied her to the door. Instead, his coachman, carrying her two portmanteaus, had gone with her. He himself had watched from the window of the post chaise as she knocked on the door. A second later, it opened and a slender woman in black, fair in coloring and not much taller than Marie, had emerged and thrown her arms around the girl, who had clung to her, obviously weeping before her mother had drawn her inside.

Rande had returned to the port, and with some time on his hands before sailing, he had repaired to the Hotel Dessein, where, he had heard, Brummel was residing since his flight from London in May. However, inquiries at the desk had netted the information that he had moved to some rooms owned by Monsieur Quillac, the proprietor of the Dessein. These being hard by the hotel, Rande had gone there and had found the Beau holding court, dressed, as usual, in the very height of fashion. He had looked as if he wanted for nothing and had never left London with his creditors hot behind him.

Brummel had been delighted to see Rande as had several of the other young blades of fashion who surrounded him. Everyone was mightily surprised that, after a mere day in the city, Rande was taking the packet to Dover rather than going on to Paris. He had not been in the mood to explain his presence there, nor had he wanted to exchange more than a few words with the Beau. Despite his indubitable charm of manner, despite his gallant attempt of keeping up appearances, there had been a wounded look in his eyes that reminded Rande unpleasantly of poor Marie.

In all, it had been a miserable five days, and more misery awaited him . . . But it would *not* be misery, he reminded himself savagely. It would afford him considerable pleasure to force his way into Brian's house and cut him to the bone with a few well-deserved slashes. It would have given him even more pleasure to flay him! A knock on the door caused him to tense and turn quickly. "Well!" he barked as his valet appeared on the threshold.

"My lord, there's a lady wishes to see you. A Miss Martyn."

"Miss Martyn?" he questioned. "I do not know a—" He paused, suddenly recalling little Miss Letty Martyn, who had spent so many hours at his bedside. But it could not be, he thought. That shy and timorous lady would never call on him without warning, and at his home. Unless . . . "Is she alone, Parker?"

"No, my lord, she has her abigail with her."

"And no one else?"

"No, my lord. She, er, seemes vastly agitated. She says as how her cousin's been abducted and—" He broke off in some surprise as Rande, flinging down the whip, brushed past him and hurried toward the stairs.

She was pacing back and forth in the hall as Rande came down the stairs. Her face was wan and her eyes bloodshot from weeping, he guessed. "Miss Martyn!" he exclaimed, coming to her side.

"Oh, my lord." She flushed red. "I know 'twas wrong of me to come here, but I had no choice. I knew no one else I could ask. I pray you will help me. I know you are to be married soon, but I am sure you can explain the situation to her. I am so worried. Brian's always been such a handful, at least so I had been told, but I never expected . . . Of course, his father, even though we are closely related . . . I never did like Cousin Matthew, and—"

"Miss Letty," he interrupted, controlling his impatience with an effort, "let me take you up to the library. We can converse better in there, where you will be more comfortable." He pointed to the stairs.

She looked nervously at him and at her abigail, a placid blond girl sitting on a bench near the door. "Rose had best go with me," she said.

"Of course." He nodded in the direction of the abigail, who had risen and come to stand beside her mistress. "Come, I will go before you and lead the way, if you do not mind."

A few minutes later, seated on a comfortable settee in the large book-lined chamber and with a roaring fire set in a large fireplace, Miss Letty said, "Such a nice room, so many books. I do love books. Jeffrey, too, was a great reader, mostly the Latin poets and sermons. He did deplore my penchant for novels, but you will be wanting to hear about poor Sheila. Oh, I do not understand him, not in the least.''

Again, it was a matter of curbing his impatience and speaking soothingly. He said, "Tell me the whole of it, Miss Letty.''

"I do not understand it," she repeated. "But they have gone to Ireland—that is, I did know that they planned to go there. Sheila was quite willing to go after he told her about your betrothal and—'' She suddenly put a quivering little hand to her mouth. "Oh, dear, I should not have said that. Dearest Sheila would not like it."

"My betrothal?" he questioned, remembering her odd reference to his forthcoming marriage. "Where had you news of that?"

"Brian told us. I do wish you both all the happiness in the world.''

"And whom am I supposed to share this happiness with?" he inquired.

She looked confused. "Why, the dancer from the opera.''

"I see," he said gratingly. "Though I am loathe to dispute your cousin Brian, I must tell you he is in error. I am going to wed no one. But Miss Corbett is under the impression that I am to be married?"

"Oh, yes, she was most surprised. She did agree to leave. She was, of course, quite put out that Brian had closed the London house without even warning her about his intention."

"Ah, and when did this take place?"

"Two days ago. It was all very sudden. I had thought we'd be in London for the Season, but no matter. He and Sir Jasper took Sheila, and while she was still sleeping—''

"While she was sleeping?"

Rose, who had been seated in a corner nearer to the fire, jumped to her feet, and giving Miss Letty an impatient look, she said sharply, "Beggin' yer pardon, sor, but she were drugged. I be sure o' that. An' they be takin' 'er off to Ireland so's she can marry the Sor Jasper. Terry 'eard 'em talkin', 'im bein' up in the stable loft where they couldn't see 'im." She turned to Miss Letty. "Beggin' yer pardon, ma'am, but I thought 'e ought to get it straight."

"That is quite all right, Rose dear," Miss Letty assured her. "Quite possibly, she was drugged, now that I come to think of it. I did think it odd that she became unconscious so quickly after that glass of dessert wine that Brian gave her . . . and he broke his glass too."

"Broke his glass?" Rande repeated confusedly.

"So's 'e wouldn't 'ave to drink none o' it," Rose put in again. " 'Im an' that Sor Jasper're as thick as thieves. They 'ad it all planned between 'em afore they come. That's what Terry said."

"I see. Thank you very much, Rose." Rande's brain was racing. Evidently, some time in the past week, Brian had learned that Marie was no longer at the Aviary. He would have learned, too, that two men had come to fetch her. They would have been described, and Brian would have guessed that he had been one of them. That would have frightened him. Consequently, he had closed the London house and ridden to the manor, where he had wasted no time in spiriting his sister away—for her protection? No, the plan was that she should marry Sir Jasper. Marry Sir Jasper! He shuddered. "Two days," he said. "That means that they will be in Ireland soon. It also means that it will take me even more time to catch up with them."

"Will you go?" Miss Letty asked.

"Yes, of course," he said decisively. "At once." He paused. "Have you anywhere to stay?"

She clasped her thin hands and looked up at him beseechingly. "I have become very, very fond of dearest Sheila. Would I be a burden if I were to come with you?"

He said gently, "I shall be traveling very fast, Miss Letty. I shall go alone and on horseback. It would be better if you remained here. My house is at your disposal."

"Oh, I could not," she murmured.

"I beg that you will." He strode to the door. "I think you should be here when I bring Miss Corbett back."

"Oh, then, I shall," she cried. "I—"

Whatever else she might have said was lost to him as he

hurried to his chamber and, without waiting for his valet, set about packing a small portmanteau. His heart was pounding heavily. "Two days," he muttered, and groaned. It would take him another three to catch up with them, and in that time anything could happen. He did not want to consider the possibilities. He would think only of finding the shortest route to Dahna!

11

BY THE TIME Lord Rande came in sight of Dahna, he could scarce see its Palladian facade, for a mist had blotted out all but a small portion of the road in front of him and had caused him to slow his horse to a trot when he had wanted to ride like the wind.

He was very near the end of his patience, and worry was a hard knot in his chest. Everything that could have impeded his progress on this journey had occurred. At the outset, his horse had cast a shoe and the blacksmith in the tiny village where the mishap had taken place was too busy to attend to it immediately. He had cooled his heels but not his temper there for an hour. Then, with night falling, he had sheltered at an inn and awakened to a pelting rainstorm that had muddied the roads and delayed him for the better part of another day.

On reaching Liverpool, he had missed the boat and had subsequently been subjected to a tumultuous crossing wherein everyone had been seasick, himself included, far too weak to continue his journey upon disembarking. He had remained in Dublin for another precious day and, continuing on to Galway, had been forced to put up at another inn for the night, having been warned that the roads were infested with tinkers and other vagabonds. In all, it had taken him much longer than he had anticipated —six days instead of a projected three, and ten days from the day Brian and Sir Jasper had left the manor. He could only hope that they too might have suffered some of his delays.

Now, however, he was finally nearing the gatehouse, an

almost indistinguishable bulk in the swirling fog. He was aware that there was more than a chance that he might be turned away by the gatekeeper, and having anticipated that problem, he had his pistol within easy reach in case the coins he was prepared to offer did not suffice.

A gust of wind smelling strongly of the sea enveloped him, and he shivered. The chill had penetrated his cloak and jacket, intensifying a pain in his shoulder that had been bothering him off and on for several hours. However that, if anything, spurred him on as he remembered the source. In the remembering, he thought of Sheila being forcibly wed to a man she hated, and he shivered again out of a deep-seated fear that he might be too late to prevent those ill-starred nuptials.

Yet surely she could not be forced into such vows! She was no cringing, frightened child like poor little Marie. Though Sheila was actually younger in years, she had a maturity that Marie would forever lack. If she had been in Marie's place, she would have defied the entire crew from the Aviary, even if she had died in the attempt. Sheila had the makings of a warrior queen, and would she be wasted on the likes of a twopenny rogue such as Sir Jasper? His teeth ground together in the rage he had been experiencing at ever more frequent intervals since Miss Letty had braved the rigors of a London journey to bring him her tale of fraternal skulduggery. She had also, inadvertently, told him something else.

Sheila had been quite willing to go to Ireland after Brian had told her about "your betrothal." Letty had blushed and looked like a child being scolded for having betrayed a confidence. And why had Brian told his sister that Rande was betrothed and why had Sheila reacted in such a manner?

Rande thought of her as he had seen her just before leaving for London. There had been tears in her eyes and he had been inclined to take her in his arms and kiss them away, and he might have so done had they not been interrupted by Miss Letty. He had actually been relieved at that interruption mainly because he had still been

comparing his situation to that of the late Arthur Bellmore.

He must have been mad, he thought furiously. If there
had been the slightest hope that Sheila cared for him . . .
And there had been, he had known that and should have
spoken, but even if he had, the subsequent events would
have intervened to thwart his plans, their plans. However,
in this latest action, Brian had happily removed any
obstacles to their match—that is, if he had not erected an
even greater wall between them. If he had, it could and
would be removed—no matter what the cost!

His hands tightened on the reins. If anyone were to ask
him what he wanted most in life at this precise moment, he
would have answered that he wanted to have these same
hands tightening around Sir Jasper's damned throat! And
now he was finally at the gates of Dahna. They stood open
and the burly gatekeeper was waiting just inside. Rande
urged his horse forward, halting at the man's grunted
command.

The gatekeeper's expression was gloomy and, at the
same time, pugnacious. "An' what would yer lordship be
wantin'?" he demanded, obviously remembering him
from that earlier visit when he had come with Marie to purchase horses.

It was on the tip of his tongue to say that he was there to
purchase more horses from Sir Brian, but he remembered
that Sheila was the owner of Dahna. "I have come at the
request of Miss Corbett," he said.

"Have you, now?"

"Yes, I am much delayed. But I believe she must still be
expecting me." Reaching into his pocket, he brought out a
sovereign and proffered it.

The man surveyed him in silence, his pugnacious expression replaced by one of pure greed as he fixed his eyes on
the glittering coin. Receiving it, he nodded. "Ye may go
in."

"I thank you." Rande rode on. He was relieved. He had
been primed for an argument and even a fight. Certainly,

he had not expected so swift an acquiescence. However, on second thought, he doubted that the gatekeeper received many sovereigns. As he continued in the direction of the house, he became aware of a preternatural quiet. The last time he had come here, men had been working in the gardens and on the lawns, calling back and forth to one another or whistling a merry tune. Of course, that had been in the spring and now it was almost the middle of October. Probably that was why the windows on the first floor were heavily curtained. The curtains had been drawn back before.

Was it his own state of mind that made him feel as if the house were deserted? Undoubtedly. Reaching the end of the carriageway, he dismounted and led his horse toward one of the posts furnished for the convenience of arriving guests. He was annoyed to find his hands trembling as he secured his mount. He preferred to diagnose his mood as concerned rather than worried, but he was worried. Despite the presence of the gatekeeper, he had the odd feeling that he was alone on these grounds. Telling himself that he was borrowing trouble, Rande strode to the porch and a second later had slammed the huge brass knocker against its plate with a force that, he guessed, must have sent echoes through the hall. He waited some five or six moments and knocked a second time, even louder. Was the door untended? Had his fears been realized?

In that same second, the door was opened and a middle-aged man in green livery said tentatively, "Yes?"

Rande found himself looking into a worried face dominated by big blue eyes that avoided his own gaze. Obviously, the servant was nervous. "I wish to see Miss Corbett," Rande said.

It seemed to him that the man paled. "Miss Corbett," the man repeated, moistening his lips with the tip of a pale tongue.

"Is she here?" Rande demanded.

"And who is it wishes to speak to Miss Corbett, Hennessy?"

Recognizing Brian's voice, Rande was filled with a plethora of emotions. Uppermost among them was a burning anger that, of course, he must needs subdue when he met this youth, whom he would have liked to throttle with his own hands. Unfortunately, Rande would have to be conciliating—conciliating to this wretch, who had taken his poor little mistress out of revenge and then had proceeded to wreck her life and now was bound and determined to do the same to his own blood sister! He said calmly, "It is I who would like to see your sister, Sir Brian."

"You!" Thrusting the servant aside, Brian appeared in the doorway. He turned a frowning face upon Rande. "How did you get past my gatekeeper?" he demanded.

"I had no difficulty, Sir Brian." Rande spoke softly, courteously. "Had you left orders for him not to admit me?"

"I left orders that I would not receive any visitors. I must speak to him, it seems. And what, may I ask, are you doing this long way from London, my lord?"

There was an ugly look on Brian's face and he spoke in an insolent manner, which made Rande long to push his words back down his throat with a well-aimed punch to the mouth. He maintained his calm with a great effort. "I came here at your sister's invitation."

"Did you, now?" Brian sneered. "Well, my lord, you should have given her some warning, not that she'd have needed it. She's not here, do you see? She'll be in Scotland by now." A mocking smile curled Brian's lips now. "She'll be on her wedding journey. She and her bridegroom are bound for Edinburgh, where he has relatives."

"She's wed, then." Rande was aware of an actual pain in his heart.

"Aye, she's wed." There was a note of triumph in Brian's tone. "She's wed to Sir Jasper Tennant. The happy event took place two days ago. 'Twas a pity you were not here to toast the bride, but I shall give her your felicitations, shall I?"

"You must do that," Rande said numbly. His mind was

racing. He longed to challenge Brian to a duel; he wanted to find the fastest way to Edinburgh and there deal with that newly married pair—or at least with the bridegroom! The second resolution took precedence over the first. His business with Sir Brian could wait. He had to find Sheila and rescue her. The fact that he would be looking for a needle in a haystack did not weigh with him. He would find them and he would spit Sir Jasper on the point of his sword or send a bullet through his heart. Looking into Brian's triumphant face, Rande longed to strangle him or at least make the attempt. However, that would gain him nothing. He was one man against a houseful of servants ready to defend their master, and furthermore, he had to be out and away. He said, "I will be going now."

"I will bid you farewell, my lord. And I will tell Lady Tennant that you wished her happiness."

Not trusting himself to answer, Rande merely nodded. Turning on his heel, he went slowly down the steps toward the post where his horse was tethered. He did not look back. He knew that Brian was still standing in the entrance watching him, gleefully enjoying his misery. His hands clenched. He longed to go back and . . . But there was no use dwelling any longer on what he would like to do. He must find Sheila, who was no longer Corbett but Tennant, and kill the man she called husband.

"My lord!"

Rande came to a startled stop and looked around. Who had called him? The cry had come from . . . whence? Not from the doorway, where, as he had anticipated, Brian still stood. He looked up and paled as he saw a spectral image —a figure in flowing white robes with long dark hair falling in tangled locks around a dead white face, its eyes sunk in dark hollows, its lips pale, its thin hands stretching out to him. "Lord Rande," it cried again, and even with her glorious coloring drained away, replaced by that sickly pallor, he knew he was looking at Sheila.

With an exclamation, he started forward and was vaguely aware of movement behind him. Then, something hit him on the head. Bright spots danced before his eyes and he fell. As his consciousness faded, he heard a long wailing scream.

Sheila crawled back through the window of her room and sat on a chair, trembling. It was Bridget, speaking through the keyhole, who had alerted her to Rande's presence below. "I'd have tried to speak to him, but the master'd've seen me. An' he's told his lordship that you are off to Scotland with yer bridegroom. Oh, Miss Sheila, it's terrible! I wish I could do somethin' to help you. We all do."

She had tried to soothe the girl. She knew Bridget's distress, knew, too, something she had not realized before: that lazy and drunken as she sometimes could be, Bridget was yet her friend. The girl had wept as she had brought her the crusts of dry bread and the water that had been given her twice a day in the room that had become her prison. "Oh, it's horrid cruel. I long to bring ye somethin' else, but he has me searched ere I come up here."

Sheila had comforted her. "I know. And I thank you."

"Mayhap it'd be better it you'd give in an' marry that Sir Jasper."

"Never," Sheila had cried. "He may keep me here for every moment of the five months that will pass before I am of age, but I'll never consent."

"Oh, Miss Sheila, you could be dead in five months," Bridget had sobbed.

"I'd rather be dead," she had averred.

Now, as she waited for her brother, she was bitterly regretting the impulse that had sent her onto the roof for a last look at the man she loved, the man who had unaccountably come to Ireland to find her. Yet, perhaps it was not so unaccountable. Probably Miss Letty had been the instigator of that journey. She must have gone to him and begged him to postpone his marriage plans—or perhaps he was already wed. And now what would happen to him? She shivered. Anything that did happen would be laid at her door. She had called out to him. She never should have called out, never should have uttered a word!

If she had not been so weak, she would have held her peace. Yet, to see him primed on Brian's lies and ready to ride out of her life forever and ever had been too much for her. Almost without volition, she had called his name. Her voice had sounded very hoarse to her own ears, but he had heard it and looked up and Tennant had struck! Tears rolled down her thin cheeks as she envisioned once more that moment when Lord Rande had fallen in the dust.

And what would happen now?

A blow like that invited a duel, but knowing Brian and Tennant as she now did, she would not put it past them to resort to measures she did not even like to contemplate. She stiffened. The key was turning in the lock. In another moment, her brother, looking insufferably pleased with himself, entered and stood against the door surveying her amusedly.

She leapt to her feet. "Why did Tennant strike him?" she cried. "What do you intend to do with him?"

"That, my dearest Sheila, depends entirely upon you. You hold his lordship's fate in your two pretty little hands." Brian's gloating smile was in evidence once more. "And in anticipation of your acquiescence, I have told dear Sir Jasper that he must fetch a clergyman. He stands downstairs in the hall, booted and spurred, awaiting your word."

"I will never give it, I will never wed him," she cried.

"I think you will when you hear of my alternative suggestion, which carries with it the opportunity of seeing your would-be guest dangling at the end of a roof or possibly sent off to New South Wales in a prison ship. They do say that the conditions aboard those vessels are very poor indeed. A great many prisoners die of scurvy or other diseases before they ever see the coast of that new country rising before them. Or they die when they arrive of the hard work and the bad conditions. All in all, I favor this latter course. It would be rather amusing to see his elegant lordship in convict's rags."

"Convict's rags!" she exclaimed. "I do not understand you!"

"But, my dear, sure you understand trespassing, sure you understand an attempted murder, charges that I shall lay against your dear friend."

"You must be insane," she cried. "They'd not believe that. He has but to tell the truth—"

"Undoubtedly, the truth would suffice in a British court, where he'd be well supplied with a lawyer and friends to attest to his sterling character, but I'll be taking him before an Irish justice of the peace who, while he holds office in a British court, will have little sympathy for the accused, there being considerable political unrest about. Were it not for our own Irish heritage, we might have seen Dahna burned to the ground this past week as was the estate of Sir Arthur Kenwick."

"Sir Arthur Kenwick!" Sheila repeated blankly. "You'll not be telling me that they attacked him."

"Aye." Brian nodded. "I was forgetting that you're a bit cut off from the local gossip—not cut off enough, it seems, or was it some little bird alerted you to Rande's presence here?" His smile had never been more unpleasant as he continued, "That girl of yours ought to be sent packing, but it seems I owe her a debt of gratitude for helping to arrive at a speedy resolution of a matter that has been growing more and more tedious. However, to get back to the unfortunate Sir Arthur, yes, his estate was burned to the ground by persons unknown. His daughter has been abducted and his wife ravished. It could have been our fate were it not that the blood of Erin gushes through our veins. And Sir Arthur, as you know, has been enjoying his Irish residence for some forty years, and his father before him. Lord Rande is a very new arrival and I fear that his lineage will not stand in favor once he's in the dock before a jury of his peers—Irish peers, unfortunately."

"You could not do such a thing," she cried.

"I could and would, unless you accept the hand and heart of Sir Jasper Tennant immediately."

"Does it mean nothing to you that I loathe him?" she cried.

"In our circles, my dear, there are very few marriages made in heaven. Consider the unfortunate situation of our late parents."

"I will deed you Dahna. Bring me the papers and I will sign them."

"We have already agreed that our grandfather's will precluded such a transfer. You managed the old man too well, my beloved. You have only yourself to blame for the outcome."

"How many times must I swear to you that I knew nothing of his intent?"

"Whether you were party to it or not, the will stands. I want Dahna. You could not love it as I do, Sheila. And once you've wed Sir Jasper, he has promised to deed it to me."

"This is your reason," she cried. "This is why I must marry him?" She began to laugh, albeit hysterically. "You fool, you blind fool, you are even crazier than I've believed to think that he'll abide by that promise."

He caught her by the shoulders, shaking her. "Stop it, stop it." He struck her across the face and pushed her back into her chair. "He will abide by it and I will tell you why and how! He will abide by it with my gun at his back as he signs the agreement. I am not such a fool as you believe. Now, do I send Rande to rot in New South Wales or do you become the sweet, blushing bride of my good friend Sir Jasper Tennant?"

She was silent a long moment, her nails digging into her palms. Her horror of the man who had been her brother's guest in the house during the days of her imprisonment and who had accepted the situation with an ease that pronounced him an even greater villain than she had originally believed, increased. Yet, if she did not consent to the match, Rande would suffer a fate even more terrible than her own. She did not doubt that her brother would stand by his word. If she closed her eyes, she could envision him in convict's garb toiling in that hot sun. "No," she cried.

"Very well." Brian turned toward the door. "I will convey his lordship—"

"No!" she cried a second time. "No, I will promise to wed Sir Jasper. You may tell him that I hate and loathe him, but if he wants me in such circumstances, I will be his wife."

"My dear," Brian smiled beautifully. "At last you have come to your senses. May I be the first to wish you happy."

"May you rot in hell," Sheila exclaimed.

"I will send Bridget with cakes and tea and perhaps a meat pasty, a prewedding snack, you might say. Also she will bring you a gown, though doubtlessly Sir Jasper would appreciate you in any garb. The poor fellow is, as I think I have told you, quite besotted. There's no accounting for tastes." He moved to the door. "I will also send your bridegroom off to fetch the parson. I think we'll have the ceremony within two hours' time."

"So soon?"

"It will not seem soon to poor Sir Jasper," Brian reminded her sweetly. "Nor to me, who have been waiting far longer to see the last of you, dear sister." Moving out of the room, he closed and locked the door behind him.

Sir Jasper was awaiting him in the downstairs hall. Joining him, Brian said mockingly, "Behold, I bring you tidings of great joy."

"She's consented at last?"

Brian nodded. "I cannot say she was precisely enthusiastic over the match, my dear fellow, but when I pointed out the uncomfortable alternatives, she saw reason. Consequently, you may fetch your cleric and make use of the license you had the forethought to procure upon our arrival."

"And what about your guest?" Sir Jasper demanded.

"I've promised his release. Have you looked in on him?"

"I have. He's still unconscious."

"I'll have Hennessy take him down into the cellars. Directly you've departed upon your wedding journey, I'll alert the magistrates as to his breaking and entering, and his threats against me and my sister. Let us pray that the population of New South Wales will be increased by one.''

"Were not time of the essence, I'd drink to that,'' Sir Jasper said softly.

"Oh, I think we may enjoy a stirrup cup before you leave,'' Brian said jovially.

"I think not, dear boy. I've been waiting too long already. I'd best forgo the libation and toast my lovely bride instead.''

"As you choose.'' Brian accompanied him to the stables and, having seen him off, strolled back into the house. Summoning Hennessy, he unlocked the small office where he had left Lord Rande.

His lordship still lay on the small bench where the two of them had deposited him. His face was pale and his eyes closed. He did not appear to be breathing.

"God,'' Brian muttered, looking back over his shoulder at his henchman, who was standing in the doorway. "He seems . . .'' He swallowed and added nervously, "You do not think that he—''

"He's very pale, right enough.'' Hennessy frowned.

"I couldn't have.'' Brian turned to Hennessy, and in that same moment Lord Rande, leaping to his feet, dealt a blow to Brian's chin that sent him reeling. Before he could recover, another powerful blow to the chin stretched Brian out on the floor.

"Arragh and that was a sweet hit,'' Hennessy cried. "Caught him off guard you did. I'd like to shake yer hand for that, I'm thinkin'.''

Lord Rande, his fists still knotted, stared at the servant in an amazement laced with suspicion. "You'd be telling me—''

"I'd be telling ye,'' Hennessy spoke quickly, "that ye haven't a moment to lose if you're to get Miss Sheila out of here before Sir Jasper, the wicked spalpeen, returns here with the parson.'' Bending down, Hennessy felt in the fallen man's pockets and extracted a key, thrusting it at Rande. "This will unlock her room. I'll show ye the way, but first we'd best lock young Brian in here, makin' sure that he's in no hurry to wake up." With that, Hennessy knotted his fist and struck Brian another heavy blow to the chin. "He should sleep sweetly for a bit," he remarked with considerable satisfaction. "Now, come, 'tis herself we must be considerin', and haven't we all been rackin' our brains as to how we could free her an' you come along an' subdue the lot o' us wi' the men ye brought with ye."

"I came alone."

"Aye, but he'll not know the difference." Hennessy winked at him. "Ah, yer a fine broth of a lad for all yer a Britisher. An' come in the nick o' time. 'Tisn't for the likes of us to stop the gentry, but we would've afore we'd have seen her wed to that Sir Jasper. But we must hurry now."

Rande could scarcely believe his good fortune. In fact, as he followed Hennessy up the long staircase, he had his hand on the little pistol he had brought with him, which Brian had not thought to remove from his pocket. Yet, he decided, Hennessy's sincerity seemed real enough. Rande could well believe that these servants, loyal to Sheila, had been, as the man said, "racking their brains" to find a way to save her without courting trouble themselves. The law would not be easy on servants who rebelled against their masters.

In another moment, he was traversing the hall. Hennessy had halted in front of a door. Producing the key, he said, "It might be that ye'll have to carry her. She's been livin' on no more'n bread'n water an' Bridget says she's that weak."

"Oh, God," Rande groaned. "And he's her brother."

"Aye, don't seem as if they could've been hatched from the same nest," Hennessy agreed. "We've always known him as a spoiled nasty lad . . . an' the Old One, he did, too. I'd be talkin' o' his worship, Lord Carlingford."

"Hennessy!" Bridget came running down the hall. She stared at Lord Rande. "Ye've come for her?"

"Aye," Hennessy said. "Ye'd best fetch her clothes."

"Oh, it's that glad I am," Bridget cried, and ran

on down the hall as Hennessy turned the key in the lock and opened the door.

"Sheila!" Rande hurried inside. Coming to a stop, he stared about him in confusion. The room was empty.

"Miss Sheila!" Hennessy exclaimed. "She couldn't have gotten out." His eyes fell on the window. It was open. "Lord save us, she'll not have . . ." He was at the window with Rande close behind him. "Ah, Miss Sheila." Hennessy leaned over the sill.

"Stay back, I warn you," Sheila shrilled. She stood on the roof, her white draperies caught by the wind, her face paler even than when Rande had seen her from below. "What have you done with his lordship?" she cried. "You promised he might go if I'd wed that monster. But he's not gone. If you do not free him, I'll throw myself from here."

"Sheila." Rande thrust Hennessy aside and climbed out the window. "My own darling, did you think I'd leave without you?"

She stared at him incredulously. "You're safe," she mouthed.

"We're both safe," he cried exultantly, and catching her in his arms, he bore her inside.

"Ye'll not be safe until ye've a few leagues behind ye," Hennessy warned as Lord Rande gently set Sheila on her feet, holding her against him.

"Dahna's mine," she cried. "I'll not run away now that I'm free."

"Sir Brian'd have it he's yer guardian, and as such, we dare not dispute him, Miss Sheila," Hennessy said. "His lordship's sent him to sleep for a bit, but he'll be wakin'."

"He's right, my dearest love," Rande said. "We must go—and soon."

Sheila stared up at him. "What did you call me?" she whispered.

"I called you 'love,' because you are my love," he said tenderly. "But we've not to speak of that now. We must be off."

"Tim'll ride with ye. He has an uncle works at the Black

Horseman, which is off the high road and away from the village. They'll not think to search for ye there, 'tis not a place for gentry an' few o' 'em knows it.''

Rande regarded Sheila with concern and anger. She was so pale and wasted. Brian would pay for what he had done to his sister, but he dared not consider punishments at this moment. "I thank you," he said. "We'll go at once. But I do not think Sheila's up to riding."

She clutched his sleeve. "I can ride," she whispered.

"No." Hennessy shook his head. "His lordship's right, you've not eaten enough to keep a bird alive, that be the truth o' it. Ye'll have to take her afore ye in the saddle." He looked at Lord Rande.

" 'Tis my intention." Rande nodded.

There was a knock at the door. The three of them tensed but relaxed as Bridget called, "Miss Sheila . . ."

"Come in, girl," Hennessy ordered.

The abigail, carrying a cloak and gown over her arm and a portmanteau in the other hand, said excitedly, "Oh, 'tis glad I am to see you freed. Here's yer clothes. I took 'em from Sir Brian's room."

"We'll wait until you've dressed," Lord Rande said. Reading alarm in her eyes, he added hastily, "I'll be right beyond the door, my angel."

"I'll hurry," she said staunchly.

As Rande closed the door behind him, Hennessy said, "I'll be fetchin' Tim." He hurried down the stairs.

Sheila was ready in minutes, and rejecting Rande's offer to carry her, suddenly ran ahead of him down the stairs. She was forced to clutch the post at the bottom and stood there panting as Rande joined her.

He said sharply, "If you've not got any more regard for yourself than . . ." He broke off, looking at her so sternly and yet so lovingly that she blinked away tears.

"I was only thinking of your shoulder," she murmured, adding, "Oh, my dear, I was so afraid for you."

"As I was for you."

"My lord." Hennessy came toward him. " 'Tis time you were on yer way. Tim's without an' waitin' for ye."

He opened the door. "The mist's grown thicker, but do not mind it. 'Tis better for ye. Hold," he added as Rande, clutching Sheila's hand, started outside. "There's somethin' you must do." He pointed to his chin. "Ye'll have to gi' me a good blow."

Rande said ruefully, "I do not like to hurt you."

" 'Twill save my life, that hurt," Hennessy said solemnly. "But let me fall near the office where ye have Sir Brian on the carpet. There's no use for me to bruise my limbs as well."

"What's this?" Sheila demanded. Receiving an explanation from Rande, she looked gratefully at Hennessy. "I'll see you're well compensated for your pains."

"To know yer safe's enough for me, Miss Sheila," he said. "Now you'd best wait here while his lordship tends to me."

Sheila flung her arms around him, kissed him on the cheek, and then went to stand beside the door. Rande, sighing, followed Hennessy back to the office and delivered the requisite blow. As Hennessy fell, Rande went back quickly and, ignoring her protests, scooped Sheila up in his arms and carried her out to his waiting horse.

"I'll strap your portmanteau behind us," he said. He tensed as he heard the sound of hooves but relaxed when a tall youth with a crop of brown curls and a wide grin rode up with Bridget before him on his saddle.

"I'll be goin' with you, Miss Sheila," she called excitedly. "You'll be needin' me."

"She will indeed," Rande agreed. "We'll hire a post chaise back to Dublin."

"But—" Sheila started to protest.

"Shhhh," he muttered. "You do not think I'd make you ride all that long way." With a teasing little smile, he added, " 'Twould be too much for the horse." Springing up behind her, he put an arm around her and drew her close against him. "Are you comfortable, my own?" he questioned.

"Oh, yes . . . so comfortable, so safe," she murmured.

"And will remain so," he assured her. He himself did

not feel quite as sanguine as he pretended. The mist was very thick. He could only pray that the young man who rode beside him was as dependable as Hennessy had insisted. Yet, despite these qualms, he could only be gladdened by the fact that Sheila sat before him almost as close as he had wanted her to be ever since he had discovered the state of his own heart.

The two of them had ridden at a fast clip, too fast for the thin little man in the rusty black garments and the white collar that was none too clean. He was holding tightly to the reins of a nag as thin as himself. Looking at the grim visage of Sir Jasper Tennant, he wished more than ever that he had been able to refuse his strange request. He had hoped that the license he had displayed was not in order, but it was and he too poor to argue.

"Ride faster, faster, Mr. Dannaher," Sir Jasper urged, seeing that the minister was falling behind.

"Sure'n if it wasn't for Sir Brian, I'd not be comin' here at all."

"You're well paid for it, are you not?" Sir Jasper snapped. "And as a Protestant in this part of the country, the pickings are mighty slim, so I've been told."

Dannaher reddened. "We do not labor for dross, Sir Jasper."

"Do you not?" His laugh irritated the minister, and his thin pinched face grew even redder.

"I did not need to come here," he muttered resentfully.

"Of a truth, you did not. I'm grateful that you did." Sir Jasper had decided to spread oil on those troubled waters. It would be difficult enough once the measly little man was brought face to face with his obstinate bride-to-be. Even at this late date, it was possible that the contrary wench would prove stubborn—but once he'd wedded and bedded her, it would be a different story. Sheila was a creature well worth the trouble she'd caused him. And the fact that she hated him was to his taste as well. By the time the night was at an end, she'd be kissing his feet.

They were coming in sight of Dahna now. His eyes

caressed the sweep of lawn; the trees, with their autumn
gold just visible in the mist; and the long driveway leading
up to the Palladian masterpiece of a house, rising like one
of the Grecian temples of old. He smiled as he saw the roof
where Sheila had crawled when alerted to the presence of
her lover. He was grateful to her for that, because her
brother's threats concerning Rande had finally brought
about her capitulation. As for his lordship, he'd be in the
cellars by now, perhaps with the rats sniffing at him, and
soon he'd be in an even darker place with the worms
feasting on him. Tennant dug spurs into his horse's flanks,
smiling wildly as the animal plunged ahead. In a very short
time he would be a happy and wealthy man, the master of
Dahna, in fact. He did not foresee any trouble from young
Brian. He could deal with the cub when the time came.

A short time later, Tennant was staring from the groggy
and groaning Hennessy to a Brian who looked in even
worse shape. The young man babbled about being
overcome by Rande while Hennessy talked about a whole
battalion of men who had taken Sheila, Tim, and Bridget
away—at Rande's command. O'Toole, summoned from
the gate, had corroborated Hennessy's tale.

"I do not believe it," Sir Jasper cried.

" 'Tis the truth," O'Toole said. "I'd not be able to tell
you how many there were."

"Where've they gone, damn you?" Brian glared at
Hennessy.

"I'd not be knowin'," Hennessy protested. "I was laid
out like a cold corpse, I was."

A stream of epithets escaped Sir Jasper. He glared at
Hennessy. "I think you're lying."

"Lyin', is it?" Hennessy caressed his bruised and
swollen face. "An' will you look at this?"

"Are you much hurt, my man?" inquired the minister.

"I am that, Father. My teeth are loosed."

"I am not an, er, father," the minister protested, "but
be that as it may, I cannot approve your language, Sir
Jasper."

"Be damned to you," Brian snarled.

"If you'd not dismissed half the staff, we'd be better off." Sir Jasper glared at Brian now.

"And whose suggestion was it that I should?" Brian retorted. " 'Twas you said you did not trust them, damn you!"

"You'd best go easy on the blame." Sir Jasper's gaze had narrowed. "If you'd not been such a weak fool and had taken my advice, we'd have been ready to go ahead with the wedding."

"You call me a fool?" Brian rounded on him. "Damn your eyes, I would like—"

"I'll not listen to this language," the minister interrupted. "Nor do I think my services are required." He stared at the two men, neither of whom seemed to have heard him, and then, thanking God that he had been paid beforehand, he scuttled out.

"Did you not think that Rande had more than one trick up his sleeve?" Sir Jasper said contemptuously.

"I do not like your manner," Brian retorted.

"And neither do I like the way you've handled, or rather mishandled, this situation. You should have whipped that girl into acquiescence."

"Damn it, she's my sister!"

"And starving's preferable to beating?"

"She'd not have responded to either. The thought of wedding you was not to her taste, Sir Jasper, and the more I think of it, I'm glad she's away from here."

"You little whelp." Sir Jasper struck him.

Taken unawares a second time, Brian staggered back and just saved himself from falling. "You'll answer for that blow, and now!"

" 'Twill be my pleasure, you young fool."

They stood on a clearing in the gardens of Dahna. It would give him considerable pleasure to shoot the villain down, Brian thought. 'Twas Sir Jasper's fault that he was here. If it had not been for him, introducing him to cards with hints that had completely failed him at the crucial moment . . . He had been a fool to trust the man, and a bigger fool to underestimate Rande—Englishmen both, and curse the day that either had set foot on Irish soil! And now Hennessy was calling the paces, and in a moment he would turn and put a hole through Sir Jasper, thus ridding the world of some of its slime.

The Black Horseman was small and off the road, as Hennessy had said, but it was also snug and clean. Fortunately its one private parlor was not occupied, and even more fortunately the establishment boasted a fine cook, who sent up potato soup and a meat pasty that Sheila found akin to ambrosia. However, she ate sparingly and also drank no more than a half-glass of wine, saying to Rande, who watched her from across the table, "I must get used to eating again."

His face darkened at the thought of her ordeal and the reasons for it, which she had haltingly explained. She looked very weary and painfully thin, but despite her pallor, she was no less beautiful to him. He said with a small shake of his head, "I've not had any siblings and have always regretted the fact until now."

"It was the will," Sheila sighed.

"It was not the will," he disputed hotly. "Such a loss cannot change a character. I am sorry to tell you this, but he must always have been the same, selfish and spoiled. 'Tis only that you could not see it until he was really thwarted."

She was silent a moment. "You're right, I expect," she admitted reluctantly. "I can remember incidents. One in particular. Stella, a feisty little mare that I adored and trained myself. She was a magnificent jumper and Brian wanted her. We were eleven and thirteen at the time, but I loved him so much I could not bear for him to be deprived. 'Twas hard for me, but I gave her to him. I'd have given him Dahna had it been in my power to do so."

"But it was not in your power and he did not deserve it, as your grandfather must have known," Rande said savagely. "Oh, my poor love"—he reached across the table and, taking her hand, held it tightly—"I do love you, with all my heart. I've not been able to stop thinking of you, dreaming of you since I left the manor."

"Nor I of you, my dearest," she said softly. "And when I thought . . ." She paused, staring at him. "But it's not true, is it?"

"What, my angel?"

"Brian said—"

He cut in, unwilling to hear from her lips what Brian had told her. "He said that I am betrothed to Marie. No, it is not true." His voice trembled with suppressed rage at both the lies and the truth of the situation: poor Marie, a shadow of her former self, and Sheila, half a shadow—both victims of Brian's stupidity and greed. "Marie," he continued, "has returned to France. She is out of my life and she never held any portion of my heart. That belongs entirely to you, my own darling. Will you marry me, Sheila?"

"Yes, I will," she said simply. "If"—a gleam of merriment danced briefly in her eyes—"you do not mind . . ."

"What ought I to mind, my dearest girl?"

"Being wed to a bucolic beauty?"

He stared at her and flushed. "I'd not be happy with any other kind," he said, and bringing her hand to his lips, he kissed it lingeringly.

"All's well that ends well," quoted Miss Letty enthusiastically when Lord Rande and Sheila returned from Ireland. They had traveled fast, and though the exigencies of the journey should have wrought ill on Sheila's weakened constitution, they had not. She was thinner, pronounced her cousin, but as blooming as when she had left. She and her lord would be married at high noon at St. James's Church on November 20, which would give her time to have her bride clothes made, even though Rande had shocked his cousin-in-law-to-be by saying that he would as lief wed her in her shift.

That the bridegroom was not entirely easy in his mind on the subject of the man soon to be his brother-in-law was a fact mentioned by neither Sheila nor Rande, but it was there, casting its shadow over her whenever she thought about it.

She had expected that Brian must pursue her; that she had heard nothing of him in the fortnight since they had returned to London did not cheer her. It only augmented her unspoken fears that at some time after the wedding and, possibly, the wedding journey, there would be a confrontation between her husband and her brother in which blood might be spilled. Then, there was also Sir Jasper, whose base action had resulted in the stiffness that was not entirely gone from Rande's shoulder and arm. If they were to meet in what could only be termed "mortal combat," who was to say that Sir Jasper, aware of Rande's intent to kill him, would not shoot first a second time.

Her fear could not be assuaged, and it haunted her whenever Rande was not with her. When they were together, her happiness at being near him precluded all other thought, but once he went away, she would envision the dueling ground and the man who was soon to be her husband, lying pale and bloodied on the grassy sward. And when Miss Letty said, " 'Tis a wonder we've heard nothing of Brian," Sheila frightened the little lady with a sharp "And God willing we shall not!"

However, they did, in the form of a letter from Hennessy, written in a copperplate hand and expressed in a manner that suggested the collaboration of some village scrivener. It began ominously:

My dear Miss Corbett:

I have the woeful task of acquainting you with the death of your brother, Sir Brian Corbett, which mournful event took place on the 12th day of October in the year of our Lord 1816, which was the same day on which you and my Lord Rande departed from Dahna.

I am sure that you will want to know what happened and I pray that this communication will prove to be properly enlightening. Sir Jasper arrived shortly after your departure, bringing with him a cleric to perform the wedding ceremony between yourself and him. When he learned what happened from me and from your brother, whom I had released betimes, he was sore put out. He began to blame Sir Brian for all that had taken place, and blows being exchanged, Sir Brian challenged Sir Jasper to a duel. Your obedient servant and Mr. O'Toole acted as seconds—I for your brother and Mr. O'Toole for Sir Jasper. In this combat, Sir Jasper, as was his wont, shot first before the count of ten and felled Sir Brian, who survived only to beg that I tell you what occurred and to beg, also, your forgiveness for his sins. Subsequently, myself and O'Toole did seize Sir Jasper, who was running away. We remanded him to the constable who forthwith did haul him off to jail. Fortunately the assizes were meeting the following week and the judge, one Mr. Rory O'Keefe, who presided at Sir Jasper's trial, did not hold with duels and, being not fond of the English, found the defendant guilty as charged and sentenced him to be hanged—forthwith. The sentence was duly carried out on October 21.

It's sad I am, indeed, to be the purveyor of such bad tidings. In lieu of being able to ask your permission, I took it upon myself to have young Brian interred in the family vault. No doubt you will want to order the stone and inscription.

May I say in conclusion that I hope Sir Brian, in meeting this cruel fate, will be absolved of his sins in regards to yourself and to others. And being gathered to his Maker, will be adjudged as having paid for his evil deeds and will forthwith go to Purgatory and not to a lower region. My sympathies upon your bereavement. I remain,

Yr Humble Servant
Patrick Hennessy

P.S. My sincere regards and thanks to Lord Rande, who struck well in my behalf.

*   *   *

Ludwig van Beethoven was a small and definitely untidy man, his hair fell into his eyes and his linen was grimy. His expression suggested moodiness, even animosity, when he bowed over Sheila's hand, listening, she feared, with wandering attention to her encomiums on his music, translated for him by young Karl Czerny, at whose house she and her husband were on this March evening.

They had come for one of Czerny's famous Sunday musicales, in which he, a well-known piano instructor, paraded his best pupils for the edification of Vienna's musical establishment.

Sheila had learned that Czerny, a musical prodigy at fourteen, had studied piano with Beethoven, after the latter had heard him play and applauded his genius. Now, Czerny was instructing Beethoven's nephew, also named Karl. Beethoven, himself a fine teacher, could not work with his nephew because of his growing deafness. Standing now in the back of the large drawing room and surreptitiously stroking one of Czerny's six cats, Sheila felt the power of the man even at this distance.

Graf Joseph von Arneth, the friend who had invited them to the recital, had explained that Ludwig's gloom had nothing to do with the performance of Herr Czerny's pupils. " 'Tis the altercation over the boy that troubles him. His temper's been sadly tested by the court battles he's been having with Joanna van Beethoven, the relict of his late brother, over the custody of his nephew.

"The dear lady's no better than she should be, a 'queen of the night' is one of the less scathing terms Ludwig uses when describing her. He feels quite naturally that she's not a fit mother for the lad. 'Tis my opinion, however, that he's no fit father or uncle for Karl, either. He's far too temperamental."

"I should not think he'd have the patience or the time to raise a child," Sheila had agreed shyly.

"He does not, but there's no convincing him of that or of the fact that he's not written anything of note for the better part of six months—mainly because of all the pother over his nephew. He considers Karl both a legacy and a duty. He also thinks he has musical talent, something with which"—he lowered his voice—"I fear Czerny disagrees, but of course, he'll do anything to please the Maestro and . . ." Von Arneth shook his head. "We must not talk of these things here. Words are carried on the wind in Vienna and blow into quite the wrong ears. Ah, I think Ludwig is leaving. He is very abrupt, you know. He's not heard half the pupils yet and . . ." He paused, realizing that Sheila's attention was wholly fixed on that departing guest.

She looked up at her tall, handsome husband. "It will be something to tell our grandchildren," she whispered tremulously, and blushed as he smiled at her.

He looked as if he might also want to kiss that beautiful face turned up to him, but good manners forbade such a display and so he merely slipped his arm around her, saying, "Shall we, too, say good night to Herr Czerny?"

"Please," she murmured with a final pat on the head of the orange cat, who stalked off, tail in air.

"You are going, then," Von Arneth inquired.

"I think we must," Lord Rande said.

"I cannot leave immediately. I will see you at the schloss." He bowed over Sheila's hand, adding, "I believe that young Czerny is much occupied. May I offer your excuses?"

"That would be kind of you, Joseph," Rande said. Nodding and smiling at some of the people they had met that evening, they made their way to the door and came out into the darkness, finding their waiting carriage a few paces down the street.

In rather halting German Lord Rande instructed the driver to take them along the Danube, dark but sparkling under a great yellow moon. He slipped his arm around his wife again and said, "I wish that Beethoven had been in a mood to play some of his famed variations. Joseph tells me that he occasionally does, even now."

"It was enough to see him," she breathed. "Ludwig van Beethoven," she pronounced his name worshipfully. "My cup runneth over!"

"And mine," he said softly. "Indeed, I have enough happiness to fill several vases, and all of them this high." He stretched out his arms. "And I owe none of it to Beethoven." He smiled down at her.

She nestled against him. "Methinks my lord doth exaggerate too much," she paraphrased.

"On the contrary." He kissed her cheek. Then, pulling her into his arms, he kissed her even more passionately. "My beautiful," he added, "do you not think it is time that we returned home?"

"I should love to return home"—she stared at him anxiously—"but have we been away long enough?"

"My own love, they will have forgotten quite . . . if anyone actually knew of our sin."

"It is not a sin," she said vehemently. "You must not believe that I consider it in that light. It would have been much more of a sin had I insisted on postponing our nuptials because of being in mourning. It is too bad that they did not know the truth, those few who thought it odd —Fiona among them, I am sorry to say—but of course, 'twas better they were not aware of the real truth."

"It is," he agreed. "Much better."

"Oh, dear, I sound as if I do not care, but I do. Poor Brian."

"I wish I could," he sighed.

"There's no reason why you should, my love," she assured him. "It's only when I think of the boy I used to know . . . His last words were of me."

"And so they should have been. It was late for him to come to his senses . . ." He paused. "But I am glad he did."

Sheila nodded. "Yes." Knowing Ivor as well as she did now, knowing, too, the tragedy of Marie, she was well aware that he was relieved he would not need to see Brian again and be compelled to seek vengeance for that and for her own ordeal. "When shall we leave?" she asked.

"Then, you are agreeable?" he said eagerly.

"I am. Five months is a long time to be away. I have enjoyed Paris and Vienna and 'twas most exciting to visit

Prague and to sit in the very theater where *Don Giovanni* was first performed—and to know that Mozart once stood in that orchestra pit. But"—she moved closer to him and took his hand—"I should like our first child to be born in England."

"Our first child?" He stared down at her, incredulity mingling with a burgeoning happiness. "You'll not be telling me that you—"

"Yes, I am. Bridget is sure of it. You know I've felt queasy these last five mornings and Bridget has told me that her sister had much the same—"

She could say no more, her words being stifled by her husband's long kiss. Then, holding her against him, he ordered the driver to take them back to the schloss. Pressing his mouth against his wife's ear, he said, "Tomorrow we'll start for home, my own darling."

"The three of us," she murmured. "We must see that he becomes a pianist."

"We must see that she becomes a singer," he insisted.

"Pianist," she corrected.

"Singer . . ." They disputed happily while the carriage bore them through the quiet streets beside the flowing river.

About the Author

Ellen Fitzgerald is a pseudonym for a well-known romance writer. A graduate of the University of Southern California with a B.A. in English and an M.A. in Drama, Ms. Fitzgerald has also attended Yale University and has had numerous plays produced throughout the country. In her spare time, she designs and sells jewelry. Ms. Fitzgerald lives in New York City.

JOIN THE *REGENCY ROMANCE* READERS' PANEL

Help us bring you more of the books you like by filling out this survey and mailing it in today.

1. Book Title: _____

   Book #: _____

2. Using the scale below, how would you rate this book on the following features? Please write in one rating from 0-10 for each feature in the spaces provided.

POOR	NOT SO GOOD		O.K.			GOOD		EXCELLENT	
0	1	2	3	4	5	6	7	8	9	10

RATING

Overall opinion of book .... _____
Plot/Story .... _____
Setting/Location .... _____
Writing Style .... _____
Character Development .... _____
Conclusion/Ending .... _____
Scene on Front Cover .... _____

3. About how many romance books do you buy for yourself each month? _____

4. How would you classify yourself as a reader of Regency romances?
   I am a ( ) light ( ) medium ( ) heavy reader.

5. What is your education?
   ( ) High School (or less) ( ) 4 yrs. college
   ( ) 2 yrs. college ( ) Post Graduate

6. Age _____ 7. Sex: ( ) Male ( ) Female

Please Print Name_____

Address_____

City _____ State _____ Zip _____

Phone # ( )_____

Thank you. Please send to New American Library, Research Dept., 1633 Broadway, New York, NY 10019.

SIGNET REGENCY ROMANCE

A FOREIGN KIND OF LOVE

When beautiful young Sheila Corbett was forced to leave her magnificent Irish estate to plunge into the London social whirl, she vowed not to be ensnared by the dashing dandies of the Marriage Mart. And when she met the notorious Lord Rande, she knew he was precisely the kind of gentleman she should avoid.

This infuriatingly arrogant aristocrat had a mistress whom he flaunted without shame. He had a skill at cards that enabled him to fleece Sheila's beloved brother Brian of his possessions without pity. Even worse, Rande was rich enough to make Sheila know it was not only her fortune he wanted, but herself as well. And most dangerous of all, she found herself shockingly tempted by tremors of love that would earn her brother's hate and leave her without a home or a heart she could call her own....

The Irish Heiress

Be sure to read these other Regency Romances
by Ellen Fitzgerald:
A NOVEL ALLIANCE
LORD CALIBAN

ISBN 0-451-13659-4